The Boys Of Hastings House

Written By

J. N. King & Cassandra Doon

The Boys of Hastings House Copyright 2023 by J. N. King & Cassandra Doon

All Rights Reserved. Printed in Australia and England. No part of this book may be used or reproduced in any manner whatsoever without written permission except in the case of brief quotations embodied or critical articles or reviews.

This book is a work of fiction. Names, Characters, Businesses, Organisations, Places, Events and incidents either are the product of the author's imagination or are used fictitiously. Any resemblance to actual persons, living or dead, events or locales is entirely coincidental.

First Edition 2023

To Deana,
Merry christmas!
And surprise...
I published a book, lol.
V-xxx

"I solemnly swear I am up to no good."

— Harry Potter

Cassandra Doon

Important Note

If you are a family member, please turn back now, We don't want to make eye contact at the next family get-together and have you wondering how we are related. If you are a friend please proceed with caution, as stated above this isn't everyone's cup of tea. We humbly understand that, and accept it. But if you do read this even after the warning just remember, We told you not to.

This book is an erotic novel, it contains Graphic Sexual content. There are trigger warnings which include:
Attempted Rape, Questionable Consent, Graphic Violence, Breath Play, Stalking, Very Explicit Situations
Etc

If you don't like any of these subjects please refrain from reading.

If you are like us, and like a good "bonking" story, then jump right in!

Love,

Cass and J.

Chapter 1

Ivy Alexander

"Ivy!" I heard my Mother call my name.
"In my room," I gave back.
I heard her footsteps getting closer to my room.
"You got in love!" She smiled at me from my doorway, her long black hair in a ponytail. I was lying on my bed, reading as usual.
"Really!" I said, jumping up and flinging the book onto the bed. I had been rereading Harry Potter for the 100th time.
I loved the thought of escaping Australia and attending a boarding school in England. It sounded so sophisticated.
I had begged my parents since I was 11 to let me go. They had always said "*no*" until now. I turned 18 soon, so that was a

factor for them finally agreeing I could go. After applying to 4 different schools, my Mother got a reply from one.

"Which one?" I ask, doing a little happy dance.

"Hastings House," she smiles. "It's 60 miles from London and only takes 80 students. You will be able to complete Year 12 there starting in September, although they don't call it Year 12 in the UK, it is called Year 13 or Sixth Form," she beams at me.

"Oh my god, Mum! That's 3 weeks away; how is that going to work? I'm only in my second last year here!" I said frowning

"Nope," she says, popping the *p*. "Your academic record is perfect. And they are happy to give you this year and allow you to start the last year immediately. Your extra work has paid off for an elite school in England."

"I feel sick," I say with a hand on my stomach.

"That's just the nerves, honey, Don't stress. You deserve this. You worked hard to get here." Mum said.

And she wasn't wrong. I did work hard. When I first started to beg them to let me go, they kept saying my academic results weren't good enough to even get in. So, I worked hard and studied harder. I had one friend here; that was it. Nerds don't have many friends, but I didn't care; I wanted to go to a school abroad, and I made it happen. I'm living proof that if you work hard enough, you can get there eventually.

"We're going to leave in 2 weeks," Mum states. "We need to get you set up and uniforms fitted; they have to measure you and then supply," Mum giggles at me. "It's oh so fancy the way they work."

"Let's hope it's better than the black pants and white polo we have now," I say, laughing with her.

Fancy should be something I'm used to, but it isn't. My parents are wealthy, and I grew up being able to get anything I wanted. But that wasn't how I was raised.

Dad comes from old money, all made in the gold rush; he now just buys and sells properties, and Mum comes from new money she made herself. She is a renowned author of Psychological thrillers, which have been best sellers since I was a baby.

Instead of growing up in mansions and having money thrown at me, I grew up moving from town to town. Dad would buy a house to renovate and flip, which meant we usually stayed in one place for a maximum of 1-2 years.

Then off we went again; over the years, the lifestyle grew on me. I loved travelling and meeting new people, I had no issues talking to strangers, and I never got the new school jitters.

The only negative side was having no friends; if I made one, I always had to leave soon after. So, I happily made acquaintances but never really got close. Probably developing

attachment issues and a reluctance to commit to anything long-term.
"Come on honey, let's go out and get some dinner. I wanna celebrate AND mourn the fact that you're leaving me for 9 months." Mum smiled at me with tears in her eyes.
I lightly slapped my Mum's arm and said, "If you cry, I'll cry. So nope, Stop it!"
Mum and I were very close. With her working from home my whole life, I got to see her every single day. And I was going to miss her like crazy. Half the reason I had to wait so long to attend boarding school was her reluctance to give me up. I didn't blame her. I will likely call her every single day.
I followed my Mum out to the car and jumped in. Mum turned to face me. "What should we get?" She said, raising her eyebrows at me.
"Italian! I need some pasta!" I said, grinning.
"You always need some pasta," my Mum laughs at me and places the car into drive.
I knew I wouldn't sleep a wink for the following 3 weeks; my excitement was too intoxicating.
Today is the day my life changed, I thought, and we headed for my favourite Italian restaurant.
The nerves, having gotten the best of me, though, I could not eat. Poking my fork aimlessly around the plate, Mum gave me a

nudge to remind me not to forget my manners. I was not at all feeling like I could eat much. Therefore, after another five mouthfuls, I put the fork back on the napkin and declared the end of my dinner.

Chapter 2

Sebastian "Fox" Foxworth

"Row faster for fucks sake!" I shouted at my best friend, Wyatt. I wouldn't let him slack today only because we had a tad too much booze last night. Usually, the drink never affected him the next day, but with the news we had received last night, his head was in a mess.

The whiskey was still burning a hole in my stomach, too, but it had made me more determined to win. It was mere practice, and we had won every race this year, but I wouldn't let Wyatt ruin our streak by slacking the moment things got shitty. "Fuck right off, man!" he gave back.

He threw his head back to remove his near-black hair hanging in sweat-drenched clumps around his steel-grey eyes.

"Just get your head in the game, Forester. And we're good." I hissed back, my knuckles turning white over the oars I had in a vice grip. A plethora of thoughts rushed through my mind as I rowed until I felt damn near sick.

In my periphery, I could see Wyatt finally pulling his weight, and for just a nanosecond, I could force a deep breath down my throat.

The news of my Mother and his Father announcing their engagement the night before had us feeling all sorts of rage and disgust.

It wasn't because we didn't want to be related through marriage; hell, Wyatt was already my brother, along with Lincoln. The three of us have been inseparable since play school.

It was the simple fact that my Mother had slept her way to the top already, stopping at my Father, who was way older than her.

As a child, I always felt like my family was like any other, but the older I got, I realised more and more that my Father was not only a good twenty years older than my Mother, but people started to ask if he was my grandfather.

When I was 15, I learned my parents had never been a typical family. My Mother just out for a steady meal ticket. She had found just that, in my Dad. Eventually, he realised this, too. He passed away six months ago from lung cancer.

Worse than having lost her husband was the fact that my Dad left nearly all his fortune to me and me alone. He had left my Mother with some money to keep her lifestyle up for a while, but she wanted more, always more, and I knew even before my Father passed that sooner rather than later, I'd have a stepfather….With a shit tonne of money.

That it would be my best friend's Dad, a nice guy at that, fucked me off to no end.

Wyatt, growing up with me, was privy to all my family's dark secrets, and he knew what kind of woman my Mother was. He had lost his shit last night; I had never seen him drink so much in under an hour.

He then went on to destroy our room. I had let him, feeling like it wasn't my place to say anything about it. Until he grabbed me by the collar of my shirt and spat in my face, "This changes nothing! Your Mother being a gold digger with her claws inside my poor Father means shit. You hear me!

You are my best friend, and you always will be"

But today, he suffered from his outburst, and I had all the pent-up rage and emotions still inside me. I knew he wouldn't tar me with the same brush, but I still felt responsible. I always felt responsible for my Mother's ways. Like I had inherited the bad gene myself. I knew it wasn't true; I couldn't care less about money or status. But having people assume you are just that had my heckles up.

The only thing I could do right now was to treat him like nothing had changed and keep my anger in check. We would devise a plan to stop whatever shamble of a wedding my Mother was planning. I didn't want Michael, his Dad, hurting, but I knew he'd be hurting more in the long run if he married my Mother. I promised Mum that once I was finished with school and Uni and settled, I'd help her out financially. Yet, that seemed to displease her as well, though. No winning with that woman.

Chapter 3

Ivy Alexander

The trip from Australia to England could have been better. 22 hours, That's how long it took, and I felt like a caged animal every minute, never able to adjust to long-haul flights. Even though we travelled in business class, it was still uncomfortable and loud. How many times does that stupid cart need to be wheeled down?
I had read 3 books by the time we landed. I cannot sleep on aeroplanes. When I was about 10 and we took a trip to Bali, Mum gave me Phanergan. She hoped it would knock me out. Nope, it did the opposite; I bounced around that plane like a kid who ate too many red lollies. God knows what was in that stuff, either. Since then, they have given up and loaded me with books.
I managed to read a whole series by one of my favourite authors. The main character had 3 boyfriends; I mean, can you

imagine it? I wouldn't say no. In fact, I hope that's in the cards for my future, I would love to have multiple boyfriends. They say you get back what you project, right? Well, I'm manifesting 3 sexy boys at once. There you go, Universe….Deliver!

My parents had set us up in a hotel just shy of the school so we could get my room set up and order my uniform. Let's talk about uniforms. I know I said I was excited to be out of plain black pants and a polo. But now that I tried that uniform on, I regretted that wish.
Dark navy blue, tailored A-line skirt, a white button-up shirt, a green tie, and a blazer. And what was with this round-brimmed hat I was supposed to wear? I fucking hoped it was optional. Me and hats could have mixed better. We tried to get as much sleep as possible, but the jet lag kept us three up for most of the night, so we decided at 6 a.m. the following day to head for the school to check me in.
The room I've been set up in was impressive. I got a single en-suite room. Mum said she didn't want me using a communal bathroom, so she paid extra for the en-suite. And by god, am I glad. I mean, seriously, yuck, who the fuck shares a shower! That shit grosses me out. I do not want to have to wear thongs in every shower I take. From the door straight ahead was a large

bay window with a windowsill big enough for me to turn it into a nice cosy reading area.

I had a Queen-size bed to the left of the room; adjacent was a small walk-in closet. An antique-looking mahogany desk graced the right wall, and next to it, I found my en-suite bathroom with a huge shower and a bath big enough for two people. A Victorian-times-looking sink and a basic toilet and bidet, nice for the price. The flooring in the bathroom was grey tiles, everything else white. Old wooden floorboards graced my bedroom, but the walls were painted in a shoddy magnolia. I couldn't wait to hang up some nice pictures, maybe even some that I took here. Thank the heavens for small mercies, the queen-size bed being my favourite so far in this room. I haven't slept in a single since I was a toddler and feared that's all you got in boarding school. By the looks of it, this school was happy to provide whatever one wanted if the money kept flowing.

My Mum was amazing; she helped me set up the room, unpack my clothes, and arrange my furniture so the negative energy could flow right back out the door. She called it Feng Shui; I called it bullshit, but hey, it hasn't failed her yet, so Feng Shu away, Mum. Maybe it will call more than one dick to my door? I mean, the Year 13 students are mixed, so I could have a male as my neighbour for all I knew. Let's hope the guys are hot here.

I might be a nerd with only one friend, but that is a life choice; I can still chase some tail when the itch arrives. I actually lost my virginity early. I was 15, and it was in a new town we lived in. I thought, 'fuck it' I'm never gonna see this boy again. And I'm thankful I didn't. It was horrible. I have learned to pick better boys since then.

Hopefully, there will be a few here with attachment issues like me and are happy to be on a rotating roster with a few others.

"Ivy," my Mum's voice pulled me from my thoughts.

"Yes?"

"You excited for your first day?" beaming at me.

Taking a deep breath, I replied, "Nervous as hell, but yes, I'm excited."

"You are going to kill it," pulling me into a hug. "Now I have to go; our flight leaves this afternoon, and your father is panicking about not making it on time." Mum laughed, a single tear smearing her mascara and running down her cheek. I was excited, but I didn't expect them to leave so early on. Knowing my Dad's emotional state, he liked to rip the band-aid off instead of dwelling on the inevitable. Saying, 'Goodbye' to your only daughter and leaving her on the other side of the world was hard on him, and he'd do his damnest to not show it. Rip the band-aid off, Dad.

We both also knew that Mum was panicking; my Mother could not be late by half a second. It gives her hives. Or so she says; I'm still waiting to see a single one.

Kissing my forehead and bear-hugging me, she headed for my door. "Have a good day, and call me every single day, or text, or even email, I don't care, just contact me every day," Mum said, blowing me a kiss

"Love you," I call to her, retreating back. Dad stepped up and gave me a similar hug, this one a tad more crushing, though. "Behave and don't end up pregnant or in jail. Love you, kiddo, and call your Mother daily!" I had to chuckle and force the tears in my eyes back down.

"Love you more, buttercup," my Mum replied and closed the door behind them both. And there I was, alone in a new city, thousands of miles from home. I hoped it wasn't a mistake coming here.

I looked at the clock my Mum set on my bedside table. It showed 8:20 a.m. The assembly started at 9. I still had 30 minutes to do my hair and change into that atrocious excuse of a school uniform. I'd carry the hat. I'm sure it's just optional.

At 8:50 a.m., I headed down to the assembly hall. Well, I hoped it was the assembly hall. I followed the map I was given. The closer I got, the louder it got, so I assumed I had gone the right way.

Walking into the massive hall, I spotted a seat at the back and sat, hoping there wasn't a seating arrangement I was meant to follow.

I looked up to the front of the hall and spotted an older man who barely squeezed into his suit, tapping the microphone. He must be Principal McRowan.

Chapter 4

Ivy Alexander

"Ladies and gents, please, let's get it together!" The guy in the two sizes too small suit barked through the microphone. He seemed friendly but definitely didn't have this horde under control. After about fifteen seconds, he gave up and carried on talking, knowing no one was listening anyway. Fucking Rich kids.

I know I was one of them, but I wasn't a privileged shit that took money for granted. I had to earn my keep. Chores, good grades, investment lessons, and how to handle money were drummed into me from the cradle.

Being a rich kid also wouldn't ever save me from bastards that wanted to simply get their dick wet. Therefore, my parents made sure I was able to protect and defend myself. I'm convinced I could've had a booming career in MMA or lightweight boxing, but my Dad put his foot down and told me

if he wanted a kid with brain damage, he wouldn't have
invested so much in my upbringing.

That was the end of that. Nevertheless, I was still a fully trained
MMA fighter with competing capabilities.

"…And so we welcome, from Australia, Ms Ivy Alexander!"

My name pulled me back from the thoughts I was lost in. Shit.
Did he just call me up? He cannot be serious…

"Ms Alexander, where are you?" he commenced.

Holy crap. My heart sped up, and my mouth became as dry as
the ground in the Northern Territory. Students around me were
looking around, and some settled on me, the new face. I had no
other option at this point. I raised my arm, "I'm here…"

"Oh, wonderful, Ms Alexander, would you please join me."

Get fucked! This was definitely getting worse.

"Come on, up you get." He beckoned me, waving his spongy
arm in my direction. Reluctantly, I got up, all the other students
looking my way. Fucking fantastic.

I cleared my throat a little, willing saliva to make a return.

I straightened my back, my long black hair in a braid hanging
over my shoulder, that stupid hat still clutched in my hands, and
very carefully made my way over to the stage the Principal was
standing on.

All heads follow me.

Nearly there, I thought, when there was commotion next to my right. I glanced at the noise and looked at three guys. Wolf whistling.

These shitheads were seriously wolf-whistling at me as I was walking past like we were on a fucking construction site!

"Reign it in boys, she hasn't even got tits." The blonde guy on the furthest to the right said, and his devilish smirk spread across his face. The other two chuckled, and within a second, some other guys joined in.

Not with me fucker, I thought, stepped a little closer, and before anyone else could notice anything being wrong, I hissed.

"Wind *your* neck in before I break it. Dickhead!"

Still clutching the hat, I saw how white my knuckles had turned, ready to unleash fury.

The guy next to him with his somewhat hypnotic grey eyes bellowed, "Feisty one," but I didn't hear any more as I strutted toward the Principal, who looked slightly fazed by me, apparently taking my sweet time to get to him.

Great start to the new school. I have to bash some heads in soon, by the looks of it.

It didn't help that the three guys in question looked handsomely delicious, and I'd rather keep their pretty faces intact, but needs must.

I used to feel self-conscious about what little boobs I had, but in the last year, I realised that breasts shouldn't be my main asset, not when I had a fire in my gut and thunder in my fists.
I also had a brain to go with it, and anyone who dared to question one would suffer the consequences….Severely.

McRowan greeted me in a friendly but now relatively uninterested manner, and before I knew it, the whole shebang was thankfully over. But the entire school knew now who I was, where I was from, and so on.
I was told to check in at the library to get my books for this semester and then head to the dining hall for lunch.
I wasn't overly hungry, so I decided to just grab a snack and head back up to my room. Having the rest of the day off, I wanted to get as prepared as I could for the next day.
My first full day at Hastings House.
On my way out of the dining hall and up the stairs, a familiar face passed. He stopped and jogged up the four steps I had taken in that time. His dark brown eyes and hair reminded me of chocolate or shit. That depended on how he was going to approach me right now.
"Ivy, it's a pleasure meeting you. I'm Lincoln. FYI, I don't mind your small rack."
Thud

That was the sound my fist made on impact with Lincoln's ribs, close, very close to his solar plexus. I winded him, and he crouched down, wholly taken by surprise.

"I'll add you to my shit list then. You already look like a pile of it," I snarled and walked further up to my room.

I know violence was never the answer, but since I wasn't even here for 24 hours yet, I had to stand my ground. Show them that this BS won't fly with me.

Glad that Lincoln and I were the only ones in the stairwell; I didn't expect any fallout. Therefore, I casually strode back to my room, closed the door behind me, and secured the extra lock my bit paranoid Dad had installed before they left for home. Home. Did I miss home?

Not yet, I wasn't going to let some pubescent wankers ruin my experience here.

I also couldn't deny that all three of them looked better than any guy I've ever seen; it's a shame the personalities didn't match.

I switched on my desk lamps and settled in to organise my curriculum.

Most of what was taught in my new classes I was already familiar with. I wasn't an overachiever, but I liked to stay ahead, and as my old school back in Australia had a similar stance to the educational board for private students than they had over here, I was able to look up what was going to be taught in year 13.

For some reason, my mind kept returning to the first three contacts I made here. The three guys that I shouldn't be interested in, At all. But for some unknown reason, they occupied my head all night. Looks can be so deceiving.

After a hot shower, my stomach decided that I had to return to the dining hall for some dinner. I couldn't wait until breakfast. In some sparring leggings and an oversized hoodie, I made my way back down for food.

Universe, not now, please, I asked. Not wanting to meet any of the three boys tonight.

Damn, did the Universe not like my requests....

Chapter 5

Lincoln Baker

She punched me.
Like full-on punched me. What the actual fuck!
Did they breed them differently over in Australia?
She didn't have a girl punch on her, either. That punch took my breath away, and I was sure I would feel it for days. Lucky punch? Or was she scrappy? Professionally trained, maybe? Either way, she made my dick hard. And by hard, I mean a steal fucking rod. One punch to the ribs and my dick wanted her. *Fuck*. I watched her walk back to her room, with her hips swaying and that peach ass on display. I wanted to shove her face into a mattress and raise her ass into the air. I bet she fucked like she hits too. Hard and dirty.
Room 28.

That was her room. I checked the number when she walked off after stealing my breath away; she better have a good lock on that door cause I was coming for her soon.

Standing up from my crouched position and readjusting my dick that was straining at my fly, wanting to be released, I walked back to our room.

We were only 3 doors down from the little Australian Princess, sharing an apartment-like room, and we had done so since we started boarding here 4 years ago.

We were subsequently the reigning Kings of the school. With our parents being Legacies, we got the royal treatment, and I wasn't complaining, it helped to keep the pussy flowing.

This was our last year, and we would all be expected to head off to university and choose a career for ourselves. That's all well and done when you know what you want to do. Fox wanted to go into property development like his Dad, and Wyatt wanted to be a doctor like his Father. Mine, well, my Dad was a criminal Lawyer, and I was currently pursuing the career path. But did I want to…. Hell no, I didn't know what I wanted, but I knew Lawyer wasn't it. A problem for another day, I suppose.

Walking into our room, I found Wyatt lying on his bed watching something on his phone and Fox playing the Xbox. Stripping off my uniform, I jumped in the shower. I needed to release some energy, the new girl being responsible for it. Grabbing my still-hard cock, I gave it a few slow pulls. My brain kept conjuring up images of that sweet peachy ass, leaving me in the dust. I imagined those green eyes looking up at me from her knees and opening those sweet pink lips of hers…. Fuck, that's all it took. Cum spurted out, coating the glass panel of the shower door. I hadn't come that quick since I was 14. I needed to get that girl under me to get her out of my head. One fuck is all it ever took for me to dismiss anything that caught my interest. And she had caught my interest all right.

Cleaning up, I grabbed a towel wrapping it around my waist. I walked out of the bathroom to get into something more comfortable than that preppy, uncomfortable excuse of a uniform.

"What happened to your ribs?" Wyatt sat up and pointed to my chest.

Looking down, I see a bruise had started to bloom. That little pretentious shit. Ivy had actually hit me hard enough to bruise.

"The new girl took a swing at me," I said, frowning at the bruise.

"You're joking! That little thing did that?" Wyatt laughed at me, throwing his head back.

"Bullshit!" Fox joined in from the couch. "You're like twice the damn height of her."

"Not joking, I told the girl I liked her small tits, so she punched me in the ribs, then proceeded to tell me I was on her shit list from now on," I say, shrugging my shoulders.

"Breed them scrappy in Australia, mate," Fox said with a terrible Australian accent.

"I think she might be professionally trained."

"Doubt it; there is nothing to her," Fox replied.

"Those uniforms hide a lot" Wyatt gave back, rubbing his chin like some old professor.

"I'll let you know when I find out."

"What, you wanna tap that?" Fox looked at me in horror. "The bitch hands you your nuts, and now you wanna fuck her."

"She probably fucks like she fights," I say, raising a shoulder.

"Just the way you like them," Fox laughs at me.

"Need some help?" Wyatt asked.

"Nah, I'll get that Aussie cunt on her knees, don't you worry," I say, heading to bed to get my curriculum for the year organised. I might be a legacy, but even I have to keep my grades high.

My stomach was hurting and grumbling.
All that alcohol the day before and lack of food wasn't a good combination. We only kept a stack of protein bars in our room. The small bar fridge we had stored cans of drinks and didn't

leave enough room for food. Every year, we intend on getting another, and every year, we forget.

"Should we go down for dinner?" I asked into the room, stretching my back out. It was stiff from sitting for so long, working out my class list and the books I needed to grab for each one.

"Yes, I'm starving," Wyatt declared, jumping from his bed.

"You coming too, Fox?" Wyatt threw a pillow in his direction

"Nah, I wanna finish this level; bring me back some food."

Walking out the door, Wyatt yelled at Fox, "Sure, you're not just avoiding Crystal?"

"Fuck off" is all we heard as we closed the door behind us. Hearing a distant 'thud' against the back of it. Clearly, the pillow now had a new resting place.

"You think Crystal is gonna be an issue this year again?" looking at Wyatt.

"Fuck I hope not; last year was enough to last me a lifetime," Wyatt huffed.

"I hope he stays away from her this year. I don't know if I can hold my tongue around her again."

"I'm not holding back anymore. Not once, I don't care. I'm done with her and her bullshit," Wyatt said, rounding the corner into the dining hall to the most perfect sight.

A round peachy ass standing in line for food.

"Why do I feel you are hungry for more than food, Linc…" Wyatt laughed. "I mean fuck that view of the back… why doesn't the school have leggings in the uniform list?" Wyatt made a chef kiss with his fingers.

Falling into line behind the Australian Princess, I leaned forward to whisper in her ear;

"Are all Australians as scrappy as you?"

Turning her head slightly towards mine, I see her blow out a breath like she was trying to keep herself calm.

"Come on, petal, play with me," I practically purr into her ear. Turning around to fully face me, she stares right into my eyes.

"I don't eat where I shit, mate."

"And I like it when they play hard to get" staring right back.

"Oh honey, I'm not the one who is hard," she says, leaning right into my body and brushing my cock with her fingertips. "FYI, I like your small dick."

She turned around to plate up her food and was gone without looking back.

"What was that?" Wyatt looked at me with round eyes.

"That right there is my Queen. Holy shit, I've met my soul mate," I managed to say while my heart beat a mile a minute.

"I think you have bitten off much more than you can chew," Wyatt laughed again. "But I won't deny she has an appeal even I want to try."

"Wanna make a bet?" I challenge Wyatt, "First one to fuck her wins, then we keep her for the year?"

"You're on. And let's include Fox; it might help to keep Crystal away if he is distracted with new pussy." He said with a smirk on his face.

"Come on, grab some food; let's sit with our new toy!" I laugh and proceed to stare at Ivy.

If only she knew what she was in for. The three of us are like dogs with a bone. We wouldn't leave off until we got what we wanted. And I wanted her. She wasn't like the usual pussy we had; it gets boring quick if you don't even have to chase. Ivy fascinated me on a whole new level; I wanted to chase and conquer her. Wrapping that beautiful silky black hair around my fist, Holding her hips from the back.

Chapter 6

Wyatt Forester

I could feel Linc getting obsessed with the new play toy already.

She had something about her that I needed to have myself.

The bet was most definitely on.

Her arse was something else, and going by experience, that shitty uniform hides quite a bit; I'm excited to find out what is underneath.

And if Lincoln is right and she really is trained in some sort of martial arts, then her body will be incredible.

I haven't had a good lay in around three weeks. Too occupied with my father's shenanigans. The fact that they dropped the *"getting married"* blow last night had hit hard. I've never once trashed our room in true Fox style, but I did. It felt good, too. Maybe it's why Fox does it on the regular?

I hope we don't think we need to stress too much about Fox's Mum and my Dad; we will sort something out. We always do. Send his gold-digging whore of a mother south. He knew Lincoln and I had his back, no matter what, and he had ours. With that thought, he and I grabbed some pasta and, like he said, headed toward Ivy's table. She, of course, had sat herself right off the track at the far back. That's where the outcasts usually gathered.

She didn't know the pecking order yet, so we entertained it and kicked two chairs back and plonked ourselves down opposite the little fighter.

Shit, she was gorgeous, long black hair, long enough to wrap around my fist; I needed to win this bet, desperately. The girls we usually entertained were well aware of us never wanting anything serious apart from a good time. It would be a privilege if we kept them for longer.

Her moss green eyes widened when she saw us coming over to sit with her, but she hid it well with a scowl and fire in her gaze. Fire that would have anyone usually steer clear of her, but not me and my brother.

We'd force her into submission. It's just another pussy, right? She looked so different from the other girls here, though; there was something about her I couldn't quite tap into yet. Oozing confidence but not arrogance and fuck, her eyes. I felt my balls tightening.

"Christ, can you guys not find some other victim?" she snarled, her cute brows drawn together.

I was already not listening anymore, just picturing her pinned against a wall with my dick buried deep inside her and her hypnotic eyes pleading with me to let her come....

Fuck.

"Easy there, petal, we're just the welcome committee. We just want to make sure you've settled in right." Linc smirked. A smirk that was maniacal, probably scary even, to people who didn't know him. I did, though, and I knew he was zeroing in on her, setting the trap.

"You should feel grateful." I leaned half over the table, close enough to see a flicker of disgust in her eyes. "Lincoln and I are legacies here, and so is Fox. You met him earlier on and threatened to break his neck." A quick chuckle followed before I carried on.

"If you stick with us, I promise you, no one will give you any trouble here, love."

She leaned back in her chair as far away as possible and crossed her arms before her chest. She was pushing those tiny boobs high enough for some cleavage under her crisp white shirt.

Kissing her teeth and sighing, she mockingly said, "Ah geez, thanks, dude, but no thanks. I'd rather take my chances with the mob."

And with that, she pushed herself up with her arms on the table, shoved her tray towards us and strutted out of the hall.

It was to be expected; she was a feisty one. What I didn't expect at that very moment was that stupid American all-star, Colt Anderson, following her, too fucking convenient. He got up and exited at the very exact moment as Ivy did.

I caught the little shit in my periphery, eyeing her up when we arrived earlier.

No way, dickhead! I thought. He could have our sloppy seconds once we were finished with her. If she even lasted the year.

Many tried before, eager for status and fame amongst our peers. It wasn't easy to survive me and my brothers, though. We fucked like we fought, with abandon.

That fact also made me cocksure that by the latest, the weekend, that little Australian Wildcat was mine….*Ours*.

The bet was for the first to fuck her, then we could all share her for as long as we wanted, but the sluts were all the same; once we let them inside our little circle, they wanted more. In the end, keeping her for the year meant we had a steady fuck at all times.

Linc's dark eyes went full-on black, watching that wildcat blow him off for a second time. That doesn't happen to him. Once, yeah, maybe, but twice and on the same day, fuck, there will be hell to pay.

"Let's eat in our room." He was fuming.

We grabbed some food for Fox and headed back. I was busy inside my head, trying to conjure a plan on how to get Ivy on my side.

I had never met someone quite as feisty as her, so I had to devise a plan. It's unnatural as none of us ever had to work for a girl before. I had lost the last two bets with the guys, which automatically built my determination.

I also needed to figure out what was happening with Colt and eliminate him immediately if he was after our cute little prize. Breaking in the Australian would make an excellent new nudge on our pillar.

We've had America, Brazil, Spain and Italy under our belt already.

You wouldn't believe how diverse this school could be, all the rich wanted to send their kids here. It made finding new pussy easy.

"Fuck man, so much money for this school, and we can't get steak regularly?" Fox seemed in a pretty bad mood. I bet my yacht that it was Crystal, the stupid bitch.

He really shot himself in the foot there, like her uncle, she was psychotic.

At one point, we thought she had tampered with the condoms and was trying to trap Fox in some awful shit.

"Send a grievance; you know how they quiver when they get them from us," I replied, trying to lighten the mood. Fox was difficult at best when he was in one of his moods.

Linc, always the "shoot first, ask questions later" guy, asked Fox outright, "You've heard from the devil then…"

"Dude, I swear she's off her meds!" Here we go again, new furniture was in our future… Again.

"The bitch cannot grasp that I want her to disappear" his face started to turn slightly red, and the deep blue of his eyes had venom inside, and off he went. The bedside lamp flew first, swiped clean off the cabinet.

"She called my daft mother to ask how her summer was and if she'd fancy *AFTERNOON TEA* sometime soon!" There goes the bedside cabinet that held the lamp a second ago.

I had to at least try and diffuse the situation. I told him last year I was done with having to replace furniture every week. If he carried on, I might as well give him my entire trust fund now, seeing how we haven't addressed our parents' new engagement.

"Listen, mate, I'll grab her tomorrow and make sure she understands that you are done with her."

His eyes rimmed red with anger, and he huffed quick breaths, but I saw he was listening to me. It started to get to me that I was the only one trying to wrangle him down from his outbursts, while Lincoln just seemed amused by them.

"What did your mum say?" Linc asked, leaning casually against our door, ready to fuck off when shit got crazier. Case in point. I threw him a look, and he just shrugged his shoulders and gave me this ridiculous Cheshire Cat grin.

We all had a temper, worse when you are a legacy and constantly have to show your dominance but fuck me, Sebastian was off the charts. As kids, we thought once he had some excellent fucks he'd mellow out, we were so wrong.

Funnily enough, though, his outburst never touched us, just our furniture or some rando's face.

But for some reason, Linc's question broke him out of his spell a bit, as he started to chuckle and slowly sat back down on his king bed.

"She asked Crystal who she even was and if she had the correct number."

We all had to laugh then.

Finally settled to eat his dinner, Fox looked up from his pasta and asked, "Was the cage fighter down there?"

Apparently, the wildcat had caught his attention, too.

Chapter 7

Ivy Alexander

Why did the hottest boys in the school have to be the biggest fucking cunts?

If they thought I was a pushover, they were mistaken.

I went to school in Australia with footy heads and hard-core bogans who would put those pompous, pampered, pretty boys to shame. They thought rowing was a sport over here, for fuck sake. We don't breed them smart in Australia, but we do produce them tough.

Fox had a bit more brawn than the other two, but different from the guys that could get me in trouble in OZ. I was sure, however, they had a stinger that would fuck me up differently. Theirs would come in the way of words; I didn't think UK boys had the exact fire I liked. The ones to punch someone out for daring to look their way. These boys here would likely write a letter to the Queen and bitch about the debacle they found themselves in.

"Hey… new girl" I heard from behind me as I exited the dining hall, the accent clearly American. Southern maybe? I wasn't sure. I was never good with accents and places. Turning around, I saw an equally handsome boy heading my way. Sparkling blue eyes, shaggy blonde hair, and very, very broad shoulders. This must be the source of the American accent, Yum.

"Ivy, isn't it?" He said, holding out his hand for me to shake.

"That's the name my mum gave me, yes," I smirked back at him while shaking his hand.

"It's a nice name; I like it" beaming at me.

"I'm Colt."

"Well, nice to meet you, Colt; what can I do for you?" I asked, putting my hands into the pockets of my hoodie. "I was just heading back to my room; you can walk me."

"Sure" he smiled and blushed slightly around his cheeks. Aw, he was a blusher; now that's my type. Sweet but big enough to kill the spiders.

"How are you settling in?" Colt asked from my left as we headed up the stairwell.

"Well, the first day has been interesting but nothing I hadn't expected."

"How so?" Colt turned to look at me with a toothy smile.

"Well, I've seen my room, the assembly hall, and the dining hall," I say, shrugging. "I've yet to walk the grounds and work out where my classes are," huffing in disappointment, I carried on, "I was given a map, so I'm gonna have to learn on the fly." Colt looked down at his watch and stated, "We have 4 hours before they declare official bedtime," holding out his arm, he smirked. "Milady, would you like a tour of the grounds before we are banished to our rooms?" throwing on an atrocious English accent.

Laughing at his antics, "I would love to, kind Sir." I reply back in an even worse attempt at an accent.

"Fuck, yours is worse than mine!" he exclaims.

"Shut up; I've been here for 2 minutes. I haven't had a chance to study the native wild animals and their secret language yet."

"Well, I hope you brought binoculars; there are a lot of pricks here, and you should keep a distance," Colt smirked at me and kissed his teeth.

"So I have noticed, in fact, I've had 3 introduce themselves to me already." Walking outside, I found the sun hadn't set yet, and the grounds looked stunning in the evening glow. I've always loved old architecture, and this place was something you would see on a postcard.

"Wow…. This place really is beautiful." I awed, whilst holding a hand over my eyes to shield from the setting sun. It was at that particular angle where it burnt your iris out but was so stunning you couldn't look away. Similar to the three shitheads that called themselves Legacies of Hastings House School, so pretentious.

"It really is," Colt said, taking in the same view. "My mom picked this place because of the building. She said it would help me with my future."

"What do you mean?" I frowned at him in question. "How can a building help your future?"

He laughed, "I wanna be an architect. But I want to bring back this old-world charm. I love the intricate patterns and shapes old buildings have. These new fancy, plain, square things do not appeal to me," Colt said sheepishly but with pride in his tone.

"So do I! I love heritage-listed buildings and old gothic mansions," I said, elbowing him. "My Mum's biggest dream was to buy a run-down mansion that is hundreds of years old and restore it to its beauty." I smiled at the thought of missing my Mum and the way her eyes lit up when she told me her future plans. "You know, places that have hidden rooms and passages; how cool would it be to find a hidden room in your house?"

Colt's face lit up with every word I spoke. "You're gorgeous, you know that?" he declared.

It was my turn to blush. "Thank you. That was very sweet." I responded.

"Don't worry about the pricks you've met so far. They are legacies here, so everyone thinks their shit doesn't stink, but it doesn't cover the fact that they are just man whores who treat all the women like they are here solely to please them" he shrugs at me as we walked through another door.

"This is where you will find all our classrooms for this year," he said, pointing towards a Victorian hallway full of doors. "We get the bottom level, leaving the younger groups to walk up the stairs," he smirked, amused that the younger kids had their classes upstairs.

"If you picked any specialised subjects, they will be in a different building. This one here is mainly English, Science, Math, etc."

"I opted for art and photography, so I'm guessing that's somewhere else."

"Yep, it is in the same one I'm in for drawing; I'll show you." He started to move away, and out the door we just came in from. Colt was easy to like. He was genuinely sweet and not a pompous twat, on the first impression. I hoped he could hold it up and that he wasn't gay; he was sexy and good-looking. Definitely up my street for a nice fling, maybe.

"Hold up, your legs are twice my length." I giggled as I ran after him.

"Sorry, I get so excited when it comes to drawing, and the classroom has some really cool drawings and paintings hanging up; I'd love to show them to you" he turned and faced me so abruptly that I bumped right into his chest.

Thud

Large, warm arms wrapped around my shoulders and neck. Fuck he smelled good, too. Like cinnamon and apples. I definitely wanted to lick him at some point.

"Shit, sweetheart, I'm sorry," he says with that American accent of his, "You ok?"

Leaning back out of his embrace, I rub my nose. "Shit, you hiding bricks under your shirt?"

"Thanks for the confidence boost, but no, I think your nose met my sternum" he laughed and rubbed his chest, "I think your nose bruised my chest."

"Shut up!" playfully whacking his arm.

"Come on, let's keep going," I held the hem of his blazer as he walked me in the direction he was headed.

"Where you from anyway?"

"Texas" Colt said, while he walked into another building, "this is the arts building; if it's art-based, it's in here. Both your art and photography classes should be here" spreading his arms

wide like he was unveiling a prize. This building suited the art department. The windows along the walls and its high ceilings were colour-stained. It reminded me of old church windows, but prettier. In no particular order, red, blue, yellow and green were blotched in a wild way inside the glass. I must see this when the sun is high and shining through, I thought. The corridor was similar to the one we just came from, but instead of the cold, musky smell, this one smelled of paint and ink. I loved it.
"How long have you been here?"
"This is my second year. Mum sent me here last year after my Pa died so I could focus on my drawing and not football." Colt shrugged, and I spotted a glimmer of sadness in his eyes.
"I'm sorry to hear about your dad. Your Mum doesn't like football?" I frown at him.
"No, she loves it as much as I did. It was my whole life until my Pa passed. Now I can't bring myself to play again," he shuffled his feet, "so I came here to get away from everyone back home, focus on my drawing, and find something that makes my life shine bright again, I suppose, or so my mum says anyway."
I felt terrible for him. It must've been hard losing a parent and then moving across the world just to find some happiness again. He also seemed so genuine and sweet that I couldn't stop myself from reaching out and hugging him. I felt him stiffen at first till he relaxed and wrapped his arms around me, too. His

apple pie scent invaded my nostrils and made me all giddy. I loved apple pie! By the way, this was going, I would take him as dessert.

But I wasn't that easy, so I tilted my head to look up at him, "Can you show me the library now? Apparently, that's where all the books I need for the year are."

I felt his chest move in a chuckle. "Come on then, you can tell me all about Australia on the walk there. It is on the other side of campus." He let go of me and then slung one arm over my shoulder, it shocked me at first, Colt was super touchy-feely, but surprisingly I was enjoying it so I didn't push him away. His arm was also warm, which I welcomed. I know September was still classed as summer here, but it didn't mean it was warm to us Australians. We went to school in 40-degree heat, with such intense humidity that by lunchtime, our school clothes were basically drenched, and it looked like we went swimming in our clothes. This weather was the end of winter back in OZ, and it had only just started to warm up for us.

"Are there really drop bears in Australia?" Colt chuckled, and I threw my head back in laughter.

Chapter 8

Ivy Alexander

Jesus wept; Colt was something else. He gave me the sort of welcome at school here that I hoped for. Not only was he drop-dead gorgeous, but he was charming, and we shared similar if different, interests in art.

He was forthcoming but in a decent, gentleman's way. Therefore, I decided not to give him the impression that I was more than inclined to a casual hook-up. Let's see what the American Dream boy had in store and if he could swoon me. Before he said goodnight in my room, he had asked if I wanted to have breakfast with him. Happily, I accepted his invitation. I was glad my first night here didn't go entirely to hell; I went for another long shower. The jet lag was really getting to me, and cuddled up in my bed with a new book, hoping sleep would find me soon.

It was 4 a.m. when I woke and looked for my phone, which must've dropped to the floor at some point. The room was pitch black, not even a slither of moon shining through the relatively thin blinds. I must've woken up because it was beyond freezing in my room. If this was the end of summer weather, I didn't want to know what the winters here would be like. I sent out a Thank you prayer to my parents for having brought two fleece blankets on top of a heavy tog duvet. I rolled myself into a human burrito and closed my eyes, wishing to fall back asleep. Unable to, I pulled up my phone again and searched YouTube for some sleep sounds.

Before I could settle back down, however, I heard the click of my door. I shoot up straight, ready to take out whoever fuck dared to enter my room. I was sure I had engaged the extra lock, but going by the noise, I wasn't so convinced anymore.

Another noise had me jump out of bed and in fight stance, when lo and behold, my door indeed opened. I wasn't a scaredy cat, but an ice-cold shiver ran down my spine regardless. Light from the hallway ran slowly across my floor, a shadowy figure emerging from the other side.

I took two steps forward and lunched at the figure. A low grunt followed by a sharp hiss came from the intruder when I had him or her in a chokehold in record time.

"Fuck sake Ivy. Let go!" A breathless Lincoln rasped. Once I realised it was him, my arm squeezed slightly tighter. He was helpless, though, and only tried to shake me off, to no avail. "What on gods green earth are you doing in my room in the middle of the damn night, you sicko." I hissed straight into his ear.

"Let go!" He said again in a raspy voice, straining against my hold.

"I will when you've passed out," I growled this time. This fucker might be taller than me, but when you have a man in a choke hold that's taller than you, you can bend the spine backwards, setting them off-kilter and, by squeezing that little bit tighter, you can send them unconscious too.

So I squeezed tighter and felt him growing weaker under me. We only tussled a few steps in my room, and I wasn't sure anyone else could hear us.

Sure, he would be out for the count in a second or two. I readjusted my grip. My mistake, as Linc grabbed my waist from behind and forcefully swung me round so I was chest to chest with him.

"Don't underestimate me, petal," he said, still hoarse.

Trying to recover from my shock that he had actually trumped me, I had no time to brace myself when he threw me on the bed.

We were both out of breath and stared at each other briefly before I was ready for round 2.

"Stop!" With his hand held out in front of me, he tried to block my attack.

"I'm sorry, all right. I just wanted to check if you were in here. I saw you wandering around campus with that dick, Anderson."

What the fuck?

"That's none of your business" I snapped, "and your unjust concern also doesn't give you a free pass for breaking and entering."

"Breaking and entering? Your door was unlocked, Princess!"

No, it wasn't. I was sure I had locked my door properly before settling down. "Bullshit" I barked. "Even if it was, it doesn't even matter. You can't seriously think you can just waltz in here!"

I was furious and ready to lay him the fuck out.

"Like I said, the door was unlocked!" He hissed back.

I was too sleep-drunk, but adrenaline pushed my heart rate at the same time; I just wanted to crawl back into my bed and drift off.

"So what do you want?" I demanded.

His eyes were dark orbs with a bit of light flowing into the room, his hands balled into fists by his side.

"I've told you; I just wanted to check if you were in your room, That's all."

"That's all... Well, as you can clearly see, I am in my room!" I spread out my arms wide.

"Now, if you are satisfied, please fuck off!"

His begrudgingly handsome face flipped a smile that had my blood run cold.

"Satisfied... Me... Not yet, not really...."

But before he could say another disgusting word, I was shoving him out of my room with threats to his life. All I got in response was his low cackle, letting me push him over the threshold. Quickly, I pressed the door shut and checked my lock twice before I could get back into bed.

I knew instantly that I wouldn't go back to sleep after this. Instead, I decided to do a quiet workout, this old building was loud as fuck if you moved around too harshly.

Between shadowboxing and push-ups, I hatched a plan to confront the prick in the morning, well, in about three hours. It was time to put this rabid dog in its place once and for all. Who did he think he was, just helping himself into my room in the middle of the night? Legacy or not, I was gonna hand him his ass.

Chapter 9

Sebastian 'Fox' Foxworth

I've not laughed as hard as I was that morning.
I woke up to Linc trying to button his uniform shirt up so damn high it was nearly hitting his chin.
That sly little rabbit nearly managed to choke him out for breaking into her room, and Linc had the red marks to prove it. This solidifies the fact she is trained. And trained well. Not many can get the drop on Linc. I mean, one, he is 6'2, taller than both Wyatt and myself, not by a lot, but still taller; he was also bigger, having come from a good gene pool.
Linc hadn't followed us onto the rowing team when we enrolled into this school. He chose to stick to academics. The kid was a tech genius in the making. That didn't mean he didn't train; he trained hard. He visited the gym with us daily and did some boxing on the side. Tried to con me into going to boxing, said it would help my temper.

Little fact: nothing helped my temper. It was all a case of being there, tried that. I was a hothead.

I was easy to anger and more challenging to cool down. Once I saw red, that was it. I needed to either fuck or fight it out. The furniture in our room seemed to get it the most unless we were out, then I would take it out on the person stupid enough to piss me the fuck off.

Except for women, I would never touch a woman. That shit was disgusting.

Wyatt was shaking his head at Linc while he explained his play-by-play of what the little rabbit had done to him.

"Why in the world did you bother to get up so dam early to check she was in her room in the first place?" Shaking my head at him.

"I saw her walking the grounds with Anderson," Linc growled.

"Why?" What was the little rabbit doing with that dickhead, I wondered

"No idea; looked like he was showing her around the school, but he had his arms slung over her shoulders when they returned to her room." I could hear in his voice that he was seething.

"She fucking took him to her room," I exclaimed with a shocked face. I am no one's sloppy seconds unless it's Linc and Wyatt.

"She didn't take him inside. He just dropped her off and left."

"We can't let that fucker near her," I growled.

"I know! It's why I checked on her in the first place," Linc looked at me with raised brows like I was an idiot.

"We better up our game." Wyatt proclaimed

They both filled me in about the new bet. I wasn't that invested in the girl when I first saw her, but I was coming around to the idea of having a new pet.

God knows I needed something to take my mind off Crystal, and I was hoping that Ivy was it. Once she was ours, we could use her for the year, the bet might be whoever got her first won, but we would then keep her between us for the year so we didn't have to chase tail all the time, I needed a new regular thing for the year that didn't have blonde hair and blue eyes. Crystal turned into a problem I didn't want to handle.

That girl was as insane as her uncle was; how she wasn't in the mental hospital with him, I would never understand. They say Schizophrenia ran in your DNA, and I was almost 100% certain she had it.

If she hadn't looked like a fuck doll, I wouldn't have touched her once. I didn't go for crazy, but I do gravitate towards anything with big tits.

"Hurry up fuck face" Wyatt threw my way. "Im fucking starving and need breakfast."

"We have to get down there before Ivy does," Linc exclaimed.

"I don't think I've ever seen you this keen for pussy in my life" I shot a smirk at Linc.

"I've never been turned down as much as she has given me the red card," Linc frowned at his feet, "girls usually throw themselves at us, but not her. Instead of turning me off her, it's made me borderline obsessed!"

"Sure, it's just borderline? I don't think you have ever chased tail at 4 a.m. for a welfare check." I laughed and threw a shoe at him. Our boy looked like he had it bad, and that was something unusual and piqued my interest. None of us ever had a steady girlfriend; we knew they were just too much trouble and work. We preferred the girls on a semi-permanent basis.

"Either way, she has set the game, and I wanna play," Linc shot back before opening the door so we could head out.

"We all wanna play," Wyatt said back and clapped Linc on the shoulder.

Walking into the dining room, we spotted the little rabbit sitting with Anderson, eating her breakfast.

"That cunt has to go!" Wyatt narrowed his eyes on Anderson.

"Agreed"

"Let's get some food and sit with our Australian Princess," Linc smirked.

That boy was like a dog who wanted a bone, and Ivy seemed to be holding one. I felt a bit sorry for her; Lincoln would stop at nothing if he wanted something, and he had set his eyes on her. We grabbed our food and hurried to sit down with the couple. Linc sat on her right, and I sat on her left, leaving Wyatt to sit next to Anderson.

"Morning, petal, how did you sleep?" Linc asked Ivy in a honey-laced voice.

"Sleep? As in the sleep I happily had until you broke into my room?" She snapped, her face scrunched up in disgust, her gaze burning a hole into Linc.

"I didn't break in; it was unlocked." Linc frowned back at her.

"It wasn't unlocked; I double-checked the lock before sleeping. This isn't school for James Bond wannabes, so stop practising your lock-picking skills on my door." She turned around and dismissed Linc.

"If you are having issues with your door lock, we can get you an electric one like ours?" I offered, trying to weasel my way in, "That way, no one can break in?"

"You also get notifications sent to your phone every time the door is opened and what code was used" Wyatt chimed in; the bastard knew what I was up to and played my game.

"Why, so you can sneak in using some crazy tech shit that I don't understand instead?" She narrowed her eyes at me. Dammit, she wasn't going to go down easy.

"If you don't trust us, that's ok. Admin has the details of the company who installed ours. Go get it and arrange it yourself." I offered instead.

"I'm confused as to why you're being nice to me now?" Ivy declared, taking a bite of her breakfast roll. "Did my small tits suddenly become more pleasing to you?" she asked in her sassy accent through a full mouth of food. Did she not learn etiquette at school back in Australia? I mean, the country was founded on criminals, so maybe not.

"I was never mean to start with. I made an observation and told my mates to calm down," I said and shrugged. "you're the one who fired up at me." Ivy just raised her brows at me.

I noticed that Anderson hadn't said a word. What was this fuckers deal? No one knew a lot about him except that his dad was an oil tycoon and that he was a star quarterback in Texas. That was it. Linc even managed to hack into the school files and still came up with nothing.

"Any input from you there, Anderson?" I threw a fake smile at him, "Are we mean?"

"Not sure, I'm still trying to work out what your angle here is. I mean, I thought you had a girlfriend, Foxworth. Crystal wasn't it?" Colt said, pointing his fork at me, "And don't you just fuck anything that jumps in your way?" He pointed at Linc, "As for you, I'm not sure, I never see you fucking around, but maybe you're just a sly motherfucker about it?" He said, looking at Wyatt, Acting all big.

He wasn't wrong, but that wasn't the topic of our conversation. We weren't mean; the girls that had gone with us, always knew the deal.

I smiled at him. "Well, Anderson, Crystal knew I wasn't interested in a relationship, but I was so good that she is still obsessed with me."

"And yes, I do fuck all the girls, Anderson" Linc smirked crazily at the fuck head, "Sorry, did I not leave any for you? Maybe it's time to find another school?"

I saw Anderson's eyes flit to Wyatt, waiting for his answer, but instead, Ivy piped in, "I'm sure you're all proud of your accolades, but honestly, I couldn't care who or what you all put your dicks in. They will never be near me, so what you do with them is your business." Clearly finished with the conversation. "Quite frankly, this bun is about to leave this sausage fest." she got up and shook her head.

"Colt, would you mind walking me back to my room so I can collect my bag for first period."

"Of course, darling." Colt smiled at her and threw us a dirty look. Tosser!

"Thank you, dear." She gave back, and her devious smile wound me the fuck up.

We watched them both leave. I turned to Linc, who looked like he was about to throw his food across the hall in a tantrum that would impress a 3-year-old child.

"What the fuck!" He growled.

"It is like she is completely immune to us. I honestly don't know what to do?" Wyatt stated with a bewildered look on his face.

This was new for us. But we never turned down a challenge.

"You don't think she is a lesbian, do you? I mean, it would make sense," I said and thought about how hot she'd look with another girl.

"The way she kept rubbing her thighs together tells me a different story," Linc stated with a sly smile.

"What?" Wyatt looked confused.

"I felt her legs move under the table a few times, so I leaned back and watched," he said, "she rubbed them together every time you made eye contact with her" he told me.

The little Australian Princess had the hots for me. Good to know.

"It's not that she isn't interested. She is simply avoiding us," he declared, "and I don't know why."

Fuck, my dick was hardening in my slacks, thinking about her legs rubbing together. If she needed friction, I could give her something to rub against.

"We need to make her trust us," Wyatt stated, running a hand through his hair, "she clearly trusts Anderson for whatever reason."

"I need to dig up more on that cunt, he is sleazy." Linc gave a look of disgust.

"Fuck come on, let us make sure she hasn't allowed him into her room" I got up off the chair and watched as Linc picked up his phone and made a call.

"Who are you calling?" I asked whilst we were walking out of the dining hall.

"The lock company, we need to get that lock on her door fixed. It really was unlocked when I walked in, and I don't trust that yank."

"Good Call"

Chapter 10

Ivy Alexander

The audacity of these shitheads was incredulous.

Their man-whore, alpha-hole attitude was pissing me off, and I needed to either have some stern words with all three or if push came to shove, kick their fucking heads in.

Whichever they choose would be all right with me, I could've efficiently dealt with their sexist comments and advances, but breaking into my room was creepy and bang out of order. These three would only learn the hard way. I was more than happy to beat the crap out of them as it was. Colt turned out to be nicer the longer you spent time with him. No nasty comments or pushing for anything. How long I could last without asking for more was the question. He was the type of guy I could set up for a regular fuck, but I was a little apprehensive wondering if he was the type to get attached or not.

He and I arrived at my door, and I needed to quickly grab my bag for classes.

I unlocked the door and held it open for Colt.

"You know you should steer clear of these three; I know what they're like."

He grabbed my chin gently, whilst tipping my head back so I could look him in the eyes.

Okay, I'm easy, but not that easy, at least take me out for dinner first.

"I bet you do, but rest assured, I can handle guys like that," I said confidently.

"Erm, I don't think so, sugar. Don't underestimate the so-called legacies in these halls. They can get away with *everything*." His voice turned ominous, and I felt a knot forming in my stomach. But my gut told me the three in question were nothing terrible, just spoiled and after tail.

Why was he making them out to be something more?

"Please don't worry about me. Like I said, I can handle them."

He wouldn't let it go.

"Come here..." he moved his hand from my chin to my arm and pulled me to the two-seater under my bay window.

"Listen, Ivy, I'm only looking out for you." His eyes grew darker.

"You seem like a wonderful girl, and with your looks, it's easy for a guy to get ideas in his head." A shiver ran down my spine, yet I still couldn't place what my subconscious was trying to tell me.

"It's really not that deep, Colt. I appreciate your concern…."
Before I could finish that sentence, my door flung open, and Linc, Wyatt and Sebastian casually waltzed into my room like they owned the place, they probably did, but that was beside the point.

"What's happening here then?" Wyatt asked, his face unreadable, but Linc, who stood to his left, had a murderous look. Fox crossed his arms over his chest and lifted his head like he was judging us, judging me.

"What are you on about? And what the fuck are you doing in my room, uninvited, again?" I pointed my finger at Linc, ready to lay into him. I got up and crossed my room until my pointed finger stabbed him in the chest. His brows furrowed, and his lips tightened; he just kept looking down at me.

Fox piped up, seeing his two best friends had swallowed their tongues apparently.

"We wanted to escort you to your first class, that's all."
Bullshit, and no thanks, buddy!

"I can walk myself, have been able to since I was 10 months old…and I've got a map to be extra sure."
Something about the boys made me have verbal diarrhoea. Usually, I had few words and more fists to give; something held me back from them, though, and I seemed to love to argue with them instead.
Standing in the middle of my room, with my finger still jabbing Linc in the chest, Wyatt and Fox drew in closer, circling me in.
"We saw Colt giving you a tour yesterday, so it's only fair we get to take you to your first class." Wyatt chimed in, the other two nodding in agreement. Linc had a wicked smile placated on his face.
I had to change tactics here. My aggressiveness clearly did not affect them.
Okay, boys, I'll play nice. And then I'll hand you your arses.
"Give me two minutes, and we can go." I declared with a heavy sigh, feeling defeated nonetheless.
"Wait, what? I thought I was taking you to class?"
Shit, I was so wrapped inside that legacy bubble that I forgot Colt was still sitting behind me.
Fox was about to open his mouth, but I was quicker.
"I know; I'm sorry, Colt. But as you can clearly see, these three here…" I swung my arms out wide toward the boys, "… can't

grasp the word no. So I'll go with them today, and then we'll nip this in the bud." Throwing a glare at them

"Well, see about that" I heard Linc whisper.

Arrogant dick.

I didn't fall for the trap, though, "Anyway, I'll go with them now, and we can meet for lunch?" Taking a step closer to Colt, he seemed furious, Too furious...

If looks could kill Sebastian, Lincoln and Wyatt would be dead bodies on my floor right now.

I could've sworn I saw something shift in Colt's eyes, and he gave back, "Sure, let's meet for lunch. I'll be waiting outside your class," and with that, he practically stormed past us and slammed the door.

"Jeez," I breathed heavily.

"Ready?" Fox asked, checking his fancy watch on his wrist. A school kid with a Breitling... spoilt fucking children. A Swatch watch would do the same *and* looked much cooler than the Grandad one on his arm.

I stomped to my desk and grabbed my bag, noticing for the first time my silver necklace was missing from it. Strange I thought I had put it there yesterday. Must have fallen off my desk, oh well it wasn't important, just a random one I picked up in the markets we walked through the first week we had arrived in London. Taking a deep breath I turn and lead the way into the hallway.

"What's the deal with you and the Yank?" Wyatt asked while we were walking into the arts building, irritation in his voice. Linc looked at me with curious eyes while Fox's steps slowed down. We had yet to speak to each other all the way down here.
"The deal is…. That it's none of your business," looking at all three whilst speaking.
"He's just a friend" I relent
Fox roared with laughter at that.
"Famous last words Princess"
We stopped at my classroom, and I wanted to give a comeback but knew it would be a waste of my breath.
"Okay, here we are, you did it. You took me to my class. Can we call it quits now?" Irritation was reflected in my voice. "I'm not interested in making this year a cat-and-mouse game. I'm not interested in anything," I pulled the strap of my bag tighter, feeling the following words coming out of my mouth were a total lie.
"We can greet each other in passing, say good morning or whatnot, but we are not friends, and that's perfectly okay."
Not to show weakness, I straightened my back and held my head high.
The guys looked at me intensely and again, not saying a word.
"Hello?" Frustration at their silence mixed with my irritation.

It was Linc who took a step toward me. His hand shot out, and he pushed a strand of my hair behind my ear. I tried not to flinch, but his gesture was too unexpected for me not to.
"I'm sorry, petal. We really can't do that. But I promise we won't be your friends." And with that, all three turned on their heel and left me with my mouth gaping wide.
What the actual fuck was wrong with them? Were they really that desperate for a beating?
Knowing that trying to decipher them would literally lead me nowhere, I turned on my heel too and walked into my very first class at Hastings House.

I had an absolute blast in my classes today; the teachers, professors and even my peers seemed all right, and no one took particular interest in me, neither negative nor positive. I was simply one of them. This was the first time I thought I had made the right choice enrolling here.
I got to chat with a girl called Lucille in one of my art classes though, and we hit it off. Nothing to go down in history, but we had such similar interests that we decided to have a quick lunch to review this semester's curricula.

I had quite a busy day and was so focused on my courses and classwork that I forgot that I told Colt I would go to lunch with him, only remembering when I saw him leaning against a wall outside one of my classrooms.

Shit.

He looked handsome as hell, though, and I hoped he wouldn't be too upset that I had dragged Lucille with me.

"Hey Colt," I gave him a quick wave, "this is Lucille; we share a few classes and want to run over our study plan quickly together."

His cute smile turned sour in an instant.

"You promised me lunch, Ivy."

"Hey, I didn't promise you anything... I said I'd go to lunch with you. I never said anything about it being exclusively you and me." Getting pissed off at his demeanour.

"Are the three fuckheads coming too?" He just barked.

From my periphery, I saw Lucille shifting uncomfortably from one foot to another.

"I think I'll just go and grab a salad..."

"No!" I practically shouted, not tolerating some guy getting pissy about lunch with me. I didn't promise him anything, nor was it a date.

Did he see it that way? Surely not, since we had breakfast together this morning.

I turned back to Colt. "Lucille and I will go over our study plan, and you are more than welcome to join us, Colt," my voice purposely cold and determined. The last thing I needed right now was another guy driving me crazy.

His eyes softened, and as if he had slipped on a mask, he gave me a cutesy smile. It made me shiver.

"Of course, I'm sorry Ivy. I had a shitty day and was hoping to talk to you about an architect expo in London next weekend." The shiver pushed toward the back of my mind, and I felt crap for flipping out on him.

"Hey, that's cool, we all had a stressful day today. Let's go get some food."

Lucille looked a bit confused, and like she'd rather be anywhere but here with us, but still plastered a small smile on her lips and trotted with us to the dining hall.

During our lunch, Colt had managed to completely ice out Lucille, and every time I tried to pay her and our planned conversation any attention, Colt pushed in with his talk about the expo. I gave a few apologetic smiles to Lucille, but in the end, she left quickly, and I had a funny feeling she wouldn't want to have lunch with me again. I felt terrible but then tried to convince myself that I had bounced on Colt this morning, too, and if having lunch and listening to his endless ramble about the expo was making up for it, I'd do it. Ultimately, he was the first here to make me feel comfortable and had taken time out of his own to show me around the grounds yesterday. He was lovely to me, and I shouldn't judge him for earlier. I, too, could snap when I had a bad day.

Despite the debacle with Colt and Lucille at lunch, I did catch myself looking more than once through the dining hall to see if I could spot Lincoln and his friends. I didn't see either of them, and I felt disappointed in my gut. Maybe I thrived on the shit they gave me; perhaps I was an idiot. It would be much easier if they weren't so good-looking. I remembered the reverse harem book I read on the flight to England and had to chuckle.

"What's funny?" Colt ripped me out of my own mind.

"Erm, nothing, I had just thought about something."

"To do with me?" He asked curiously.

"Uh, no, my parents." I lied, his eyes showing disappointment.

"Ready for class?"

"Yep, but Colt, you don't have to take me to every class now. I'm sure you have your own tight time schedule."

"I wouldn't want to expose you to the three musketeers if I can help it. So, if *you* don't mind, I'd like to take you to your class."

I didn't know if I liked protective Colt, but I went along with it. It seemed harmless enough.

We got up and brought our trays back and then headed for the exit, only to bump into…guess who.

The air seemed to turn from neutral to hostile in an instant. Colt, ignoring the guys, grabbed my arm and tried to pull me away out the double wooden doors.

"Anderson, she doesn't need a crutch, don't you think?" Fox snarled, clearly annoyed at the sheer presence of Colt.

"She doesn't, *no*. But she doesn't need you guys harassing her either." Colt bit back.

That must've triggered something in the guys, and before I could blink, Fox had Colt by the collar of his shirt.

"Mate, I'll have you in the hospital in two minutes if you don't buck up your ideas here…"

This wasn't going to end well. Linc and Wyatt flanked Fox, and I could already see fists flying. That would usually excite me, but this wasn't a ring, and I had no interest in being called into the Principal's office.

"Let him go, Fox!" I interfered and put my hand on Fox's arm. He jerked his head to me and eventually let go of Colt, who straightened his shirt immediately and spitted daggers with his eyes, his fists clenched by his side.

"What a way to act! Especially around a girl! Classmate, you have real class." That seemed to infuriate Fox all over again, but this time, I caught it in his face early enough, grabbed Colt by the arm and started walking. I looked at the guys and said quietly but sternly, "You guys really need to leave me alone!"

Then I turned back to Colt, and we headed out.

What I didn't like was that Colt seized the opportunity and took my hand that was on his arm and snaked the other around my waist.

I didn't want a punch-up in the dining hall, but I also, for some reason, didn't want to be touched by Colt right now… Not at all.

Chapter 11

Sebastian 'Fox' Foxworth

Anderson was dead.
I was gonna kill him.
He was a snake in the grass and needed to go.
"Linc, find out more on this Anderson fuck wit. We need him gone. Now!" I almost bellowed at him
"I'll find something," Linc replied, "but let's hurry up; we have English, and Ivy is in our class."
Thank god for compulsory lessons. Linc managed to pull Ivy's class timetable off the admin computer this morning after that disaster of breakfast.
He now knew where she would be and when.
"Linc, send us all a copy of her timetable, we need to keep an eye on her."
"I'll do it now" Linc replied, and I felt my pocket vibrate with a text.

"You got English and Math with her," Linc spoke from behind me as we walked to the main building.

"Wyatt, you got English and History."

"What did you get?" Wyatt asks Linc

"Just English, but two of my classes are in the building next to her art ones, so I can keep an eye on her from there."

"How is the progress on the door lock?"

"Locksmith should be there now, changing it out. Admin will give her the starter code and paperwork so she can then program her own code into the app on her phone," Linc smiled.

"She seemed confident that she had locked the room last night; I wonder why it was unlocked?" I asked Linc, "Can you get into any security footage and find out?"

"Security is still the only place I've yet to hack," Linc said, displeased with himself " but I'll double my efforts."

I was sure he would. Security was the hardest one to get into here at Hastings House. They were so thoroughly checked and maintained, that breaking into the system was something Linc had yet to manage in all the years we had been here.

It was something that bothered him on the regular.

"I might just set one of my own up, facing her door and hall" Linc announced. "that way, I can monitor it at all times."

"Use my account," I said as we walked into English and zoomed in on Ivy sitting at the back.

Linc and Wyatt had plenty of money, but their accounts were monitored by their parents. But my dad was dead, and I inherited it all, So I had full access to my accounts without any issues. We always used my funds for anything that the parents would question and didn't need to know.

I walked right up to Ivy and took the empty seat behind her, Wyatt took the one next to me, and Linc stood in front of the girl in the seat next to her. Leaning down, he put on a sinister smile. "Do you mind if I take your seat, kitten?"

"Of course not, Linc," she beamed back at him. He fucked her last year, and she had been trying to get back into his pants ever since; Linc said she was a shit lay, and her gag reflex was so bad she couldn't get passed the knob without nearly vomiting on him.

"Thank you, sweetheart," he said as she packed up her things and changed tables, flushing bright red.

I watched as Ivy crossed her arms, placing her hands in her armpits like she was trying to trap them under there.

Leaning forward, I whispered to her, "Wouldn't you like the same power over the sheep?"

Turning around to face me, she whispered to me, "I would rather swallow razor blades than allow myself to drop to your level," she looked at me with so much disgust. Doesn't everybody want power? This girl was a conundrum.

Linc leaned over his table and swiped up her phone. "Excuse me?" she yelled in shock, trying to snatch the phone back. He just turned the screen around to capture her facial recognition to unlock the phone.

Ivy climbed out of her seat with her hands balled into fists. "Fucking cunt... hand it back!" She whispered to him.

Just then, the teacher walked in, "All right, class everyone, please take your seats."

I saw Linc smirking from his seat as he typed away at Ivy's phone.

Ivy took her seat and lifted her hand in the air.

"Yes, Miss Alexander, isn't it?"

"Yes, Sir, it is. Could you please tell Linc here to hand back my phone?" She said in a sweet voice, "I know that I'm new here, but taking someone else phone seems a bit unethical" She continued.

"Mr Baker... Do you have Miss Alexander's phone?" the teacher asked him.

"Yes, sir, I was just helping to upload the school's app so she has a phone copy of the school grounds and timetable. Walking around with that paper copy isn't safe. What if she lost it and was unable to find her way." Linc lied sweetly, "Sorry if I offended you, petal" handing back her phone. The deceit written all over his face.

"Well, as nice as that sounds, Mr Baker, please refrain from taking other people's belongings without permission, please."
"Yes, sir," Linc replied, with his best put-on facade.
I cannot help but chuckle. Oh, these games were fun. I hadn't had this much fun in ages. The little rabbit will be ours.
Ivy snatched back her phone and placed it in the pocket of her blazer. Shaking her head at Linc, she settled down for the lesson.
"All right, class, I'm Mr Murphy," the teacher started writing his name on the board. "I know most of you know me from last year, but we do have a new person in our class today."
Grabbing a bundle of books, Murphy piled them on the desk at the front of the class. "Take one and hand them around, please," he instructed.
"I've given you a copy of the book Wuthering Heights by Emily Bronte. Has anyone in this class read the book?"
I watched as Ivy's hand rose into the air and no one else's.
"Argh, Miss Alexander, did you enjoy the book?'
"Yes, Mr Murphy, it's one of my favourites."
"And why is that?"
"Because it's one of the first books written back in 1847 that portrayed morally grey men and the poor hold on mental health the world had in that time period. It also shows us love, passion and vengeance. The social status of one person to another and

the lengths one will go to for someone they love." Ivy said with so much passion I wondered just how smart this girl really was.

"I completely agree," Mr Murphy stated. "I'm very interested to read your essay, which will be this semester's work."

Wyatt turned to me, "Did you understand any of what she said?"

"Nope," I say, popping the P "but I'll be sure as shit googling the fuck out of this book tonight."

Chapter 12

Ivy Alexander

Snatching my phone really pissed me off. These 3 had some gall and were starting to push my boundaries.

I had let all the other shit slide because I'm just a girl after all, and by god, were they handsome with their broody, possessive eyes, towering height, and toned muscles for days. But it seemed they didn't want a casual hookup. Instead, it felt like they wanted to torment me, and I'm not into that kink. Squeeze my throat, spank the bad girl in me, make me choke. That's what I need, but this bullshit, no thanks.

When the bell suggested the end of class, I turned to Fox, "I need to talk to the three of you. Now!" then I got up and left. With quick steps, I marched outside the building, hoping they'd follow me.

I crossed the Victorian Garden that connected the two main buildings the classes were in and the even older-looking fountain that stood in the middle, it was a rainy and grey day, perfectly accompanying my mood. I spotted a giant horse chestnut tree to my right, concealing half the science building and aimed for that.

I yanked my bag off my shoulder and threw it to the ground. Rambling in my head how I would tell the three shitheads how to leave me alone without beating the living daylights out of them on school grounds. Always remembering my father's words 'Your brain is your most powerful weapon kiddo, not your fists!' I chuckled quietly to myself at the next part 'unless it's a guy who deserves it!'.

Well, Dad how about three?

It didn't take them long.

They had found me easily enough. Wyatt was the first to approach me, flanked by Fox and Lincoln. I wouldn't give them a chance to speak first, and as soon as I thought they were in earshot, I began my rant, desperately trying not to look at them too much. These stupid uniforms looked way too good on them. The fabric of their blazers stretched from their muscled backs and shoulders.

Fuck.

"Listen, I'm sure you all had enough fun pissing off the new girl. But it is seriously time to look for a new target. I just want to get this year done and keep my head down...."

I didn't get further than that as Linc broke the rank, swiftly he moved in front of me and grabbed my chin. My mind lost all its balance in the nano-second it took him to do this. He leaned down so close that our noses touched. I felt his minty breath fanning my face. A small shock wave ran from my crown to my toes and exploded between my legs.

Get it together Ivy!

For fuck sake. What was it with these boys?

His thumb traced my jaw, and like I was under hypnosis, I let him.

"We're not trying to piss you off, Petal." His lips were dangerously close to mine. Before they could touch me though I snapped back into my body and only saw one way to get out of this. Apparently, peace talks were fruitless.

I raised my eyes to his. From this close, I could see flecks of gold dancing inside the chocolate brown tones of his pupils.

For God's sake, get it together Ivy.

I took a deep breath, keeping his intoxicating scents of Cologne and mint breath at bay.

I lifted and strengthened my left arm, fistballed and ready to dish out a devastating blow to the liver.

But before I could make contact, another hand gripped my wrist, holding me in place.

"Not so fast, wildcat."

Wyatt had my wrist in a tight grip, not to hurt but to stop. He stepped closer to Linc, and I could smell his scent too then. The smells clouded my mind, invading every cell of me.

My back was now pressed against the chestnut tree, and I had nowhere to go.

I knew I could get myself out of this situation, but for some reason, I couldn't think how. My subconscious was telling me not to fight.

But I needed to put an end to it all. Didn't I?

"Let's GO!" I hissed.

All good that did, was the two of them stepping even closer. Too close.

"I will if you promise to keep your fists by your side." I felt Wyatt's breath close to my ear.

I nodded hesitantly.

Wyatt slowly lowered my arm to my side but didn't let go of my wrist, his grip loose.

Still, too quick for them I shoved Linc back and stepped out of the circle to my right, aware to not get too close to Fox who was standing in the same position as earlier, looking unimpressed as always, though his blue eyes lit up when I brushed past him.

"That's enough!" I shouted.

"I really don't want to fight any of you, Physically or mentally." I looked from one set of eyes to the next, amusement in all three pairs, which engulfed me in rage.

"I will though, if you leave me no choice. Just leave me alone!" there was a small shake in my voice, not wanting them to actually leave me alone for unknown reasons but for them to stop bothering me with petty shit like stealing my phone.

"What are you trained in?" That was all I got as a reply. It was Lincoln.

At this point, I was sure I was plain stupid when it concerned these three as I willingly answered, "I'm fully trained in MMA and Boxing."

"Competitively?" Fox asked.

"Yes, But I don't compete, it's more of a hobby," I replied in a stern tone.

"We sure as hell won't hurt you Wildcat" Wyatt said, taking a step further away from me to show he wasn't a threat of any kind to me.

"I know you won't because you can't" I sighed, the adrenaline leaving my body quickly, "you guys need to back off, as I will hurt you if you don't," I sighed,

"I gave into your little game, I entertained your bullshit now I'm out"

I went to grab my bag that was lying behind me where I had left it, only for Wyatt to pick it up first and handing it to me. He smiled like he had never had before, cute and genuine.

"We're not playing games..."

"We just don't trust that prick Anderson and want to make sure you're safe." Fox chimed in.

I choked up a sarcastic laugh

"I think you know that I can keep myself safe."

I looked around the garden for the first time since I picked the spot to confront the guys and noticed that it had a static flow of students but none paid us any attention, despite what had happened between us or two of them practically pinning me to the tree.

I wondered just how much power these legacies had at this school.

If I had witnessed similar scenes back home, I would've interfered. Not every girl is like me, and three guys against one girl is more than a problem that anyone should interfere in. Apparently not here, Not when it involves the Legacies.

"Why don't you prove to us that you can keep yourself safe?" Linc asked and pulled me back from my thoughts.

"What?" I spat.

"You know, you can show us what you've got in a safe environment." His devilish smirk trying to overshadow his face again.

"We have a fully equipped gym, with a ring for sparring and one for wrestling." He explained

"We also have the keys… The gym wing was sponsored by my parents," he carefully stepped closer to me, ready if I pounced. I wouldn't give him the satisfaction. I stayed calm and steady where I was.

"You want to fight me?"Linc asked

I felt gobsmacked by his proposal.

"No silly, We said we won't hurt you in any way shape or form." Wyatt stepped closer too, his voice hushed and convincing.

"We pretend like we want to attack you, one by one, and you put us on the mat. If you can do this, we might consider backing off. What do you say?" He asked.

"You can't be serious? You really want me to beat you three up for no reason?" I laughed, not believing what they were proposing here.

"Nah, don't kick the shit out of us, just fight us off, Simple. We won't hurt you, but will act like we want to attack and hurt you." Fox smiled showing me his white set of teeth, also stepping closer to me. "Get us away from you and you've won, one by one." He repeated.

I mulled the idea over in my head for less than ten seconds "OK but don't come crying when I hurt you or your egos. I will not hold back, I never hold back!" I said with a straight back, then smiled at them and made my way to the next building. Knowing I overstretched tea break and was most definitely way too late for my next class.

Chapter 13

Wyatt Forester

I normally loved class. Call me a nerd. But today I wanted out.

We had 2 classes left for the day then I got to see my Wildcat again. That's what she had become to me, a complete distraction. Girls were meant for a fun time, not much else. But this one got under my skin, it wasn't even about winning the dam bet, my mind was completely enthralled by her. I wondered what it would feel like to wrap that long black hair around my wrist while I took her from behind.

I felt my dick twitch in my pants, A total fucking distraction. I wasn't sure if I was happy or pissed off about this new development.

Maybe fucking her would get her out of my system faster?

I adjusted my dick in my pants as discreetly as possible while I sat through math. There was something beautiful and simple about math that always appealed to me.

The numbers just always made sense, the same with chemistry and biology. I struggled with everything else in life including girls.

The girls I sought out off-campus were not the type you took home to your mum. They were the type you paid money to. The type that would allow me to hurt them, and wouldn't call the cops on me the next day. I struggled to get off the traditional way, I needed the pain. I needed to feel pain and to inflict it. Nothing else worked.

Thankfully being a legacy meant we were allowed to go off-campus, as we pleased. We had designated car parks in the staff parking area and fobs to open and close the gates. I didn't chase tail at the school like Fox and Linc, but I was able to leave the campus at least once a week to go pay for it.

It had been over 5 days since I went into town. We always arrived a few days before school officially started, to get settled in. And I used this for a few stints to town, but not this week. The little Wildcat had me wanting to stay on campus. It had been a mere two days and Lincoln and I were obsessed with the shiny new toy. The fact that she made my dick twitch on the regular had me wanting to investigate further. Maybe, just maybe she will be able to handle me…. I wonder if she would like Shibari? I felt my dick lengthen in my pants at the thought. Shit I needed to think of something gross….

Looking around the room I see the bleach blonde head of Crystal and yep that did it, dick was a limp noodle again. That batshit crazy bitch was a turn-off for me. Not because she looked gross, it was her demeanour and attitude amongst her insanity.

We really needed to do something about that bitch soon. She was going to be an issue in the future I could feel it in my gut. Thankfully the class passed quickly, I needed to get to the last class of the day and save a seat for my Wildcat. We had a history together, My new favourite subject.

Math and history were in the same building, so it was only a matter of changing rooms. I took advanced math, so there weren't a lot of us in this particular class. How Crystal managed to grasp math but nothing else in life always boggled me. Packing up my books I started to rush out the door.

"Wyatt?"

Turning to see Crystal looking at me "Yes, Satan?" Her face grimaced, clearly, she didn't like me calling her by her real name.

"Do you know why Fox isn't messaging me back?"

"Why don't you just ask him?" I replied shortly.

"I would but he isn't messaging me back like I said," she stood there with such entitlement in her face and her arms crossed under her boobs. The first few buttons on her school top were unbuttoned, so you could clearly see her cleavage.

"Well, talk to him at breakfast, or lunch, or dinner?"

"He told me not to approach him, so I haven't," she frowned, "I was hoping it was just for the day, then he would come and find me, but he is ignoring me completely"

"Then there is your answer, Crystal, he does not want to see you or talk to you. You pushed your luck last year, practically stalking him, but he was decent to you and explained that you two weren't an item. Then you kept trying to get involved, even calling his mother. What exactly did you expect to happen?" I shrugged, "Anyway I'm done with this conversation" I said and walked out the door.

As I said, trouble, she was going to be pure trouble.

Walking down the hall to the History classroom, I saw my Wildcat was already inside and seated. Thankfully there was a seat behind her.

Sitting down behind her, I heard her sigh loudly.

"Hey, Wildcat!"

She turned in her seat and looked directly into my eyes, holding my stare "Yes."

"Are you ok? You look a little stressed?"

"Oh you know, it's just my first full day of classes, I have 3 stalkers and I cannot find my history book that I swear I placed in my bag this morning, and on top of that I missed tea break so I'm hungry." Her face was genuine, nothing mocking or sarcastic in her tone. Her green eyes were stunning. I had a hard time not looking at her with anything less than desire. How could a girl do that in the course of two days, I asked myself I leaned down into my bag, pulled out a protein bar and handed it to her. "Note to self, carry snacks," I said with one of genuine smiles. She must realise that I wasn't an enemy.

"I normally have snacks but I haven't been able to stock up today," she frowned, "thank you."

She unwrapped the bar and ate it in three bites. I kid you not. I normally hate the way people eat, it annoyed me, but with her, I even found that cute. Fuck, she was getting under my skin and I didn't know how to handle that. "Note to self, carry extra snack for hangry Wildcats," I gave her a smile.

"Shut up stalker." She blurted, her claws were out again.

"Here," I said, not giving in to her comment but handing her my history book, "you can borrow mine for the lesson."

"It's ok you will need it"

"I'm a legacy, trust me, the teacher won't even notice I don't have one, plus we can share," pushing my luck I gave her a wink.

"Thank you," she said quietly, with a slight flush staining her cheeks.

I wonder if her ass would glow the same pretty pink colour? I felt my dick responding to my train of thought again. Shit this needed to stop, Im not a blushing 15-year-old virgin anymore.

I needed to have a chat with myself and Lincoln. Being like this around a girl never happened before, and by the looks of it, he and I both had the total hots for her. Linc had also made everyone aware that Ivy was off-limits. His little minions ran the grounds fast to spread the word.

This all felt so different to our conquests before. Off limits, full legacy protection and our total attention in under a Week. It definitely was a new record we set, there was just something about her eyes…

Chapter 14

Sebastian 'Fox' Foxworth

The kitten was coming around. I never thought we could pull this off, but apparently, challenging her to fight made her compliant; who'd have thought?

The guys and I weren't trained fighters, but coming from where we did, being Legacies and quite athletic inclined, we never shied away from a fight. If I can say so myself, a good punch-up was never wasted on us; we always came out on top. This was gonna be different, though, fighting a girl. Well, not really fighting but actively seeking out a girl in a manner that is abhorrent to me, regardless of it being real or not. But we had to make do with what we got, so we could get somewhere with her eventually, and that was by fighting.

I bet she was already skipping across the school halls, looking forward to kicking the shit out of us. Little did she know that it was all part of our plan. A plan to make her trust us and eventually pick one of us to fuck, Our bets were starting to be downright mental.

I wasn't feeling that feisty kitten, but a lay is a lay, and a bet is a bet. So, of course, I'd put my all into it. You never know, maybe she was good at it, despite the tiny tits. And I had to put some distance between me and crazy girl Crystal. Shit, that girl was out of her mind. I never promised her anything, apart from causal hookups, but before I knew it, she roped me into a somewhat relationship.

No lie, she was a stunner, but that was all there was to Crystal, nice tits, lovely arse and some banging lips to go with her blonde hair. Besides her schizo side, she was highly shallow too, and nasty, horrible even if things didn't go her way, and that had put me off even more than her being mentally unstable. It was the combination of it all.

Ivy was a beautiful girl, too, no doubt. I just wasn't too interested apart from the bet. I had too many other vital things occupying my mind. My gold digger of a mother, to be exact. How I would fix that mess, I didn't know. But I had to try *something*.

I'd find a way.

When Ivy had left us earlier, we had to follow her…again to establish the rules. She was OK with them all, just looking hungry for blood. Thinking about it now, we should have made a rule for her to fuck one or all of us if she couldn't fight us off. She seemed eager to get violent with us. But Linc thought that would be too extreme.

We had to win her trust, he'd said.

This felt all too similar to the long-winded bet we had back in year 7. Who could gain the most muscle within the term? It was a tie, but fuck me, did that shit go on and on. Granted, it helped us to lay some groundwork, though. You wouldn't catch us skipping a day of the gym now.

Ivy's demands were that we had to act like typical peers until the bout. Whatever that meant, but I could see Wyatt's eyes lighten up. He wanted her, clear as day, and he'd probably do everything in his power to get her. Again, the why was my biggest question. He knew no one who wasn't paid to do his sexual bidding. Why, all of a sudden, was he fixated on a girl like this was beyond me. Maybe he unlocked a new kink with her; he sure as hell wasn't going to turn her into a sub.

The teacher walked in late for my next lesson, and I realised that I had spent most of that time waiting on the teacher, thinking about her. *Ivy.*

Fuck.

Ivy was actually being decent and friendly, retracting her claws, ever since we agreed to all act normal until we could have our little bout. She overlooked, or at least tried to ignore, that we were indirectly still stalking her, thinking we did it because we wanted her to be safe at this school and maybe be friends with her, Such a naive little girl. We were the predators, and she was unmistakably our prey. As per usual, we weaselled our way in; she just had to take the bait, and by loving fights so much, it was as easy as ABC.

Nonetheless, I caught myself too often watching her, especially when she smiled.

I put it down to not having sex for about a week now. Who in their right mind stays celibate for a stupid bet?

We do. We are the morons who always have to take things way too far, we had told her under that tree that we'd meet her two days later outside the gym after the last class.

I needed this to hurry up; she had sat with Anderson daily for lunch and dinner. That kid needed to go. He was the reason why this fiasco started. Linc couldn't stand to think of the little rabbit with him.

Thankfully, that time was nearly up, and I was getting myself ready in our room. Gym shorts and a white tee with the sleeves rolled up. Our looks had to be on point for what we were about to do.

Linc had some black active-wear joggers and a black tee on, while Wyatt dressed in our rowing t-shirt and grey sweats.

We knew we looked good.

We're coming for you, kitten, and there's no way you won't fall into our trap, beating or no beating.

A bet is a bet.

Chapter 15

Ivy Alexander

These punks were up to something. I didn't trust them as far as I could throw them, and that wasn't very far. Since our little "chat" they had been nice. I wasn't an idiot. I knew it was for show. I just had to work out why and beat them at their own game.

I was finally going to get the chance to beat the ever-loving shit outta them, and I would enjoy every fucking second of it. I wasn't going to hold back. I might actually put a little bit of effort into it.

After following the map that I now had on my phone using the app Linc had put on, yes, that fucker did something useful; I strutted confidently to the gym and found the three boys on the mat stretching.

Fox was wearing gym shorts and a white T-shirt that hugged his arms and was currently doing a cross-body stretch on his arms. He looked lick-able.

Linc was in all black, Joggers and a T-shirt. Did they purposely buy T-shirts that were one size too small? It was tight and showed off every dip of his abs. The abs were not notable in their school uniforms, no wonder the girls followed these boys around like lost puppies.

If I wasn't currently in this mess with them, I would have joined the sheep. Looking to my left, I saw Wyatt lying on the mat wearing another tight t-shirt and grey sweats. He wasn't stretching; he was laying flat with his arms under his head, but the bulge in those sweats was so much more pronounced in that position, Holy hell, in a handbasket. I was screwed. How the hell did I fight off three boys when all I wanted was to allow them to touch me, grab me…. Shit, I could feel my core heating at my thoughts. I needed to get it together. I needed to beat the shit outta these delicious boys and get back to the main reason I was at this school.

Walking over towards them, I saw Wyatt's eyes turn in my direction, and the smile that spread across his face was to die for. I had to look at the floor; there was no way I could've kept my cool if I kept looking at that face.

"Wildcat," Wyatt exclaimed and sat up off the floor.

Linc spun around so fast I worried he would have gotten whip lash from the movement.

"Petal!"

Looking at Fox, I waited for his greeting, too. I didn't get one. He just continued with his stretches. Jerk.

Walking over to the mat, I sat down myself and started stretching out my hamstrings.

"Are we going to fight on this mat or use the ring," pointing over to the other side of the gym where a boxing ring was set up

"What do you want to use?" Linc asked me.

"The ring doesn't have enough room for me to throw you around" I smirked, "so let's use this mat."

Linc's eyebrows disappeared into his hairline. "you think you can throw a 6 foot 2 giant like me around?" He said, pointing at his chest. "I'm not usually chauvinistic, but goddam girl, if you can do that, I'll keel at your feet!"

"Oh, I can do that and more," I laughed at him, "just let me warm up; I'm not pulling a muscle lugging your fat ass."

"Gonna end up giving me a complex if you keep talking like that," Linc frowned and grabbed his ass cheeks. "I hope you know just how tight and sculpted my buns are."

"I'm sure they are," I mumbled as I lay my whole body flat on the mat, with my legs spread wide.

"Fuck me!" I heard Wyatt exclaim from his seated position.

Rolling myself forward, I pulled my legs behind me and pushed up into an upward-facing dog; laying myself back flat, I grabbed my ankles and lifted up backwards into a perfect bow pose.

"Oh, for god's sake, the girl's a pretzel," I heard Fox mumble and the rustle of clothing. I wondered if that fucker just adjusted his dick. Maybe he wasn't as unaffected as he wanted me to think.

Finishing a few more stretches, I jumped onto my feet and declared, "Let the games begin!" Clapping my hands together, I asked, "Who wants to go first?" I threw a blood-thirsty grin in the boys' direction. The blood was pumping in my veins, and my adrenaline was climbing.

I loved a good fight.

It was on a level with a good fuck.

"Me," Fox walked forward, "but I want you to turn around and close your eyes."

"OK," I said and shrugged my shoulders. Turning around, I closed my eyes. I heard the other two walk off the mat and sit on the bench seats that lined the walls.

I could hear Fox moving around behind me as he reached for me and placed his hand over my mouth, then wrapped his arm across my chest.

It's a classic kidnapper move.

Tipping back, he started to drag me away from where I was standing. I did the opposite of what he expected, and I went dead in his arms, completely limp. The extra weight caused Fox to stop moving, allowing me to get my feet back under me. I bent my knees and jumped, so the top of my head smashed into his chin, causing him to let me go completely. I quickly turned around and throat-punched the dickhead. Grabbing his throat, Fox dropped to his knees, trying to catch his breath.

I looked over to where Linc's eyebrows had utterly disappeared into his hairline, and Wyatt was readjusting his dick. Fox caught his breath, those blue eyes of his fuming, but he sat down and kept his mouth shut, still coughing slightly.

"Who is next?"

"Me!" Wyatt jumped up quickly.

Instead of walking over to me, Wyatt went into an attack move and just started running at me.

Wyatt might be the shortest, but he wasn't small.

What he clearly didn't calculate was that we played rugby at school for PE. I can tackle like a pro.

Instead of running away, I crouched and ran back at him, grabbing him around the middle. We collided in a heap of groans, and the air left my lungs. Propelling myself forward, I managed to tip him backwards and crashed his back into the mat.

Quickly, I scrambled up on top of him and pinned his arms to his sides with my thighs. I felt the hardness of his dick under my ass and gave a little wiggle, making him groan. "You are clearly the winner here, wildcat." He said and gave his hips a fast push upward. "Now get off me before I can't promise you I'll behave."

"OK, Linc, your turn," I said, looking up at him.

I felt Wyatt's hands grab my hips, and he pushed my ass down on his dick harder and groaned once more. Raising my eyebrows at him, I leaned down and whispered in his ear, "If you wanted to get into my pants, all you had to do was ask!" I nipped his ear lobe with my teeth and jumped off him.

"Fuck me." I heard Wyatt growl as he sat up. "wildcat, that was insane."

"If you think that was insane, you should see what I can do naked," I laughed at him sarcastically. His grey eyes widened with amazement, and he shook his head.

"Come on, Linc, show me what you got," I gave him the universal 'gimme' sign with my hands.

"I wanna try something a bit different," he declared, walking over to me.

"I wanna kiss you and see if you can fight me off when I start to force myself on you," he smirked.

I smiled back at him, shrugged and said, "OK," walking right up to him.

Standing in front of him, I placed my hands on the front of his T-shirt and leaned up on my tippy toes, tilting my head back as I put my lips over the top of his. God dammit his lips were soft and full.

Licking the seam of his lips, I felt them part to allow me entry. His arms grabbed my hips, and he pulled me closer to his body. I could feel his dick hardening against my stomach, so I lifted my hands up off his chest and wrapped them around his neck. God, he tasted amazing. His signature smell of mint hit me, but no gum was to be found. Did this tough giant eat mints? Like actual mints for fun? I wondered if he had one of those tiny "Fisherman's Friends" bags in his pocket.

Wrapping his hands over my ass cheeks, he lifted me so my legs had to wrap around his waist. This new angle meant our faces were level with each other.

He started nipping lightly at my bottom lip while devouring my mouth with his. I must admit to myself, this was hot. I meant so dam hot I'd be using this to get myself off with later.

Linc lowered himself to his knees and laid me flat on the mat, grinding himself on my heat. This was the moment I needed to take control. But did I want to? No, No I did not. But I had to.

I bit his bottom lip so hard I heard him yelp and pull his head back from mine. With the new angle, I could drive the palm of my hand into his nose without damaging that pretty face too much.

He yelped even louder and hurried off to stand above me. I took the opportunity to sweep my legs under his, sending him crashing to the ground. Quickly, I climbed over the top of him to wrap my legs around his neck and squeezed. I felt a light tap on my thigh. That didn't take long fucker.

I looked up over to where Wyatt and Fox were sitting. Wyatt rubbed his dick through his sweats, and Fox was sitting there with his eyes narrowed on me. That fucker had a severe issue.

"Petal" Linc said from the floor where he was still lying. "Can you please get me my gym towel? I think you broke my nose?"

Looking down at Linc, I saw blood pouring from his nose, "Oh fuck, yes, sorry," I blushed and jumped up. Wyatt threw me a towel, and I turned back to hand it to Linc, who was then sitting up with his head held back.

"I'm really sorry about that," I said, pointing at his face with a grimace.

"I hope I didn't do any lasting damage."

"Petal, it's not the first bloody nose I've had, and I'm sure I will have plenty more in my future," he mumbled from behind the towel.

Fox stood up from his chair, scowled at me, and walked out the door.

"What's his issue?" I asked as I watched him disappear.

"What isn't," Wyatt replied

Chapter 16

Sebastian 'Fox" Foxworth

Oh, this girl, This damn fucking girl.
I needed to leave immediately, or something would've happened. Something I wasn't and probably never will be ready for.

She looked so fucking hot in her gym attire, and when she started to warm up, I thought my dick was going to explode in my pants. However, the way she finished me off in less than a minute was by far the biggest turn-on. It made me feel things that I sure as hell wasn't capable of feeling.

The damn sex ban must be getting to my head, for fuck sake. I needed to fuck... Her... Soon.

When she told Wyatt that all he had to do was ask her, I was ready to lunge at her. Take her there and then, with or without my best friends joining me. I wondered if she was just feisty-mouthed or if she actually meant something by it.

Fuck, this girl got into my head, and I did not like it one bit.

I started sprinting through the school, up the stairs and to our room. If I didn't get some release soon, I'd probably bash some idiot's head in.

The thin line between lust and violence in me was blurring. With full force, I opened the door to our room and headed straight for the shower.

Stripping off my clothes, I felt my cock straining painfully against my boxers. In a rage, I tore them off and stepped under the hot stream.

I held on to the wall to my left, my head under the water and gripped my dick forcefully. I closed my eyes, and all I could see was her.

Down in the gym, stretching like a contortionist, beating us easily. Her smile, her laugh, her moss green eyes.

It took all but three hard strokes to my dick, and I exploded. Shooting my cum all over the tiles, I moaned roughly and tried to make it last. I pictured her on her knees right in front of me in this shower. My balls drew up higher, and I managed to draw my orgasm out for a few more seconds.

Breathing heavily, I cleaned myself up and tried hard to clear my head, but by the time I was done, my thoughts were still with Ivy, and I was rock fucking solid again.

Something was wrong with me.

I needed to kill someone. Jacking off apparently didn't solve the issue.

Stepping out of the shower with a massive lob on, I heard the door open, and the guys entered.

They were quiet. Too quiet.

I swung a towel around my waist, pushing my cock down as best as I could and opened the bathroom door.

Fuck me sideways.

She stood right there in front of me.

"What the fuck!" I bellowed, clamping the towel around my waist tighter and looking at my brothers for answers.

"Sorry, Sebastian since you just ran away like a scaredy cat, I had to come up here to talk to all three of you." She explained with her eyes wandering down my half-naked body. By god, I hoped she didn't see my rock-hard dick.

"I don't like to repeat myself." She carried on with a sickly sweet voice laced with sarcasm and venom.

But I saw that spark in her eyes regardless while they trailed down my body.

Clearing her throat a little, she turned her back to me, thank fuck, and stared daggers at the other two. Linc's upper lip was smeared with dried blood from his broken nose; I had to chuckle to myself. We underestimated her.

"Listen, I want you to back off now. We had a deal, and I've beat you fair and square."

A smug smile on her petite face. Wyatt wanted to interject, but she raised her hand and held her palm out in his direction to tell him to shut up.

"I wasn't finished, cunt!" She spat, more venom in her voice. Fuck did she really hate us? We didn't even do anything that bad to her. We were just messing around. Every girl in this school got the same treatment, even if she was already so very different to all the other bitches here.

Wyatt and Linc's eyes widened, but they stayed silent.

"I don't mind if we talk every now and then. I don't mind being decent if you show me the same respect." She turned to me. "But the bullshit stops now, or by god, I swear I will really badly hurt you. This was just a taster."

This time, she didn't storm away. She needed our answer. One we weren't going to give her…

Chapter 17

Ivy Alexander

I just stood there like an idiot, waiting and waiting. Nothing, not a dam peep, came out of anyone's mouth.
Taking a deep breath, I turned on my heel and walked out.
I legit had no patience for fuck heads.
Walking to my room, I swiped my fob on the fancy new lock the administration had installed. I knew for a fact it was the boys. Why, I wasn't sure, was I grateful for the extra protection? Yes, but I was still mad that they did it without my permission. Gaining a girl's permission seemed to be something these cunts didn't understand.
Maybe if I rode Wyatt's disco stick, they would fuck off. I'm sure all they wanted was to get into my pants. They looked like the one-and-done type. They looked like my type. But I would never tell them that.

I was packed with energy. I needed to either fuck or fight, and since fucking was off the table, I thought maybe I could head back down to the gym and burn some steam off.

Grabbing my phone out of my pocket, I send a quick text to my mum asking if they managed to find me a new trainer. I needed to train daily. My body craved the burn of the exercise and the flood of endorphins.

Pulling the app for the map back up on my phone, I headed back down to the gym. This place was huge and built like a rabbit warren. I don't think I would ever be able to walk the halls without getting lost. All I needed was for the stairs to move, and I could imagine being at Hogwarts for real. Do they have a room of requirement here? I sure could do with one!

Reaching the gym, I found the door locked. Fuck, I forgot Linc said he had a key to it, I sure as shit wasn't going to head back up to get the key from him.

A run around the grounds would do instead.

Looking back down at the map on my phone, I took the hall to the right, which should have led me outside.

I could do a few laps of the grounds and return for dinner.

Opening the door to head outside, I heard my name being called.

"Ivy!" turning around, I saw Colt jogging towards me.

"What's up, Colt!"

"Where're you off to?" Colt looked me up and down, and a tiny glint entered his eyes."

"For a run, you?"

"Can I join?" He asked with that sweet smile of his. I couldn't deny that he was good-looking, but something in my mind kept going back to the three shitheads that wanted to make my life miserable. Colt, I saw him as a friend and nothing more.

"Of course you can, but I'm not much of a talker when I run," I declared back and took off in a slow jog.

"That's cool, I was heading for a run myself," he stated.

That's when I noticed he had running gear on, tights under shorts and a tank top.

"Wanna show me the best place to run then?" I gestured with my hands while setting a brutal pace. I needed to feel the burn today. Anything to get my mind off those three boys.

"Sure can, follow me; I'll go slow so you don't get lost," he said with a challenging smile. What was it with the boys at this school thinking they had to take it easy with me or underestimate me completely

"Please don't. I need a good run!"

Smirking at me, he said, "Sure thing" and started sprinting.

Fuck yes, this was what I needed.

Colt led me around the grounds and pointed out landmarks on the trip. The school had a forest out the back of the building;

Colt mentioned they had running paths there, too. The way the trees swayed in the autumn wind was beautiful. We went past the lake where the rowers trained and past the staff parking lot. I saw three cars that very distinctly stood out, A BMW X1, an Audi RS GT and an Audi A5 Cabriolet.

I knew without a doubt the boys owned these. The rest of the car park still housed some nice expensive cars, but none were new and this year's models. I had been browsing cars myself the last few days. Mum told me to pick one out so I could go off campus and check out London on the weekends.

I wondered who owned which.

Rounding back to the front of the school, I saw the doors to the main hall open and quickly checked my watch. It was dinner time. We had run around the grounds for a good hour already. And as promised, Colt didn't speak much at all. Just mentioning the areas we passed. It was refreshing to just run and push my body but also take in the gorgeous scenery. This school definitely had that English charm you see in movies. It was as old as time by the looks of it and picture-perfect.

"Wanna grab dinner?" I asked Colt. After the debacle the other day, I thought it'd be the polite thing to do.

"Most definitely," Colt replied and slowed his pace.

I was drenched in sweat. Shit, I had to walk into the hall looking like a drowned rat. Fuck it, I wasn't here to make friends.

Pulling my hair out of a ponytail, I flicked my head upside down to re-tie it up into a messy bun. It might look half-decent. Walking into the hall, I saw the boys sitting at their regular 'I'm so fucking popular' table as I lined up for food with Colt behind me in line. Turning, I saw he was just as drenched and sweaty as I looked.

"Do you know what's for dinner tonight?" I asked him.

"Well, it's Thursday and that means it's pasta day"

"I could murder a pasta!" I replied with anticipation.

He laughed and bopped my nose with his pointer finger. "Well, hurry up and grab a tray then."

Grabbing a tray off the stack, I checked what was on offer. The pasta looked like Bolognese, not my favourite, but it would do. I grabbed two bread rolls to go with it and four packs of butter. As well as a bottle of water. With the amount of calories I burned daily with training, I was used to eating rich foods. I remember when I started training. Skinny like a bean pole, my trainer made my parents up my food intact. I found it really hard at first, but now I can consume large amounts of food and fast, too.

Sitting at one of the free tables, I quickly unzipped my gym top and shrugged it off my shoulders, leaving me in a tight razor-back crop top. I tied it around my waist and got stuck into my dinner. I was freezing my tits off. The weather in Surrey was so damn cold. I knew my tiny nipples were stiff peaks and entirely noticeable for everyone, but fuck it, wearing the sweat-soaked top was a lot colder.

I managed to get about halfway through my pasta when I felt a warm zip hoodie being placed around my shoulders. Looking up, I saw Wyatt draping it over me. It smelled divine.

Leaning down, he said in my ear, "You looked a little cold, wildcat; just give it back later." And he walked off back to his table. I could see him still wearing those 'fuck me' grey sweats. Grey sweats should be illegal.

"If you were cold, I would have gone and gotten you a jumper," Colt said, frowning at me.

"I wasn't that cold, but now that I have it, it's best I put it on so I won't get ill," I replied while pushing my arms through the sleeves and zipping the hoodie up. God, it really did smell incredible. If I pulled it up to sniff it, that would make me look like a complete idiot, so I refrained from doing so, but it was hard not to.

"But why would you wear the dickheads jumper?" Colt continued, still frowning at me.

I just shrugged. "Why not?"

"I don't understand you; one minute you wanna bash them, the next you take their sweater to keep warm?"

"So?" I snapped, his attitude throwing me off again.

"So! It's fucking weird," Colt growled back at me.

"Why do you care?" I raised one of my eyebrows at him

"I suppose I don't," Colt snapped and stood up, pushing his tray towards me and storming off.

I watched him walk out the hall. That kid had major issues, I had come to realise. One minute, he was lovely; the next, he was harsh and weird. It was definitely not easy being his friend, but I'd still try.

Fuck it, I was chasing after him, I was starving and I didn't mind sitting alone. Tucking back into my dinner, I was suddenly joined by non-other than the three dickheads.

"You okay, petal?" Linc asked.

"Why wouldn't I be?"

"Anderson seemed to be mad at you for something, that's all." Linc gave back, bumping his shoulder as a friendly gesture into mine, "Just wanted to make sure he wasn't giving you a hard time."

"The only people giving me a hard time at this school are you" I snapped back.

"We're not trying to give you a hard time. We're trying to be your friends." Wyatt joined the conversation.

"You have a funny way of showing it," I glared him down "but thank you for the jumper. I didn't realise how cold it really was in here."

"Anytime, Wildcat."

"Why do you keep calling me Wildcat?" I asked Wyatt.

"Because you remind me of one. You bite, scratch and purr all at the same time."

I didn't miss the innuendo in that sentence. Maybe Wyatt will be down to scratch any itches I have in the future.

"Princess."

I turned my head to the left and looked at Fox. Nicknames were the thing I gathered by now. "Yes, Fox?"

"Did you want to watch a movie with us in our room tonight?' He deadpanned.

My eyebrows shot right up into my hairline.

"You're kidding, right?"

"I don't kid" Fox replied, staring me down.

"Um… No…. But thank you." I replied, "I want to get a start on that essay for English, but maybe another time." I tried and failed to give Fox a sympathetic smile.

"Actually, I wanted to ask you about that book…" Fox started, but a blonde bombshell sat down next to him at that very moment.

"Fox, can I talk to you, please" she smiled at him.

"Seriously, Crystal, I have said *No* more times than I care to" he turned vicious eyes towards her, "In fact, I've told you to stay the hell away from me. I've asked you not to call or message me, and I've asked you to not contact my mother, yet here you are again." His voice started to tremble, and I saw the strain on his throat. That girl must hit a nerve with him in the worst way.

"But I need to talk to you…" she frowned at her lap.

I could tell it was all just an act; she was clearly an ex of his or something like that, and he clearly couldn't stand her. I've never spoken to her before, but I've seen her and her little clique in the halls and bathroom. She wasn't the sharpest tool in the shed, I figured. Either that or she was too clever and calculating.

"Seriously, Fox, I need to talk to you" She kept trying to get his attention. I was watching Fox and felt that he was about two seconds away from flipping out.

"Okay, well, I'm here. Talk quickly," he looked at her with anger and disgust in his beautiful blue eyes.

"In front of everyone?" She gestured to the rest of us.

"Yes, Crystal, here is just fine."

"Okay… well, I'm pregnant" she spat out in a rush, "it's yours." She looked at him with hope in her eyes.

Of course me, being me, burst out laughing, and four sets of eyes turned to me in shock about my outburst.

"What's so funny?" Crystal spat, fuming.

"Oh honey, you're so not pregnant!" I exclaimed while still chuckling. Poor Fox, he looked like someone just slapped his face with a rotten fish. I guess he does not wrap it then, filthy boy.

"Excuse me?" she rose from her seat and tried to intimidate me by hovering over me.

Linc leaned back in his seat, crossed his arms and settled in like he was enjoying the show...

Wyatt was sitting there with his eyes ping-ponging between me and Crystal.

"I heard you in the bathroom yesterday telling your friends you were glad your period finally finished, and now I understand why you came tonight. You can't fool a man into being pregnant if you're bleeding."

With that, Fox turned and faced Crystal, getting up, "Is that true?" He levelled her with a deadly stare.

"I… um…. You're going to pay for this, you slut." Crystal looked down at me, grabbed the water bottle off my tray, and poured it over my face. I turned quickly but not quick enough and ended up with most of it all over me. I jumped up and grabbed her by the collar of her shirt. "Listen, you silly bitch," I started to shout in her face, I heard Linc next to me starting to clap. "Ohhhh girl, you're gonna get it now" he sang at Crystal. "Watch what you're doing, as this was your one and only strike!" I hissed at her further.

Lincoln was wrong. I was not going to touch her. Instead, I let go of her, wiped my face with the sleeve of Wyatt's jumper and ran my tongue along my front teeth, seething with fury in my gut.

I was going to smash her face in, just not right in that moment. She was a lot smaller than me. If I hit her, I might actually do some damage. I was only here for twelve months. I didn't want to be thrown out over a blonde-haired bimbo.

Instead, I turned back to the guys staring at me, "Good night, boys; I'll leave you to deal with your girlfriend, Fox" I stated, turned on my heel and causally walked out of the hall.

The guys didn't say a word, at least not while I could still hear them.

Walking back to my room, I felt the hot prick of tears behind my eyes. I don't care how tough I think I am or how tough I want the world to think I am; being treated like this hurt nonetheless.

I ran out of the dining hall and across the garden with the cobblestone walk paths to the dorm building and up the stairs to my room. I used the fob for my lock and closed the door behind me as the tears started. I hated it when people got to me. The boys were dicks at the best of times, but me still being so drawn to them, Colt making it hard to like him, and now Crystal was a little too much. I could fight, sure, but that didn't mean I was a beast. My loud mouth was the wall I had put up so no one could see I had feelings, too.

I removed my gym gear and hung Wyatt's jumper on the radiator attached to the wall. Hopefully, it would dry quickly. Then I headed for the shower. I scrubbed my hair and myself, and then I sat on the floor of the shower and sobbed, Fucking boys. This was why I root and boot. This shit is just too complicated for me. And ex-girlfriends are nothing I wanted to get in the middle of, either.

Once the tears had stopped, I got out of the shower, wrapped my hair in a towel and dried my body off. I walked out into my room butt naked to get dressed. Gosh, it was cold. I had to put the heating on higher.

I grabbed a pair of pyjamas out of my drawer, quickly got dressed and checked if Wyatt's jumper was dry. Thankfully, it was, so I threw it back on and pulled his collar to my face. The smell of him soothed something in my soul.

Climbing into my bed, an early night might do me some good. I could start that essay on Wuthering Heights the next day. I curled on my side and closed my eyes as my phone beeped. Grabbing it off my nightstand, I saw a text from my mum. She found me a trainer. He'd be here daily from Monday at 5 a.m. So early morning training sessions it was. I was excited to get some of these frustrations out of me.

I closed my eyes again and drifted off to sleep, wrapped in Wyatt's scent and thinking about the boys.

Chapter 18

Lincoln Baker

I think I've cracked my petal now, she was all tough exterior, but when that psycho bitch Crystal threw the drink at Ivy, I saw her eyes. I saw a speck of defeat in them. I was sure we all had pushed her to her limit. That prick Anderson left her in an angry bout, too, fuck knows what that cunt is pissed about now. He needed to go.

Ivy stormed out of the dining hall, and I had a bitter taste from it.

Fox was still arguing with Crystal, so I pulled Wyatt over and told him what I had in mind. It was risky, but the whole Ivy thing wasn't going to plan anyway.

Wyatt was, of course, on board, so we got up and left. I felt shit for leaving Fox behind with the crazy bitch, but he needed to put a stop to her once and for all.

Wyatt texted him what we were about to do while we were heading upstairs, and if he could, he'd join us, I'm sure.

The key fob worked perfectly. Thanks admin.
I wasn't nervous but uneasy. I needed to do what we were about to do, but losing her for good if this went south was an unsettling thought. With only the light on Wyatt's phone, we entered her darkened room.
The slow, soft breaths from her bed to our left told us she was sleeping. Fuck, what were we doing?
Couldn't stop now, though.
I gestured to Wyatt to close the door as quietly as possible and made my way over to her bed.
I felt a tight squeeze in my chest, seeing her lying there so sweet and petite. Shit, that girl got me good. I crouched down to her level, careful to not wake her just yet.
As Wyatt approached me, he, too, crouched down, and his eyes told me everything I needed to know. She got to him, too.
I counted to three with my fingers for him to see.
1, 2, 3
Gently, my hand rose to her face, and I traced a finger along her cheek.
"Petal, It's me, don't freak out."

I should've thought this through better as in a nanosecond, I had her fist flying against my jaw, and she had sat bolt upright. For fuck sake.

"Hey…shhh…hey, it's okay Wildcat, it's just us. Calm down," Wyatt soothed her.

Not so sleepy anymore, she sat on her knees, furious and out of breath from the scare we just gave her. I noticed her eyes were red and puffy. Had she been crying?

Her voice trembling, "How in the actual fuck did you get in here? Why are you in here?"

No excuse would smooth this, so I was blunt and honest with her.

"I saw that Crystal got to you, and we were serious with the offer of a movie night. So I thought it'd be okay to come to check on you and see if you wanted some company."

"Didn't I beat your stupid arses, so you would stop doing just that?" She asked in a sarky tone, but I didn't see the usual venom in her eyes. Her teeth raked over her bottom lip in thought, and I wanted to pounce on her.

I had this unexplainable, desperate need to touch her, feel her, smell her. Taste her.

"Fuck a duck," she sighed heavily and covered her eyes with her hands.

"What movie do you guys want to watch?"

Bingo!

I would lie if I said I wasn't surprised she caved so fast; I was ready for another round of punches and snarling.

I sat there looking a little stunned until Wyatt broke the silence.

"Harry Potter?!"

Silence again.

"I love Harry Potter," she finally said back, her hands still covering her face like she didn't want to see or be seen.

"So do I. Which part is your favourite, or should we start with the Philosopher's Stone and watch one every night?"

Her hands dropped into her lap, "I won't get rid of you, will I?" It was more of a statement than a question.

"No, Wildcat, I don't think you will."

At that moment, the door slowly opened, and a rage-filled Fox stomped in.

We all turned our heads to him.

"Good job, we laid the groundwork here, dude, or she would've killed you for prancing in here like an elephant on steroids." I barked at him.

He just shook his head, and I took the hint. Crystal made him fucking mad. Was he being in here a good idea? When he was in one of his rampage moods, he loved to destroy furniture or people's faces.

To brace her from the shit storm that was about to be unleashed, I quickly kicked off my shoes and sat on the bed next to Ivy, who sat with her back to the wall now, her duvet pulled up to her chin.

But nothing came. I watched Fox looking at Ivy, the lights of the TV that she had switched on illuminating the room.

She looked back at him, and something had passed between them as the fire in his eyes dimmed, the frown smoothed out. What the fuck!

In the meantime, Wyatt had taken off his shoes and sat beside her on the other side, flicking the remote until we landed on Harry Potter on demand.

Ivy turned very still when we sat next to her. I couldn't even hear her breathe. Her eyes were fixed on the TV.

Fox walked over and kicked his shoes off, too and then, as casually as if he'd done it a million times before, laid across Ivy's bed in front of her feet. Which she pulled up even further to not touch him

She was sandwiched in between the three of us, still as a statue. And that's how we started to watch the movie.

Around the time when Hagrid came to get Harry off that shitty island, I felt her relax next to me. Slouching down a bit to get more comfortable, but still very aware not to touch Fox with her feet.

The longer the film played, the more the tension had left the room.

When Harry joined the Quidditch team, I started to draw tiny circles with my finger on her hand. I couldn't help it. She didn't flinch; she pretended it wasn't happening and kept her eyes glued to the film.

I took my chances and ventured further, up her bare arm. The goosebumps came immediately, and from my periphery, I saw her face blush a little.

Wyatt, knowing me better than I knew myself, took the cue and gently reached out to her duvet-covered leg. Tracing it up and down. At this point, she gave up I thought, as she started to ease herself into our touches ever so slightly. I ventured up her arm to her neck, causing more goosebumps, but she didn't blush this time. She fucking closed her eyes. That squeeze in my chest came back. Something about this girl…

I took a chance and pushed her a tiny bit forward to reach her shoulder, stroking every part of the exposed skin. She let go of the duvet, and it fell below her tits. Through the thin fabric of her top, I could see her perky nipples. Fuck me.

I tried not to get distracted and carried on with my soft assault on her skin, Wyatt on the other side of her doing the same. It was intimate, definitely way more intimate than my brothers and I ever were with a girl together before. Usually, without very little foreplay, we fucked a girl, and that was that. With Ivy, it felt different. I felt different.

Her eyes still closed, she leaned her head toward me, and I gave her my shoulder to rest on while stroking the back of her neck. Wyatt took a gamble, brushed the hair from her face and shoulder and leaned down to kiss her neck. The way I could feel her shudder beneath me had my dick so hard that I was worried it would punch through my pants.

All the while this was happening, Fox lay still in front of us, watching the film. At one point, I thought he had fallen asleep, but a shift of his head, balanced on his hand to look at us, disproved it.

We didn't go any further that night; Wyatt and I just made her feel good and safe with our strokes on her soft skin. She gave us little moans as barter, and I swear I have never heard anything so erotic in my life. Fox never got involved, however, and I wondered what his freaking problem was.

By the film's end, Wyatt and I had worked her into a pliant, soft kitten, and she fell asleep on my shoulder. I knew she was exhausted. I was okay with her being asleep. I was okay with what happened between us. I was aware that it also changed everything now.

Chapter 19

Ivy Alexander

"Beep, beep, beep, beep" Reaching out to grab my phone with closed eyes to turn the alarm off, I collide with something warm. Something that wasn't my bedside table. Quickly leaning back, I ran into something warm behind me, too.
"Morning Wildcat"
"Wyatt?" I ask, confused, opened my eyes and looked dead straight into steal grey ones.
"What are you doing in my bed?" I looked at him dumbfounded.
"We all fell asleep watching the movie," Wyatt stated as he wrapped his arm around my middle and snuggled back into sleep.
Looking to my left, I see Lincoln asleep.
"Beep, beep, beep"

I elbowed Linc, "Lincoln, hand me my phone."

I watched as his arm shot out; he patted away at my bedside blindly until he reached the phone and handed it to me. Looking down at the screen, I saw a picture of me and Linc. One from when I beat the boys up in the gym. It was me kissing Linc…

"Um, Linc, I think this is your phone," I handed it back with a small shriek. "Can you please hand me mine?"

Linc's hand shot out again, this time he got my phone and passed it back to me.

"Here, Princess," he said in a heavy, sleepy tone, then settled back into sleep.

What the ever-loving fuck was going on? Did I wake up in an alternate universe? Don't get me wrong, waking up with two boys in your bed was what I would call a good night, but I didn't say *they* could stay. And what the fuck was Linc's phone wallpaper about? I could only guess one of the boys took the photo when we were in the gym, but why was it his wallpaper? I had more questions than answers today. I needed a run.

Sliding out of Wyatt's hold on me, I slipped off the end of the bed, grabbed my running gear from the wardrobe and headed into my bathroom to get ready.

When I emerged, I saw Wyatt was gone, but Lincoln was still fast asleep. I didn't bother to wake him. What was the point? He clearly had a fob to my room; letting himself in and out didn't seem to be an issue for him, so fuck it. I just left him there as I walked out my door and closed it behind me.

From my periphery, I saw Fox coming out of their room and turned to look at him. He was dressed in training gear. He just looked at me and smiled.

Like actually smiling at me, I clearly woke up in a different universe. There was no other explanation.

"Princess," he said in greeting, nodding in my direction, "did you wanna join me for a run?"

I held my hand up in the universal stop sign.

"Stop. Just stop." Taking a breath, I looked at him.

"Clearly, I've woken up in Narnia "cause I have two boys in my bed, and now you are being nice…"

Fox laughed at me. Like a full-on heartfelt laugh. Fuck, it was super cute. The way the morning light hit his face through the window as he laughed, illuminating those blue eyes. They were shining bright like the ocean.

"Princess, if you haven't worked out that those two idiots like you, then maybe you're not as smart as you seem."

With that admission, he just walked past but stopped before he reached the stairwell to whistle over his shoulder, "Come on, hurry up. I gotta be down to start row training in ten minutes."

Oh great, we're back to normal now. I'll follow along like a lassie.

"Did you just whistle at me?" I asked him, "I'm not a fucking dog!"

I sprinted to catch up to him, why I didn't know, I was clearly broken somewhere.

He turned his head when I caught up and looked down at me.

"Listen, I wanted to say thank you for yesterday; I would have believed the girl was pregnant if you hadn't said something," he said while rubbing a hand over his neck. Clearly saying Thank you to someone wasn't something this legacy was used to.

"No need to thank me; she clearly misses a few marbles. I can see the original appeal, though she's very hot."

"I was only thinking with my dick when it came to her." He sighed. Wow, blunt honesty. I liked him like this.

"Well, admitting you have an issue is the first step," I smirked.

"Has anyone ever told you, you're a prickly bitch?" He replied

"All the time," I shrugged "but I don't care."

With that last statement, I took off in a jog, heading towards the river, with Fox hot on my tail.

After fifteen minutes of silent running, another person joined us, Wyatt.

"Morning, Wildcat," he said, his dark hair wet from the shower.

"Morning" I puff back " I take it you are here for row practice?"

"Sure am."

"Wanna race?" I asked and took off in a sprint towards the shed by the river that housed the rowing equipment I gathered. I needed the pain of running to clear my head; these three were starting to consume me, and I needed a break.

Actually, what I needed to do was fuck them out of my system and move on.

Just as the river shed appeared, I saw blonde hair zoom past me. Fuck, Fox was fast.

Suited his name.

The second his feet landed on the shore of the riverbank, he turned around and raised his arms in the air like he just won a marathon, bowed at us.

Stopping next to him, I leaned over to gather my breath. "Dude, you're fast!" I said to him, inhaling big gulps of air.

"These long legs come in handy," he joked.

Not two seconds later, Wyatt skidded to a halt next to us. "Shit, I'm gonna have to up my cardio. I cannot have you two beating me," his face in a dumbfounded expression.

I shook my head at him, "Anyhow, I'm off, gotta finish my lap," and turned to run off.

"Wildcat?" Wyatts called.

Turning around, I looked at him.

"Have breakfast with me?" He looked at me sheepishly.

I looked at Fox, who was standing next to Wyatt, his eyebrows drawn together like this wasn't typical Wyatt's behaviour. Was he telling me the truth before when he said Wyatt and Linc liked me? Did I want them to like me?

Maybe, I thought to myself and just headed off without giving Wyatt an answer.

I needed a bit of space to think.

Taking off the way Colt had shown me, I continued running, trying to sort out my thoughts.

First, I was going to ask Linc for my fob; I didn't particularly appreciate knowing they could come and go from my room as they pleased. Second, I would set some boundaries, like staying over in my room, in my bed. I hadn't approved that. I didn't mind it, but I hadn't said it was okay, either. Third, I needed to get off campus this weekend; I needed some new wrappings for my hands for boxing on Monday morning. I also needed to check out car dealerships and get to the shops to stock my room with protein bars. Wyatt handed me one nearly every lesson we had together, claiming he liked me nice and not hangry. The ones they had in the cafeteria were horrible. I needed my favourite type, or ask Wyatt where he got his from.

Maybe I could ask Wyatt at breakfast time? The thought of having breakfast with Wyatt made me nervous. The boy was hot. All that messy dark hair that was the perfect length to run your hands through, and the size of his dick, oh yes, that one I remember well after he pushed my core over the top of it in the gym. Fuck me, I was gonna have to take care of myself when I finished this run. It had been a long time since I had burnt off that kind of steam.

My brain was in a crazy overthinking mode. Maybe my period was due soon, and that's why I was so indecisive and all over the place.

God, I needed to get my head together. Clearly, this run had clouded it further when I had been trying to clear it instead. Turning the corner, I saw the ornate double doors of the housing building coming into view and Colt, dressed in this running gear, standing to the side having a heated discussion with Crystal. I never thought these two were friends.

Who knew that boy was so hot and cold?

Running past him and Crystal through the doors, I headed back up to my room, only slowing down so I wasn't full-out jogging through the halls. It only took me a few minutes to reach my room in my haste state. I ran the fob on the pad, opened the door, and found Linc still fast asleep and snoring slightly in my bed. He did look cute, all spread out on my bed like that. His body was so tall his feet were dangling off the end, and his head was a bit further down from the headboard.

Walking over to him, I poked him in the shoulder. "Lincoln, you gotta wake up, dude; we got class in an hour."

He opened one eye and looked up at me, "Nope, I'm taking the day off" and closed his eye again.

"Okay, well, take the day off in your own bed," I poked him again.

Whipping his arm out, Linc grabbed my hand so fast I didn't see it coming. And that was saying something. It made me wonder if he had been holding back on me this whole time. That he was faster, more agile and powerful than I had thought. His body sure looked like it.

Pulling me into him by my wrist, he grabbed me around the waist with his other arm and pulled me down on top of his resting form. I let out the sound of a strangled kitten as it happened.

"Linc, what the fuck?" I managed to grumble from where my face was smashed into his chest.

"Just stay here with me," he grumbled back. Oh boy, his scent was all-consuming, Cedarwood and leather. His body felt incredible against mine, and I had to work really hard not to give in. He was counting on it, I was sure.

"Dude, I'm all sweaty and gross from running; I also didn't say you could touch me." I lied.

"I know, but I don't care," he replied as he shoved his nose in my hair and took a big breath.

"Dude, what the fuck, that's gross. I stink," I exclaimed, trying to push up from where Linc had managed to pin me to his front. I could feel his morning wood poking me in the belly from this position. It felt big, like 'holy shit that is too big for me' big. I tried wiggling around for a minute until I realised wiggling was what he wanted. So, instead, I just went limp. If I couldn't get out of the hold, what was the point in moving around on top of that log between his legs?

"Stay in bed with me today, baby." He mumbled while maintaining the iron grip he had on me.

"I have class."

"So? They don't care if you skip a day or two."

"I didn't fly across the ocean just to wag school. I actually came for the education." Determination in my voice.

"Please," he asked so quietly I wasn't sure I heard him correctly.

"Why do you want me to wag so badly?" I asked him.

"I just want to spend the day with you," he replied, and my heart rate picked up, I hoped he couldn't feel it.

"You do realise tomorrow is Saturday, right? We have no school on Saturday and Sunday, can't we hang out then?" I asked.

"Of course, we can, and yes, I would love to hang out with you for the weekend," Linc declared as he let go of my body and sat up in bed.

Throwing his legs off the side of the bed, he walked straight out of my room, called back, "See you at breakfast," and closed the door.

Oh my god, he baited me into spending the weekend with him.

That manipulative shit.

He played me, and I walked right into it.

He was clever, too clever. I had to remember that in the future.

Chapter 20

Wyatt Forester

Ivy was falling into my trap deeper by the minute. The issue I had with it was that I kept forgetting about the bet at times. I had to keep my head in the game. But her stupidly beautiful eyes and how they looked at me had me feeling things I don't usually feel.

She agreed to breakfast in her own little way, and this weird feeling in my gut had me on edge. I felt odd, lighter. If this bet wasn't settled soon, I would have to go to London to get off. Again, though, this unknown feeling inside me piped up, and it made me regret even thinking about going back to that place. I was probably coming down with a cold or something. There was no other explanation for this weirdness inside me.

I scared off some year 10s to get a table by the heaters. Ivy would probably be cold, and the last thing my libido needed was to acknowledge her perfect, perky nipples. The thought of them alone made my cock rock solid and straining against my trousers. This bet needed to be won this weekend or else.

Before I even saw her, her scent invaded my nostrils, making my hard-on painful. She had the sweetest smell about her: vanilla and honey. It was intoxicating.

My mouth began to water, and my thoughts trailed to her pussy. How she'd taste. How she'd squirm when I had her bound…

"Hey" Her voice pulled me back.

Readjusting my dick under the table, I turned my head to look at her.

"Morning… Again… Hungry?"

She looked at me and followed down to where my hand was fumbling under the table to sort my dick out before I got up and showed the whole school at breakfast what I had packing.

"You got crabs?" She asked in the most sarcastic tone and winked at me with a wicked smile. Those green eyes shone bright. I desperately needed to fuck her out of my system, fast.

"Funny, but no, I wasn't scratching, just rearranging positions. Bit tight in there." I teased back. She looked unimpressed, rolled her eyes at me and turned to walk up to the food counter. I had a quick thought of my old maths teacher in Primary school, Ms Wendall, and thankfully my cock went soft instantly. I got up and followed Ivy to the line. Out of my periphery, I saw the door fling open and Linc and Fox waltzing in. I bobbed my head to show them what table I had chosen; Fox beelined for it immediately and sat down in a slump. Linc joined me, and we both had to push another few year 10s out of the way to stand behind Ivy in the queue. Linc turned so his back was facing the tables and no one could see him running a finger sideways along the small of her back.

Wildcat flinched and turned to him with a glare, "I thought we covered the touching without my consent?"

Linc put on a sheepish face that was probably panty-melting to every girl in this school, but no, not to my wildcat. "You didn't mind last night…"

Checkmate.

She thought about a comeback for a second but only replied quietly, "Let's not do this in public" and stepped forward as the line had moved along.

We all grabbed some food, and I grabbed some eggs and fruit for Fox too. He must've been in one of his moods again if he didn't line up with us.

As we sat and started eating, Ivy asked me about the protein bars I had supplied her last week.

Fox's mind absent but still listening to our conversation, explained to her where they were being sold and that the three of us could take her this weekend to stock up.

Surprisingly, she agreed without a fuss, and the mood changed into a comfortable one; even Fox had taken part in our conversations.

By the end of breakfast, we also agreed to carry on our Harry Potter movie marathon, continuing with the second film, The Chamber of Secrets, that evening. When we told her we could get her into the HP studios with a special VIP tour, Ivy nearly jumped out of her seat ecstatically and made us promise we'd take her. The dynamic between us had changed drastically, and it felt so natural. Just Fox was his usual distant self, but he didn't give her any hassle, so I took that as a win.

What got to me the most during the breakfast was the looks she gave us. Sweet, seductive and hungry. Like a changed person, she seemed to finally let us in.

The day passed quickly, and I caught myself rushing around, eager to start our movie night in Ivy's room.

I was just about to head for the shower after I had come back up to our room after the last class when Linc hauled us in for a chat.

"Does Ivy seem different, or is that just me?" He'd asked.

Fox nodded, chewing on an apple, "She probably wants to fuck us now of her own volition. Like every girl does."

"I don't think that's just it." I said, "She sort of fits into our little circle."

Linc piped up, "He's right. She doesn't act like the girls that throw themselves at us. She seems to fit us like a glove."

Fox shrugged his shoulders, ever totally uninterested. However, I did notice how he looked at her. He might think he can pretend to be anything but interested in fucking her, but I know my brother. Sometimes, I know him better than he knows himself. Being brothers officially by marriage soon was still something he and I had to sort out, but as our parents proclaimed they weren't going to rush into marriage but instead wanted a summer one next year, I was hopeful for now, we could solely focus on rowing, school … and…Ivy. Fuck, this feeling in my gut was agitating.

I needed to address one more thing with them before we went forward.

"So, no matter who wins this bet, are we still all right in sharing her after?" I looked at my two best friends with certainty in my eyes.

"Sure," Fox replied immediately, acting like he didn't care.

Linc nodded, getting dressed into his sweats and tee for the evening ahead.

"Absolutely," He said after putting on some sneakers.

With that being agreed on, I headed for the shower.

In anticipation of the evening ahead but knowing I couldn't push for sex with her just yet, I had nothing left, but to do it myself under the shower.

I thought about her in front of me, on her knees, her arms tied neatly behind her back. Waiting eagerly for my commands. My cock was painfully hard, and leaning with my back against the wall, my shaft in my hand, I pumped. My visions of her in my head changed from her being underneath me, moaning my name, to looking at me with pure lust in those beautiful eyes. And I shot my cum all across the shower floor, grunting. Angling the shower head so I could wash it down the drain, the picture of her underneath me wouldn't leave my mind, and I set myself the goal of fucking her by latest next weekend. My hunger for her was too intense. I needed to fuck her out of my system.

That *peng* in my gut exposing my own lie.

I quickly dried and got dressed, eager to start the evening. The responsiveness of Ivy to my touches last night made me hard again. Of course, I wanted to fuck her bad. But there was something about just stroking her skin, her tiny sighs and the goosebumps. I needed that again.

"Let's take her to Guildford to get some protein bars tomorrow. I've overheard her talking about getting a car; we should take her to look around for that, too. I need to get off school grounds for a while anyway. This place is giving me cage syndrome at the moment." Fox explained to us.

"Sounds like a plan." Linc and I replied in unison.

Then, the three of us headed out.

Chapter 21

Lincoln Baker

Some might think sharing a girl with your best friends is wrong. I mean, we have shared a lot of pussy before, but not one we actually liked until Ivy.

And that's the truth of this situation now, we liked Ivy; well, I know I did. In fact, I wanted to keep her, as in keeping her as my girlfriend. Even Wyatt, with his kind of kinks, wanted her, and the closer he got to her, the more I knew he was starting to feel the same. Fox was going to be the issue. Fox didn't keep anything permanently. Crystal was the closest he had ever gotten to a girl before, and even then, it was pure sexual attraction. He never once spoke very friendly to her, never took her out, never did anything with her other than fucking. He was different with Ivy, but I was curious if he could maintain it long-term.

Only time will tell.

We headed over to Ivy's room at 6 p.m. as we had planned; Wyatt grabbed some snacks we had stacked in our room and a few cans of soda. We were due a trip into town to grab more, so this weekend's trip was working out to be fruitful.

I knocked on Ivy's door this time and waited for her to open it.

"Now you knock?" She opened the door and tilted her head like a puppy. She wore the cutest matching shorts and singlet set; you could see she had no bra on.

"I was trying to respect your boundaries, Ivy," I said as I leaned down to kiss her cheek. I watched as a flush creeped up her face instantly. God damn, she was cute.

"Well, come on in and make yourself at home," she said, swinging the door wide.

Wyatt laughed. "Gosh, your inviting friendliness is scary."

"Come in, kind Sir" she replied, "please take a seat. Would you like a cup of tea and a finger sandwich?" The atrocious attempt at an English accent had me doubling over in a fit of laughter.

Wyatt looked at her with his eyebrows drawn so low his eye's were about to close, "Has anyone ever told you, you suck at accents?"

Laughing, she grabbed a pillow off the floor and threw it at him. "Yes, actually, all the time!" she started laughing. Fox shook his head but chuckled, too.

With that, we all settled in and put on the movie. It turned out the night before was a fluke with Ivy being so quiet. Because she just about quoted the whole Harry Potter film out loud word for word. What surprised me the most was that Fox joined in a few times; I wasn't sure he even realised he had done it himself. We had taken the same seating arrangement that we had before. Wyatt on her right, me on her left, and Fox at our feet. We had the perfect position to continue with small touches and drawing patterns on her skin. Every touch was rewarded with goosebumps or small hitches in her breath. It wasn't until Wyatt leaned in and kissed her softly on her lips that she let out a small moan.

The moan drew Fox's attention; he rolled over and looked at us, reaching out his arm to run his finger up her leg toward her knee. A slight shiver ran through her body, and she let out a much louder moan.

Taking that as my cue, I leaned in, ran my tongue around her ear lobe, and nipped the flesh. I noticed she was rubbing her legs together to gain some friction on her pussy, the little mouse was loving this attention.

"Did you want me to help with that?" I asked, running my hand up her thigh and towards her heat.

"Yes," She breathed.

Then she groaned as Wyatt brushed his fingertips over her stiff nipple.

Fuck me, I was gonna cum in my pants like this.

Fox sat up and grabbed both her legs to spread them wide, placing one of her feet on his left hip and the other on his right. Opening up her legs for easier access.

"Is it normal for you to share a girl?" She asked as Fox started trailing his hands up the inside of her legs.

"We have before," he answered her.

"But only in one-time occurrences, it's different with you. We wanna keep you." I whispered into her ear.

"Keep me?" She asked, with a look of confusion on her face.

She was about to ask another question when Wyatt ran his hand right over her pussy. A loud moan wrung from her mouth, which I captured with my own. Licking her lips, I asked for entry.

She opened them, allowing me to massage her tongue with my own. Her moans grew deeper, making me pull away from her mouth so I could watch how Wyatt was making her feel.

He pulled the crotch of her shorts to the side, revealing no underwear, as I had guessed. He traced a fingertip up and down and then between her slit, opening her slightly and running gentle circles around her clit.

She started squirming and bucking her hips to meet Wyatt's touches. She was so responsive.

Fox placed his arms under her knees, drawing her further toward him and giving Wyatt better access. Who then pushed a finger into her core, "Fuck. Oh God" she moaned and rolled her hips. Wyatt gave her slow pumps, adding a second finger, rubbing tight circles on her clit, and I could tell Ivy wasn't very far off her climax. Her breaths came quicker, and she grabbed my arm tightly for purchase. Her eyes were closed, her bottom lip between her teeth. That sight of her alone drove me wild. But Wyatt wasn't generous to her; he pulled his fingers out before she could fall over the edge. He then lifted them to his mouth and sucked them clean.

"Wildcat, you taste so damn good," he said as he leaned in to kiss her so she could taste herself. Her nails dug into my arm; she needed to get off.

Fox reached forward, stroking her sensitive skin on the inside of her thighs. He had that look on his face that hunger; he needed her just as much. She lifted her head to him, and with her eyes, she showed him how desperate she was for his touch. He dropped her feet that were placed by his hips, got to his knees and, without another warning, plunged two fingers inside her. She bucked, and I thought for a moment she'd lift off the bed. He had her writhing. But Fox was unkind to her too, and after a few shallow pumps, he let her go too. As Wyatt, Fox lifted his fingers to his mouth to taste Ivy. If looks could speak, we would have discovered right there that Ivy had clawed her way inside him.

I couldn't hold myself back any longer; I needed to know what she tasted like. I ran my hand down into her shorts; I felt the clean-shaven pussy, and her wet heat. Pushing a finger into her, I found her drenched. I added a second, then a third as I finger fucked her. I pumped into her much slower than Fox had, wanting to commit every bump, every grove of the inside of her pussy to memory. I hooked my fingers, and that was her undoing.

"Oh god, Linc." she moaned, "Go faster!"

Wyatt reached down with mine and circled her clit, inviting tiny cries of pleasure to emit from her. No more than a few seconds until I could feel her core tightening.

"Please don't stop," She begged and rolled her hips to meet every thrust of my fingers.

Wyatt started to lick and bite her nipple while rubbing her clit faster. That's all it took, that small bite of pain and she fell. Her pussy walls tightened around my fingers, making it hard for me to push them in.

Once we had worked her through it, and she was nothing but a shaking form, I pulled my fingers free and licked and sucked them clean. Wyatt wasn't lying; she tasted fucking amazing.

"Fuck" she breathed, as she slumped against the wall with her back.

"Three is definitely the magic number!" she mumbled.

Just as I was about to answer her, there was a knock on her door.

"Are you expecting anyone?" I asked, looking at her limp body, aftershocks convulsing through her still.

"Nope," she said quietly, not fully back with us.

"I'll get it." Fox jumped up and opened the door, only to find Crystal standing there, her eyes blown wide as she realised Fox was standing in Ivy's doorway.

"What the fuck are doing in there?" She tried to push past him into the room, but Fox threw his arm against the door frame, blocking her view inside.

'None of your business!" he smiled at her and tried to close the door.

"Bullshit. None of my business," she screamed back. "You are mine, you hear me? I have a right to know what you are doing in the skank's room!"

Before I could stop her, Ivy jumped off the bed and walked to her door. "What do you want, Crystal?"

"Well, I was actually looking for Fox and came to see if you knew where he was! Why is my boyfriend in your room, slut?" Crystal spat.

"Well, you found him. But call me a slut once more, and I rearrange your face. Now, fuck off." Ivy raised her brows at Crystal, but her voice was steady and calm.

Crystal gave Ivy her best resting bitch face, one that pulled most of the sheep that followed her in line, but not Ivy. She just glared straight back. Ready to pounce if Crystal made one wrong move.

"Do hurry up; I was watching Harry Potter, and the Basilisk was busy slithering through the pipes," Ivy said so nonchalantly it made me laugh.

"Oh great, you're all in there" she pointed into the darkened room towards my laugh.

"Seriously, Crystal, get it over with; what do you want? I was busy." Fox exclaimed as he crossed his arms.

"I came to tell you that your mother was very interested to hear about our pregnancy" She smiles like the nut job she was.

Fox leaned in so close to Crystal you could almost mistake it for a kiss and said, "As I said yesterday, I don't believe you; I also don't care; even if you are, it's not mine, so find someone else to leach off!"

Without hesitation, Crystal swung back to slap Fox across the face.

Ivy instantly grabbed her hand mid-air, twisted her arm backwards and pulled her wrist halfway up her back to restrain the girl.

"Ouch, you fucking slut, let me go!" Crystal cried out.

"With pleasure," Ivy replied sarcastically, pushing Crystal forward. She landed on the carpet out front of Ivy's room on her knees, barely catching herself as she descended.

Turning on her heel, Ivy walked back into her room and grabbed the door handle. Fox took a step back so Ivy could slam it shut on Crystal.

"You really gotta deal with that bitch." Ivy mumbled and rushed back to the bed to take her place between me and Wyatt.

"Hand me the popcorn, would you," Wyatt spoke like nothing had happened.

And that was when we all curled up on Ivy's bed and finished the movie. The only difference was Ivy kicked us out when it ended and told us to find her in the morning so we could head into town for supplies.

Chapter 22

Ivy Alexander

Fuck. If I hadn't kicked them out, I would've let all three of them go to town on me.

Not being shy at all with my sexuality but also not too slutty, I thought it best at the time to have them leave. Being alone and not fully satisfied made me regret my decision quickly.

I wasn't sure what was happening, but I was convinced I wanted them all.

I was also infamous for making very rash decisions, and not two minutes later, I had my phone in my hand and texted Lincoln. I had noticed that sly mother fucker had added all of their contacts in my phone the day he stole it in class.

Another three minutes later, there was a knock on my door. I was prepared that it might be Crystal, so I asked before opening the door. Thankfully, it was Lincoln. "What's up, petal?" He asked. But I wasn't in the mood to talk. I was in the mood for him. Without giving him an answer, I grabbed the top of his t-shirt and yanked him into my room, pressing my lips against his. He didn't try to get away from me, quite the opposite. His lips played around mine, his tongue licking the seam of my mouth, asking, begging for entry. His big hands grabbed me around my waist, lifting me up. I locked my legs around his middle, Never breaking the kiss. At this point, the foreplay seemed to have been the days of us tormenting each other, not wanting much more. Or so I thought.

Linc broke the kiss, and out of breath, he began, "Not so fast, princess." His hands squeezed my butt, and I felt his hard cock pressed against my core. I started to wiggle, wanting more, but he placed me back on my feet, "We're not doing the 'wham bam, thank you ma'am thing here, petal!'

"Why not?" I protested.

"Because I like you, and like I said before, I want to keep you."

"What do you even mean by that Linc?" Getting agitated now, "You want me to be your girlfriend? I'm not doing that, mate!"

"I never said that either." Grabbing my chin and pulling me close again. His forehead leaned against mine, his eyes boring into mine. My knees started to buckle. I also felt a bit more for him, but I would never tell him that!

Him telling me that they wanted to keep me had me weak, but I'd never show them that. No guy would ever have that leverage over me, let alone three guys simultaneously.

I wanted sex, and I wanted it now, with him, then with the others. Preferably, no strings attached from my side. That couldn't be so hard now, could it?

"Can we not just fuck and see where this goes?"

His low chuckle made me feel a little stupid, and I quirked my eyebrow at him in dismay.

His fingers stroking my cheek, he said, "Yes, I want to do that, but I want it slow."

Good lord.

Not knowing what else to say, I pushed up on my toes and started our kiss again; he didn't stop me this time.

Grabbing the hem of my top, he pulled it up over my head and threw it behind him onto the floor while we stepped closer to my bed.

I had the back of my knees touching the side of it. Our kiss intensified, and I felt lost inside my own head. He grabbed the small of my back and slowly lowered me onto the bed, with my head stretching slightly backwards. He took that opportunity to trace his tongue along my neck. When he reached my chin, he blew softly on the slick trail he had left. Fireworks were exploding inside me, and I needed to feel, smell, and touch him. Now!

My hands were tracing his muscular back, his grip on me so tight that I didn't have to worry about losing my balance.

Once he had laid me down, he shrugged out of his tee in record time, hovering over me again.

His eyes were like magnetic pools I lost myself in.

"Fuck. You are beautiful," a shiver running down my spine at his words.

My hand reached up to his dark hair, tussling it.

"You're not so bad yourself, Mr Baker," he smiled and if I had panties on, they would've melted right off me in that very moment.

Ready to not waste any more precious time, my hands wandered to his jeans, and I started to pop his buttons while Linc traced kisses down the side of my neck, gently biting the soft skin behind my ear. Moans escaped me, and I had to pull myself together and concentrate on getting him out of his jeans. He helped me, and by the time he was out of them, I had ripped my shorts off of myself.

He was huge.

He was significantly more oversized than I expected, but I was eager to see how well he fit inside me. My feral side was taking over; I grabbed his cock with my hand and started slow pumps.

The growl that came deep from within his throat had my head spinning. There was nothing that turned me on more than a guy that makes noise. I was not too fond of a silent one.

Grabbing my hips again, Linc pushed me further up the bed, and I lost his cock from my hand.

Without a warning, his hands went under my knees and pushed them up and apart. I was spread wide for him, and from the hungry in his eyes, I could tell he liked what he saw.

"Lay back, this will take a while." He practically growled at me.

I did what I was told and suddenly felt his finger tracing my slit, slowly spreading my slick lips.

His head lifted slightly to look at me. "Are you wet for me?"

I nodded erratically, grappling the sheet beneath my hands in desperate anticipation.

"Let me see." He whispered against my core, his breath touching the sensitive skin between my legs.

His finger plunged between my lips, and a moan escaped him. He ran his finger up to my clit, and I grabbed the sheet tighter. Running circles ever so slowly against my clit had me whimpering. I rolled my hips to match his movement and to add more friction.

He replaced his finger on my clit with his thumb, and I felt the tip of his tongue at my entrance, teasing me with tiny circles.

"Shit. More!" I begged, bucking my hips toward him.

His other hand found my hip, and he pushed me back down. "Shhh" I felt him say against my core more than I could hear him. The vibration of his voice made my knees tremble.

His tongue licked its way up from my entrance to my clit, stopping there to lick and suck.

I knew it wouldn't take me long now; I was that crazy about him making me cum.

I felt two of his fingers pressing against my entrance, easing in. "You're so fucking tight petal!" He said between licking and sucking my clit.

That turned me on so much that it didn't take much longer before I felt all my muscles clench.

Euphoria took over while his fingers stroked my walls. He must've felt that I was close as he hooked his fingers and rubbed my sweet spot until I shattered beneath him. I convulsed, sucking his fingers deeper into me.

My moans grew louder, and not wanting to wake the whole wing, I covered myself with a pillow.

Linc didn't let up, though, rubbing that sweet spot inside my pussy until I rode that last wave of my climax.

When he was convinced I was back down from my high, he withdrew his fingers, moved them up to his mouth and sucked them clean.

Seeing him like that made me need him inside of me.

I pushed up on my elbows and reached for his neck between my legs. I pulled him up higher for a kiss.

I could taste my arousal and cum on his tongue.

He pushed us both down without breaking the kiss, positioning his cock by my entrance.

And without any warning, he pushed inside me to the hilt. He was bigger than any guy I had before, and it took my breath away for a second.

"OK?" He asked, and I nodded after a second, adjusting my position.

He started moving, pushing his veiny dick deeper with every thrust.

But it wasn't a quick fuck; it was hard, slow and intense.

"I need you to cum for me again, princess," he spurred me on. "I need to feel you squeeze me tight."

The room was quiet, only our soft moans and skin slapping to be heard. I wrapped my legs around Linc's waist to feel him deeper.

He hit spots inside of me I never felt before, and with two more hard thrusts, I went over the edge. I squirmed underneath him, moaning and panting.

"Fuck, Linc" I breathed out, my lips trembling, my back arching.

I felt how I clenched around him.

"God, Ivy Fuck, look at me," he growled.

I had my eyes shut tight, riding the waves of my high.

His face was so close to mine when I opened them that I could barely make him out.

But he lifted his head slightly and stared into my eyes with such intensity that I felt a squeeze inside my chest that made me blink a few times. All I wanted to do was keep them shut.

His hands were wrapped behind me, holding my shoulders to keep me in place.

"Look... At... Me." His husky voice demanded, and I focused back on his stare.

He gave a few more deep punches and then stiffened. With a loud moan ripping free from his throat, his eyes never leaving mine, he came deep inside of me. Breathless, he collapsed on top of me.

Chapter 23

Lincoln Baker

"Fuck, petal." I moaned into her neck. That was possibly the best sex I've ever had, and I've had a lot of it. It wasn't even crazy insane sex. It was plain missionary. But the connection we shared and my feelings for her felt much more intense than I had before.

Since the little Australian Princess had arrived, I had been totally consumed by her. I hadn't even noticed any other girls at the school since. This was totally out of character for me. But to be honest, I was digging it.

I know she said, *"Can we not just fuck and see where this goes?"* And I agreed at the time, but I was keeping her. She was ours. If the others didn't want her long-term, that was okay because I did. She was mine; she just didn't know it yet.

"Okay, you gotta move, you're squishing me," she mumbled into my neck.

"Sorry," I laughed and pushed myself up. Reaching down, I grabbed my dick and slipped out of her, and that's when I noticed I wasn't wearing a condom. Fuck.

"Um, petal, we didn't use a condom," I said with shock, anxiety already building in my gut.

Pulling her own eyebrows together, "Shit, I honestly didn't even think of it at that moment" she rushes out, "fuck I hope you're clean!" She glared at me.

Laughing at her, "Oh Princess, I'm clean; I've never fucked anyone bare, not once." I was starting to realise this was more than likely why it felt so dam good.

"Neither have I!" She stated

"Please tell me you're on the pill, petal; I'm too young and hot to be a dad just yet!" I groaned, sitting back on my feet as I kneeled before her.

"Of course I am. Have been since I was 14; I know condoms are like 99 per cent safe, but that one per cent is too much of a chance for me," she said as she pulled herself into a sitting position.

"Also, what does *hot* have to do with being a dad? If you hand a regular-looking guy a baby, he instantly looks better…. Hand a hot one a kid, and every woman's ovaries will explode," she smirked at me.

"Really?" I frowned

"Wanna test it out?" She teased me.

"Nope," I say, popping the p.

"Thank god! I don't want kids… Fucking ever!" She announced as she climbed out of the bed and walked towards her bathroom. Flicking on the bathroom light, I saw my cum running down the inside of her leg, and it made me proud. My cum, marking what's mine, I thought.

Oh shit, these thoughts and feelings were not good. This was all new territory for me.

I jumped off the bed, followed her into the bathroom, and slid into the shower behind her.

In this light, I could see and appreciate her body better. Her tits were small, like barely a handful, her stomach so toned I could make out the start of a six-pack pecking through her skin, her ass round, leading down to thick at the top thighs. It was apparent she did boxing and MMA. Her body was a toned weapon that hid well under clothing. Fox kept referring to her as a rabbit, A meek little thing. He might be very wrong on that front. She was more like a wolf wearing sheep's clothing. We all needed to watch out if we wanted to keep her *forever.* Fuck did I just think forever? I thought once I had fucked her, she would be out of my system a little bit. Turned out she had just burrowed herself in deeper.

Wrapping my arms around her body, I pushed us both under the stream of hot water.

Leaning my face down to hers, I placed a small kiss on her lips. "Just so you know, Wyatt likes his water this temp… me not so much," I said as I stepped back and leaned out of the scolding spray.

She looked at me confused, "Why do I need to know the temperature of Wyatt's shower water?"

Smirking at her, I stated, "I told you we share."

"Yes, you did; I didn't realise you meant it together and separately."

"Petal, did you think just cause I fucked you, the other two would back off now?" I laughed at her, "No way, this will make them hungrier."

"And here I was thinking the books were nothing but fantasy," she said quietly and shook her head.

"I think I would like to read these books," I said cocking my head at her.

Laughing at me, she replied, "Oh, I dare say you would like to."

"Can you please pass me the soap? I wanna go to bed."

Leaning down, I grabbed the body wash off the bottom of the shower and pumped a few pumps into my hand. Instead of allowing her to wash her own body, I went to work cleaning her myself. I wanted to run my hands over every inch of her with the lights on. She enjoyed my hands roaming over her body and titled her head back with appreciation.

After we showered and dressed, Ivy tried to kick me out again. That wasn't going to happen. Nope, I was going to wrap that Australian Princess up in my arms for the night; she could kick me out in the morning.

I wanted a few more hours with my petal until I had to go back to our room as the crowned victor of this little bet we had.

Chapter 24

Ivy Alexander

It was barely 1 a.m., and after the great sex I had and the hot shower, I felt exhausted and needed sleep.

Linc refused to leave, adding to my confusion. I liked him, but I wasn't one to get attached or have false hope.

Every boy could talk the talk; that's why I wasn't giving Linc's words any truth.

I couldn't lie, though; when I had him there so close, it felt nice.

The sex was good, sweet and intense. Just like he was.

Arguing with him would not get me anywhere, so I let him stay.

After he insisted on washing and drying my body, I pulled out some shorts and an oversized tee and crawled back into bed.

Like he'd always been my bunk buddy, he put his boxers back on and climbed in next to me.

"I wish you wouldn't smell so damn good," he whispered into my ear, pulling me closer so my back was pressed flush against his chest.

"Mhm," I gave back. Sleep was already tugging at my conscious mind.

When he started to stroke my arm, moving over to my lower belly and drawing tiny circles all over, I was done for. My heavy eyes closed.

But before I went wholly unconscious, I heard him again, "Sleep beautiful and get used to this."

I woke with my face nuzzled into Linc's neck, one leg and arm draped over him. His arms held me tight, and his face was buried in my hair. Fuck this felt good, too good to keep.

Lincoln must've still been asleep as his breathing was even and deep. I savoured a few more minutes of laying with him, thinking this was what I could have, but then I faced reality and started wiggling out of his embrace.

"Stop," he murmured against my head, "it's not time to get up yet." His grip on me tightened.

Shit, I thought, he was so good at playing this game, and it was so easy to fall for it.

I couldn't, though, "I need to pee," I declared, and after one more tight squeeze, he sighed and let me get up.

I rushed to the bathroom, pretending to be busting for a wee. In actuality, I needed space. I sat on the toilet seat, mulling over my next move with him and the other two. Casual sex was ideal, but with three, it was a bit more tricky, and as I was starting to catch some feelings, it would turn into a disaster. Urgh It wasn't as straightforward as I hoped, and I couldn't conclude.

The other option would be to cut them off.

I knew I couldn't do that either. Fuck. I was in a mess.

A slight knock on the door pulled me back from my thoughts.

"You okay? Can I come in?"

"Sure," I replied, standing up and turning the water in the sink on to wash my face.

Lincoln stepped inside and looked at me through the mirror. His hair was beautifully dishevelled, and my lord, did he look good in his boxer shorts. He was so toned, with abs for days and the prominent veins in his arms and hands making me all weak in the knees again. I had to splash more water on my face to hide the blush creeping up.

In typical Linc fashion, though, he wrapped his arms around my waist from behind and kissed my head softly.

"What's going on? Are you regretting last night? I hope not, as you were the one that had me come over…"

"I know, I know," I replied, letting a heavy breath out.

"It's not that." I began looking up at him through the mirror, "I don't normally do this". I said, gesturing with my hands between us.

"Ah, I see. You fuck and bounce?"

"Usually"

"Okay, well then, it's time for you to learn not to bounce." He said, turning away to shower, leaving me gaping at him. So easy for him to declare this shit, and I had to follow.

It was way too early for this crap, so for now, I let it slide.

After breakfast, we got into Fox's car and headed to the nearest town. Yer, that fucker drove the Audi A5 Cabriolet. I just knew it; he was totally the convertible type.

We decided that London would be a trip for another time when we had all day to spare. Wyatt and Fox had a rowing meet later and couldn't miss it.

Fox was in the driver's seat, Linc in the passenger seat, and Wyatt shared the backseat with me.

I could feel that the mood had changed around us.

I was sure that Linc had told his two best friends what happened last night; he had my text message to prove it. Now, I felt like I had done something wrong.

The guys didn't treat me differently, but I sensed a shift had happened.

In silence, we drove the twenty minutes to Guildford. By the end, I started to fidget, the shift in mood and atmosphere getting to me somehow.

Wyatt kept looking at me throughout the car journey but didn't say anything until he caught me fidgeting.

Without a word, he unbuckled my seatbelt and pulled me onto his lap.

"You okay, Wildcat?" He whispered while brushing my hair off my shoulder to gain access to my neck.

I nodded, and he began to run his nose up the side of my neck, placing tiny kisses behind my ear whilst stroking up and down my arm. I felt so out of place; this wasn't me, but I couldn't help but enjoy his touches, feeling a little vulnerable for the first time.

Fox parked the car at an underground car park, and we got out of the vehicle. I straightened myself, hoping I wasn't still blushing from Wyatt's touches.

Lincoln came over to me and helped me into my coat that Mum had sent me and arrived a few days ago after I complained about how flipping cold it was here already.

He flung his arm around my shoulders, and we walked to the elevator that would take us to the mall.

We shopped a little, buying a tonne of protein bars for me and a pumpkin-spiced latte and walked out onto the high street.

It was a beautiful and very picture-perfect English town. The medieval buildings alone made me feel like I finally reached Harry Potter country.

When we were done shopping, downing two pumpkin lattes and gawking in awe at all the buildings, Fox declared it was time to go for lunch. He had been the quietest all morning, only speaking when spoken to directly. He caught me a few times staring at his handsome face and oh-so-muscly physique; I just blushed and looked away. I hated how he made me feel. How they all made me feel, but I was more comfortable with staring at Linc and Wyatt, not blushing right away. Linc now had carnal knowledge of me anyway, and damn, I hoped Wyatt would, too, very soon.

They basically offered themselves to me on a platter, and I'd be stupid to decline. The worries from this morning were gone from my mind with the lightness of our shopping trip. Nevertheless, I could still feel the shift in our dynamic, but even that I ignored for now.

I wanted to feel free and happy today. I made the journey across the pond because of a good education and exploring England with friends. And yes, have heaps of sex.

What else could a girl want?

The boys led me to an intricate small building that looked like it popped out of Diagon Alley and held the door open.

I walked in and was speechless. If it wasn't out of HP, I sure as hell just walked into a Tudor-esque tavern.

My eyes grew wide, and my mouth agape. I looked around like a kid in a candy shop.

The boys, amused by my gawking, greeted the middle-aged guy in a black shirt and purple bowtie behind the bar. Wyatt took my hand and led me to a table at the back of the building that was reached by walking over cobblestones and wood planks that had to be at least 800 years old.

We sat at a modern round table that was more booth-like but still all wooden.

A candle was lit in the middle of the table. I was in heaven. I wanted to take pictures and send some to my parents but decided against it as the boys were busy fumbling with the menu cards.

And I could not resist the smell that wafted around in this place. Homemade *'stick to the bones'* pub grub mixed with medieval wood, fire, patchouli and beer. I wanted to live here!

The boys all had a Soda with their lunch... I had a tea and picked chicken and leek pie with mash and veggies for lunch. My food was porn on a plate.

The conversation at the table was mainly about school work, the rowing team and the gym. The boys noticed that I wasn't in a talkative mood, more engrossed in my excellent food and the building I was having it in.

Once finished, a lovely elderly lady cleared our table; whilst acting like the guys were her boys in the sweetest motherly way, Wyatt asked if I wanted to carry on with our HP marathon after their meet in the evening.

Full of happy hormones, I said yes, that was the plan anyway and blurted out that we should have a proper sleepover this time.

At that point, I was sure I was under some English spell, Idiot. Oh well, I had all their fingers and one of their dicks fuck me already, and I wasn't able to keep my feelings at bay whilst being in such a lovely place, so at this point, it was what it was. The guys, all too cheery about my idea, made plans to stop at a grocery store on the way back to school to get some snacks.

I was in deep shit here.

When we left, Fox helped me into my coat this time, but he didn't directly look at me or say anything, Ever the broody gentleman.

And that was precisely what drew me in.
It seemed I had a thing for morally grey boys….

Chapter 25

Ivy Alexander

We arrived back at the school at around 2:30 p.m., and the boys had to be at the rowing meet at 3 p.m. So I thanked Fox for driving me into town and the other two for coming along and for the lovely lunch. I had until 6 p.m. to get a head start on this English essay. It wasn't like me to put off schoolwork; by my standards, I had slacked off a lot.

Linc had offered to walk me to my room and was so sweet and gentle-like.

"You sure you don't need a study buddy?" He dropped his bottom lip at me.

"Linc, I don't need a distraction. I need to focus, and we both know *you are* a distraction." I said while I poked him in the chest.

"I'll see you at 6 anyway. I'm sure you can find something to do for three hours." I raised my eyebrows at him.

"I could be doing you?" He mumbled, then leaned in to kiss my lips before turning on his heel and heading back to his room. How was I meant to focus now?

Turning around, I swiped my fob and walked inside my room. The movement reminded me that I still needed to ask Linc for the fob to my room. I really needed to remember to get that...

I quickly changed my clothes into some yoga leggings and Wyatt's hoodie. Yes, I had yet to give that back, and I was starting to wonder if he would think it was weird if I asked him if I could swap it for another one that smelt like him. This one's smell was starting to wear off. Stage 5 clinger coming in hot.

Grabbing my laptop, I pulled up the map and followed it to the library, hoping the book on Emily Bronte was still on the shelf.

Walking into the library, I was assaulted by the smell of old books. Holy shit, it smelled amazing in here; the libraries in Australia smelled good too, but the books we had were nowhere near as old as over here, and the smell portrays it. I had no idea why, but the musty old book smell made me so happy.

Smiling to myself, I used the computer to locate the book I was looking for and searched for it. Thankfully, the library seemed quiet today, as I got lost about six times before finally finding it. I'm known to mutter to myself when I'm frustrated, and I just had a whole conversation with myself that would have been embarrassing if others were around.

Grabbing a desk with a window view of the grounds, I got to work on my essay. I found myself lost in the world of Heathcliff and Catherine. I was so engrossed in my work that I didn't notice that Crystal and her posse had walked into the library.

"So not only are you a slut, but you're also a nerd?" Crystal stated as she came to stand in front of my desk.

Looking up at her, I noticed just how pretty she was, long blonde hair, blue eyes, tiny waist and massive tits. I could see why Fox fell into her honey trap over and over.

"Can I help you?" I looked her dead in the eyes. I found looking anyone dead in the eyes and holding eye contact can usually make them uncomfortable enough to leave you alone.

"Yes, you can," she said as she bowed closer to me and showed off her impressive cleavage.

"You can fuck off back to Australia and leave Fox alone," she said sweetly.

"Oh, of course, I'll get right onto that," I said sarcastically as I closed my laptop and stood from my chair. "I've got five and a half terms left, then I'll be gone." I smiled sweetly back at her.

"Fox isn't yours!" she spat.

"Oh honey, I know, and I also know he isn't yours either; I'm fairly sure he has stated many times that he wants you to go away." Rising to her bait.

She walked right up to my face, spat on my cheek and yelled, "You are a fucking slut!"

Oh… Hell… No…. This bitch needed to be taken down a peg. Placing my laptop and bag back on the table, I shoved my hands into her chest and sent her flying back onto her arse.

"I'm only going to say this once, leave me the fuck alone. I don't care about your issues with Fox; I don't care about your territorial need to cock your leg and pee all over him like a bitch in heat. Just stay the fuck away from me!"

Turning on my heel, I reached out to grab my bag but found Crystal had reached out simultaneously and grabbed my laptop. She opened the screen and bent the whole thing back, snapping the screen from the base. Ruining all that hard work I just put into my essay and losing all the work I had done for other subjects.

This bitch was dead.

I snapped out before I even had the time to pull my punch a little. My fist collided with her face so quickly and forcefully that I felt her nose break on my knuckles. Shit. Hopefully, her parents can buy her a new one.

Clapping came from behind me. "Two trailer park girls go round the outside, round the outside, round the outside." Linc sang while twirling his finger in the air.

"Did you seriously just quote an Eminem song?" I looked at him in total confusion.

He just shrugged, "I mean, was I wrong?" One side of his mouth tilted into a wicked grin.

Fucker.

"Lincoln, she just punched me!" Crystal cried from the floor and started to crawl towards him and her minions that had stood there like statues, "You need to help me; she is crazy!"

He looked down at her and said, "Fuck off, Crystal, you had that one coming" and turned to face me, grabbing a hanky from his pocket. Linc wiped at the spit off my cheek.

"You okay, Petal?" He looked at me with concern in his eyes.

"Yes, let's get the fuck outta here!" I grabbed my bag and looked at my broken laptop on the floor.

"That yours, Petal?" Linc looked down where my poor laptop was bent backwards.

"Yep."

He scooped it up for me, "Come on, Princess, we got a movie to watch." He slid his arm across my lower back and led me out of the library.

We walked in silence. I was quietly seething in anger. I would love nothing more than to go back and smash her face into the ground. But I know if I do, I'd do much more damage to her than she could ever do to me.

Linc stopped at his room instead of walking to mine.

"I'll see you at six." I sighed and tried to wiggle out of his arm.

"Oh no, you don't," he said in a low voice; he swiped his fob on the door and pushed me inside.

Walking into the boys' room, I first noticed that it wasn't what I expected at all. All the furniture was mixed-matched. Nothing matched at all.

And it was so tidy, it was a little concerning. Three boys lived in this room, yet nothing was out of place; the beds were all made with precision.

Frowning, I looked at him, "*This* is your room?" Pointing to the beds, "Do you have a cleaning service that comes in daily?"

Laughing at me, he announced, "Nope, Wyatt is a complete neat freak, and after sharing a room with him for many years, the habit has rubbed off on us all."

"Honestly, if anything is out of place, Wyatt will just whine and whinge about it, so it's easier to maintain his level of cleanliness than fight him over it" he shrugged at me.

Guiding me over to his bed, Linc placed my laptop on his desk and pulled a mini screwdriver from one of the desk drawers. He then proceeded to put a headlamp on his head and unscrewed my laptop's base.

"What are you doing?"

"I'm going to pull your hard drive out and place it into a new computer so I can grab all the data off it," he said like I asked a stupid question, all this while wearing that damn headlamp.

I would adequately laugh at him if he didn't look so cute.

"Can you really do all that?"

"Petal, this sort of stuff is fun to me," he turned and smiled at me while blinding me with this light.

"Shit, sorry," he exclaimed and went back to my laptop.

"So you're a tech nerd." I grin, "Gonna go work for MI6 and be a super spy?"

"Nope, my dad wants me to be a lawyer like him, so I'll be a lawyer like him" he sighed.

"Why can't you be what you want to be?"

"It's just not how the world works for kids like us."

Just then, Wyatt and Fox came crashing into the room, having not noticed me sitting on Linc's bed yet.

"Shotgun shower first." Fox bellowed and pulled his shirt over his head while entering the bathroom.

Holy hot damn. Fox without a shirt was like a dream come true.

"You're drooling." Linc teased me

With his words, Wyatt and Fox turned to face us, me sitting on Linc's bed and Linc at his desk.

"What are you two doing in here?" Fox asked harshly.

"Sorry, I'll just go," I answered back.

"No, you're not," Wyatt stood before me.

Fox just turned on his heel, walked into the bathroom and closed the door.

"What brings you to our humble abode, Wildcat?"

Chapter 26

Ivy Alexander

"I had a run-in with the humble queen bitch, and she thought it a good idea to destroy my laptop. And here I am watching the wunderkind trying to salvage my schoolwork." I had just finished my sentence when a loud bang came from the bathroom, like a punch-the-wall sound, followed by a clatter and a few more blows.

It made me jump, and Wyatt sprinted the few steps to Linc's bed to take my face in both hands.

"Don't worry, it's just Fox letting off…Steam" he proclaimed. My eyebrows reached my hairline, and I gave him a questioning look.

Linc turned in his chair to face us, still with that ridiculous lamp on his head, "He might make her disappear if this continues." He said more to Wyatt than me, but I understood the innuendo regardless. Then he turned to his desk, took off the headlamp and grabbed something off of another laptop: a USB stick.

"It's all on there, petal, nothing's lost."

"Oh shit, thank you!" My voice was a high-pitched sound filled with excitement. I was glad to not lose the handwork I had put into my school work, but sure as hell was I going to make Crystal pay for this.

I jumped off his bed and grabbed the USB stick off him.

"I'll see you guys in a bit?"

Looking from Linc to Wyatt, then to the closed bathroom door where nothing else was coming from but the sound of the shower.

"Of course! We'll be round in a few." Wyatt reassured me.

When I left, I heard them both talking about Fox having to get his shit together concerning me.

I shouldn't be eavesdropping.

Back in my room, I showered and changed into something more modest, feeling a bit off kilter after Fox's rampage, check PJ bottoms and an oversized HP sleep shirt.

At 6:10 p.m., my door opened; of course, after we had sex, Linc felt he didn't have to knock anymore. Prick.

I was sitting on my bed with my phone, texting my Mum. Wyatt and Linc looked relaxed and dressed in what you could call lounge slash sleepwear and black tees; they smiled at me, showing me their pearly whites and took their usual spots next to me. Fox, however, looked like he was ready to maul someone to death, too, wore check lounge bottoms and, again, a white tee. Fuck me sideways; he was sex on a stick, but his face spoke a thousand words. Words of fury and torment.

He didn't look, let alone smile at me. That made me scoot up a little higher, my back pressed against the wall and pulling my feet as far back as possible not to touch him. He noticed my movements and finally looked at me. I couldn't believe it, but all that vexation clearly displayed on his face before melted away, and lo and behold, he gave me a hint of a smile before he laid down again by my feet. And then, with one hand, he grabbed my ankles and pushed my feet under his ribs, like they were placed the night before.

I didn't say a word, just letting him do what he needed to do.

"Nice spread, Wildcat," Wyatt said, pointing at the snacks and bottles of water I had arranged on my desk.

It made me smile and broke the ice a little.

We started the third HP, Prisoner of Azkaban, and by the time Harry had boarded the bus, the guys' hands were caressing my skin again.

It was Wyatt, though, that kept my attention the most. He kept kneading my right shoulder with his knuckles, and gosh, did that feel good. It was so good that I was close to offering him my other shoulder.

By the time the credits rolled, we had gone through most of the snacks but still felt hungry.

Fox lifted himself for a stretch off my bed with his arms over his head, his tee lifted, giving me a dizziness-inducing peak at his abs; he asked if we wanted pizza.

Of course, everyone wanted pizza.

Fox ordered, and we unanimously decided to watch the fourth HP, The Goblet of Fire, as it was still reasonably early.

The boys were their usual affectionate selves, but they didn't go any further like the night before; I was pleased with their restraint but also pissed. Wanting, needing to explore this odd constellation further. When I started to fidget during the 4th movie and after a helping of pizza, Linc's hand shot down and grabbed my left thigh with such strength that, for a second, I thought we were about to fight.

He looked down at me, his eyes nothing but black pits and scooped me up in one swift motion, placing me onto Wyatt's lap.

"Hey there, Wildcat, fidgeting again?" He wrapped his arms around me like he did in the car in the morning. It didn't take him long to graze his fingers up and down my arms, his touch making me squirm instead. When he pushed my butt between his legs and started working on both my shoulders, I was literally done for. Occasionally, Linc would lean over to peck me on the lips like he needed reminding of something. Fox was still stationary at my feet, only throwing me a glance ever so often. But his hands stayed by himself tonight. He could fuck right off, I thought and made sure to enjoy the other two's attention even more.

By the end of our second movie of the night, I was all jelly and needed sleep or to get fucked, but I was sure I wasn't going to get the latter, so I asked how we should sleep and got up to get ready for sleep and to take a pee break. Thank goodness for the queen bed I had in my room. Otherwise, the four of us would struggle to get some shut-eye.

Sorting myself out and brushing my teeth longer than necessary, I heard my door open and close, but voices were still coming from my room.

I brushed my hair and finally made my way back out when I noticed that one boy was missing, and two were already in my bed playing on their phones.

They left me in the middle with my pillow.

"Where's Linc?" I asked whilst trying to climb into my own bed, careful not to waltz into a pair of balls.

"He had to quickly check something on his computer. He'll be back in a few." Wyatt said and got comfy on his side, facing me.

Fox was still on his back with his phone in his hand. I was about to tell him *if he'd rather be out of here than go* when Wyatt grabbed me around the waist again and pulled me flush against him, his chest to my back. I was still looking at Fox when Lincoln returned and got comfy next to Wyatt, but with a distance between them. He pushed back up before turning my bedside lamp off and leaned over Wyatt to gently kiss me. "Good night, Petal."

Feeling that connection between us, I leaned more into his kiss and stroked over his hair with one hand. He made me feel so cared for and safe, and after mulling it over in my head a million times, I wanted him to know I was choosing not to bounce.

I was sure he felt it as he intensified the kiss until Wyatt broke us up, "I seriously can't breathe anymore down here. Lay down, both of you!".

Linc chuckled, and I smiled like the Cheshire Cat and laid back between the calm and collected Wyatt and the broody, cold-as-stone Fox. Who was still on his phone, apparently unfazed by Linc and my antics.

I snuggled back into Wyatt's chest with my back and told Alexa to play some random calm playlist.

My eyes found the side of Fox's face again, still on that fucking phone, but I couldn't look away from him. He kept pulling me in like a magnet.

All the while, Wyatt stroked my upper leg and the other tightly clamped around my middle. I was yet to push my butt closer to him, worried about what I would come to find between his legs, but also curious if he was hard or not. I wasn't soaked, but laying there between these flipping hot and handsome guys had an effect on a girl. The little play the night before and then the sex with Linc pushed all the right buttons within me.

Wrapped up around my thoughts for a while, I didn't realise for a few seconds that Fox had turned his head to face me. At this point, I was staring at his neck but also into space. When I caught on that he was looking at me, our eyes met, and a faint smile quivered over his lips, those baby blues of his shining bright in my moonlit room. "Night, Angel." He whispered, and if I hadn't seen his lips move, I could have sworn I had imagined it. He then turned his back toward me and went to sleep.

Fuck a duck, that boy was driving me insane.

And I was left in the arms of Wyatt; for any ordinary girl, one guy would be more than enough. I wasn't normal, though, and I didn't want ordinary; the need for all three was growing by the day.

Without actually realising it, I had started to wiggle my lower half a bit, and Wyatt's hold on me tightened, "Shh, Wildcat, you don't want to poke the bear now, do you?" It was more of a challenge, I heard in his voice than him trying to get me to stop. I liked bears, I thought and wiggled again.

I desperately wanted him to make the first move and make something happen here. Without being too provocative, I pushed my butt closer against his crotch, and I heard his breath hitch. But he took the bait.

One of his hands trailed down my hips and my thigh, grazing his short nails against my skin, making me erupt in a shiver and endless goosebumps.

My head leaned back, and a small moan escaped my lips that seemed to spur him on. His other arm let go of my waist, too, and his hand found my throat; ever so gently did he hold on to it whilst his other hand on my leg now sought my heated core. The anticipation was like an electrical current running through me. My breaths short, I gave that final push against him, and fuck did he feel big under his lounge pants, hard and thick. My next soft moan led him to push past my very short shorts, and he had me. My hips started moving, so desperate for friction. His mouth was against my ear. "I'm not like any other guy, Wildcat. If you give in to me, I'll let you in, but don't take that offer lightly."

Not a clue what he was on about; just horny as a bitch in heat. I grabbed the hand he had in my pants and pushed it closer to my pussy. He needed to give me what I was craving.

"No going back now" his hushed whisper reached me again, and in one swift move, two of his fingers plunged into me. My hips bucked, my back arched, and I exhaled sharply.

His fingers pumping in and out of me in a torturous slow rhythm. Until I was sure, I was going to lose my mind. My fingers dug into his wrist under my shorts.

Then, the hand on my throat wandered to my mouth and nose and shut my air supply off. He had my next breath choked inside my lungs. Taken by surprise but turned the fuck on by it, I came after another two pumps of his fingers, entirely shattering around him. My pussy clenched greedily for more while my lungs felt the slightest twinge of a burn.

Chapter 27

Wyatt Forester

I was naturally selfish, but I did not want to take things any further with Ivy.

I was curious if she would respond to my type of touch; so far, so good.

Breath play was one of my favourites; now I just needed to see if she could take a crop. I had a feeling she would love it.

"Fuck Ivy," I breathed into her ear, "you clench my fingers so good."

With those words, Fox rolled over and stared at her; I felt her body stiffen at his sudden movement. Fox was a bit of a wild card. He would either join in or stare her down until she submitted to him. His alpha hole nature wasn't one many could handle.

Fox leaned forward and kissed the tip of Ivy's nose. "Go to sleep, Angel," and he closed his eyes.

Poor Ivy, she wasn't going to have fun with that one.
Pulling my fingers free of her pussy, I placed my fingers into my mouth and sucked them clean.
"Did you know you taste sweet like honey?" I Stated
"NN No?" She stammered, and I could have sworn she blushed.
"Well, you do, and it's my favourite flavour," leaning forward to kiss her mouth. I shoved my tongue past her lips so she could taste herself.
"See, sweet like honey," I mumbled against her lips.
"Ah ha" she moaned back breathlessly.
Pulling back, I settled behind her and wrapped my arms around her middle. 'You heard Fox; go to sleep, Wildcat" As I nestled my head into her neck.
I started to draw small patterns on her thighs until I felt her body soften and her breathing deepen. I wasn't sure what was happening between Ivy and me, but it was something I wasn't used to. I didn't usually use the girls on campus as they couldn't handle my type of fun, but Ivy called to me like a siren. I was starting to think that even if she wasn't into my kind of fun, I wasn't sure I could let her go.

That morning, we got up and went for breakfast in the hall. Fox and I had a mock race for rowing later on, and Ivy wanted to finish off her schoolwork. Linc had bought and ordered a new laptop yesterday and had it delivered to the school this morning. He was going to stay and study with her until it arrived. I suspected he mainly wanted to see the smile on her face when she received it. He had given her one of his spares to work on for the moment, and she had no idea he had bought her a new one. He was falling hard for the Wildcat.

I was starting to think we all were in some form, but I wasn't ready to address those feelings yet.

"Hurry up fuck face," Fox glared at me from the door.

"You're sitting over there staring off into space, and we gotta get down there in ten minutes."

"Fuck off," I growl back, throwing him an angry look. That's just how we were with each other.

"I think my mum is going to be here this morning, too," he sighed and it explained his extra shitty mood.

"Fuck!" this was bad. Fox hadn't seen his Mum since we came back to school.

The whole *"our parents getting married shit"* was too much of a mess for us to even begin to address.

"She isn't bringing my dad, is she?" I ran my hand through my hair, pulling at it, the slight pain easing the uncomfortable feeling in my gut about possibly seeing our parents.

"She didn't mention it, but that does not mean shit." He had walked back into the room and fiddled with his phone.

"Why is she coming? She hasn't been to one training session or race since we started going here?" I stated while lacing up my running shoes.

"I suspect she is here to discover the truth about Crystal." Fox shrugged.

'Fuck me, we really need to do something about that skank. She ruined Ivy's laptop and now has a personal vendetta against her. Let alone shouting around being pregnant with your kid, that's some high-level bonkers" I shook my head at him, still not comprehending how nuts Crystal was.

"I know! I'm not sure Ivy is strong enough to withstand Crystal's games." Fox frowned, raking his teeth over his bottom lip in thought.

"I think she might be much stronger than we give her credit for, Fox." I jump up and hurry to the door with him. We're going to have to jog to get to training on time.

"Oh, I know she is strong physically, but can she withstand Crystal's mind games and bullying?"

"Let's hope so!" I said, thinking about ways we could protect Ivy from Crystal.

Once we had arrived at training and pushed our shell into the water, I saw Fox's Mum walking to the shore, hand in hand with my Dad. Great, just what I wanted on a Sunday morning.

"Super, dumb and dumber are here." Fox pointed at our parents, his face turning into a grimace.

"Come on, let's burn some of the steam off and win this race," I said, pulling him with me.

"Wanna see if we can beat everyone by a length this time?" Fox challenged.

If there is anything Fox loves, it's winning. He will push himself to breaking point to win something. It can range from a stick of gum to a race. You can guarantee he will put the same amount of effort into both. Lincoln and I were surprised he didn't go all out with the Ivy bet; it was very out of character for him. Linc suspected it could be that, for once, the guy had caught some feelings. I was not convinced. However, when Linc fessed up that he had slept with Ivy and ultimately won the bet, neither of us acted like we usually did. We acknowledged that she had sex with one of us, but it didn't make a difference in pursuing her more. That's how deep she had her claws in us. Making a bet near enough redundant between us. Link mentioned that we were bound to catch some feelings at some stage. It was apparently Ivy for Fox and me; we never saw that coming. It was an odd feeling, good and weird at the same time.

"Well, come on then you dick, row!" I shouted to Fox, placing my oars into the water and started the small paddle to the starting line.

I wished Ivy was here to watch us race; I would have loved to see her face at the finish line… what the fuck was wrong with me. Since when did I give a shit about a girl watching me row? Maybe I needed a trip to the Rathbone Villa again soon to get it out of my system. But that thought had my gut twisting; it was telling me that it was the complete opposite of what I really wanted.

Looking back to where our parents were standing, I saw Crystal walk up and start talking to Fox's Mum. Shit… I turned to look at Fox, who caught sight of his Mum and Crystal, and his face displayed pure fury. His complicated relationship with his Mother and the girl who imagined a full-blown romance with him was pure terror to my best friend. Two women set out to make his life unnecessarily complicated.

Fuck I thought, no way were we winning this race now.

"Im going to fucking kill that slut." Fox growled from his seat behind me.

"We can deal with her after the race," I turned and glared at him. "Let's just win this, then put a leash on that mutt."

Turning back to face me, Fox just nodded and clenched his teeth together. This was going to be a bad race.

Blowing out a breath, I readied myself for the horn. We propelled ourselves backwards the second it went off; Fox was screaming with every spin of his oars, clearly taking his anger out on the water. At least it wasn't our furniture this time.

The race was short, only a quick five-minute straight line. We made it in three. I was wrong; Fox being angry while rowing might be a good thing. We beat our record time by a minute, and our coach was dumbstruck.

Climbing out of the shell at the shore, we secured it by the river bank, and I heard Fox mumble profanities, most definitely aimed at Crystal and his Mother.

Our parents walked over with huge smiles on their faces.

"Oh honey, I should come and watch you row more often!" His Mum, Vera, beamed at him.

"Thanks," Fox said between gritted teeth while shuffling his feet.

"Amazing, boys!" My Dad beamed at me and held his fist for me to bump. I love my Dad, but man, he was too soft. The looks he kept throwing at Vera made me want to vomit. Was it that hard to see she was just sucking his cock for his cash? Maybe he did know and didn't care.

Crystal then appeared and slid her arm into Fox's while beaming at his Mum. Her face was a mess, and there was tape over the bridge of her nose; she had a black eye and swelling underneath. Ivy did a number on her, what a good girl Ivy was.

Fox pulled himself immediately out of Crystal's reach, fuming. "Seriously, Crystal, fuck off!" he growled.

"But baby, I was just here to tell your parents about our pregnancy," her lips in a pout, her face a picture of innocence. That girl could win awards for her acting.

"You're not fucking pregnant, Crystal, and if you are, it's not mine. Get some help for your issues!" he yelled at her, his fists balled at the side. I was getting ready to intervene and drag him away if need be.

"Fox!" Vera howled. "Seriously, this isn't the time or place."

"Mum, it is. I want the whole school to know that, for one, Crystal isn't pregnant, and second, it's not mine even if she were," he said, raising his voice so the crowd could hear him. His eyes moved to Crystal, making sure he had her full attention.

"I'm done playing your games, Crystal. You need to leave me alone, or I will make you regret ever meeting me. I've tried nice. Consider this your last warning. Oh and stay the hell away from Ivy!" he turned on his heel and stormed off. Crystal's mouth was a thin line, but her waterworks were turned on, and she, too, stomped off, thankfully in the opposite direction.

"What the hell is going on here?" My Dad asked in a confused tone.

I sighed, still watching Fox in the distance, ensuring he aimed for the housing building and not anywhere near people he could smack.

"Crystal has been telling everyone she is pregnant with Fox's kid. She also thinks they are a couple, but Fox hasn't touched the slut in months. If she were pregnant from him, she'd be very far along. But that tight stomach of hers says a whole other story." I explained, tired of this shit show.

"Please watch your swearing," my Dad retorted, shaking his head, "I'll write an email to the board and see what I can do, But I don't think there is a lot we can do other than partition for her to be tested for a pregnancy if her parents sign off" he shrugged and pulled his phone out of his fleece-y coat.

Fox's Mother, ever the sly one, smiled at me," Don't worry honey, I'll get to the bottom of this for you" and hugged me. "Make sure Sebastian keeps away from her. We don't need any more trouble." I nodded and gave her a flat smile.

I didn't know whether to be happy knowing she was going to destroy Crystal or scared for her. Vera was brutal and cunning, the connections she had reached very far and wide. I was a little relieved that she would help us handle it; we had more important things to focus our attention on. It was our last year of school, Uni applications, rowing and last but definitely not least, Ivy.

"Thanks for coming," I said to the both of them, "are you sticking around or heading off?"

"Sorry, son, but we have to head back; I have surgery booked for the afternoon and need to prep." He smiled and reached out with his hand to clasp my shoulder.

"You did well in that race. I'm proud of you, Both of you. And I can't wait to see you in action next time."

"Thanks, Dad, it's appreciated." And with that, Vera and my Dad went their way, and I went toward the housing complex. Knowing full well, I was about to walk into a trashed room.

Chapter 28

Ivy Alexander

Having Linc help me study definitely took my mind off of the night before. Damn, I had it bad. I felt like I had fallen right into their trap; I just couldn't help myself. Wyatt was so different yet the same as Lincoln. You could tell they had been the best of friends for many years; the distinction was that I could feel the dominance oozing off of Wyatt and wanted it. The way he restricted my breathing had me rubbing my legs together under the desk.

"Any exciting thoughts there Petal, or memories…?" Linc teased in a deep voice, which had me rubbing my legs even more.

"Nope," I lied, shaking my head. Even though he didn't say anything to me, unlike Fox last night, I knew that Linc was also awake when Wyatt gave me that amazing O.

How quickly my time at this prestigious school had turned into a never-ending wet dream, and I was here for it.

"You gonna focus on your work, or would you rather go upstairs and I make you quiver underneath me?" Linc said casually, his beautiful eyes glaring with devious thoughts.

I had to close my eyes tightly before budging and taking him up on his offer.

"No, Linc, I'm fine, thank you very much!" I said sarcastically and stuck my head back into my book.

Before I could have another thought about how these boys made me feel, the doors to the study hall flew open, and all heads popped up.

It was none other than the furious and broken-faced blonde that came about to make my life here a little more challenging. I either beat her up so bad that she would end up permanently in medical care and land myself most definitely in prison, or I had to call my parents and get them involved. I wasn't overly happy with either choice, so sticking to the long game for now, it was.

"You little whore!" I heard her scream whilst marching up to me. Yep, I was the whore she called out for.

Linc stiffened beside me and clamped his hand on my thigh to tell me not to get up. Tough luck there, mate; I wouldn't hide behind a guy.

I then saw him grab his phone and text as fast as I'd seen anyone type a message.

I wrung myself out of Linc's hold and stood, walking round my chair toward Crystal. I heard Lincoln say something, but I focused on the girl who wanted my head on a stick.

"What is your fucking problem, cunt?" I hissed.

That seemed to infuriate her even more, and her feet moved faster until she stopped before me.

Linc got up, too, but kept his distance.

"You have gotten into Fox's head and made him believe that I'm not pregnant! You poisoned him against me. For that, you'll pay," she snarled, raising her right hand to lunge at me.

Again, tough luck as I saw it coming a mile away and blocked her silly attempt at smacking me. I held her wrist in a firm grip, having had enough of her shit.

"Listen here, you silly girl, the number I did on your face will be nothing compared to what I will do to you if you don't leave me the fuck alone!" Tightening my hold on her as she wriggled to get free.

Every student in the study hall was now on their feet watching us. Linc just stood a few steps away from me, watching too, but with a look that suggested that if Crystal made one wrong move, he and I would have to battle it out who'd put her in a hole first.

Crystal was just about to spew more when the door opened again. Fuck me, a hulking Fox sprinted through with an equally pissed-off-looking Wyatt on his tail.

Fox reached us and was about to grab Crystal when another player entered the game. It was none other than Colt.

My oh my, how many pawns were in this game?

"Sebastian," he shouted, "I will not stand by and watch you hurt a girl." Great!

"We all know she isn't....Stable." He carried on, referring to her craziness, I assumed, not knowing it was common knowledge.

"I wasn't gonna hurt her, arsehole," Fox replied in a shaky voice. At this point, I wasn't sure if he would've or not.

Fox stopped in his tracks, Wyatt right beside him, when Colt moved over to us out of nowhere; I didn't realise he was in here, too. The guys formed a perfect circle with Crystal and myself in the middle. I was as calm as ever, but my mind was going a hundred miles an hour; Crystal kept escalating, and something needed to happen without me or any of the guys getting into trouble.

Crystal had started crying at one point, but I couldn't feel sorry for her. Lying to a guy about a pregnancy was a total no-go in my books.

Her jealousy, though I understood.

Colt stepped closer, carefully taking Crystal's arm that I was holding, his eyes telling me to let her go.

I did, and he wrapped his arm around her shoulders, her sobs uncontrollable now.

The guys just stood there watching like the rest of the student body in the room.

Crystal leaned her head against Colt, and he walked her out, speaking in a hushed voice.

After the door closed, the other students returned to work like nothing had happened, probably knowing they should keep their heads out of legacy business.

Fox took a step toward me, "You all right?" Looking me up and down.

"Of course."

He gave me a slight nod and a piss-poor attempt at a smile, then turned around and walked off.

That boy was going to be the death of me.

Hot… Cold… Colder….

I heard Wyatt and Linc take a deep breath simultaneously while I slumped back into my chair. This was all getting too complicated, and I wondered if it was best if I took a few steps away from the boys for a while. At least until Crystal was dealt with.

Like he could read my damn mind, Linc piped up, close to my ear.

"I hope you are not thinking about backing away from us because of her."

He grabbed my hand, "We will deal with her, just don't bounce."

That tiny word had become a code between him and me.

I nodded, though still unsure of what the best course of action would be.

Wyatt had sat on the chair on my other side and scooted closer. His fingers tucked a strain of hair behind my ear and stroked my cheek gently like I was some wounded kitten. For the first time in my relatively independent life, filled with fights and bruises and knockouts, did I allow myself to feel vulnerable? They made me feel vulnerable.

"Wanna get out of here?" He asked, and I looked at him and his drop-dead gorgeous grey eyes.

My chest tightened again with this feeling, like something irrecoverably was bound to happen between me and the guys. Something I never thought I wanted, let alone needed.

Chapter 29

Sebastian 'Fox" Foxworth

I was done. Crystal needed to disappear.
This was my last year of school; so far, it had been filled with nothing but drama. The little Australian princess was supposed to be the fun we needed to finish out this year. But Crystal was determined to ruin everything.
Storming into our room, I grabbed my phone out of my pocket and called my Mum.
"Sweetheart," she greeted me.
"Mum, I need a favour," sighing down the line. This was my last resort; calling my Mother meant I was out of options.
"I assume you need help with Crystal?"
"Yes," I replied, knowing that Wyatt had mentioned something to her already.
"What type of help do you want, dear? Are we hiding a pregnancy? Or are we getting rid of one?" She asked like she

didn't even listen to me when I shouted at everyone by the river that Crystal was not pregnant from me.

"She isn't pregnant!" I bellowed through the phone, "I haven't touched her in months!"

"I can petition the school to have her tested?

"Yes, I need this cleared up now, Mum; she is a piece of work," I admitted.

"Where has this girl even come from? I didn't even know you were seeing anyone."

"I wasn't really, I just hooked up with her a few times, and when I found out she was sleeping with the rest of the school at the same time, I told her fuck off."

" Language, Sebastian! Is this the same girl who rang me the other week?"

"Yes, the one and only" I sighed again running my hand over my face, "She is insane and thinks we're in a relationship, which we are not and never have been!"

"Okay, okay, calm down, I'll deal with it," Mum said. "Send me her details, and I'll get it sorted out, but Sebastian, I expect to see you at home for dinner next weekend."

Always a ploy with her "Sure thing, Mum, can I bring someone?" I asked quickly.

"Yes, of course you can, darling", surprise in her voice.

"Anyone I know?" I could hear her smile when she asked.

"No, she just started here this year," I replied, not wanting the third degree.

"What do her parents do?"

There she is, my Mother was the real snake in the grass. If Ivy's parents were wealthy, which I assumed they were, my Mum would get her claws into her.

"I honestly don't know mum, I haven't asked"

"How well do you even know this girl then?"

"Well, enough to know I'm bringing her to dinner next weekend." I growled, "Anyway, Mum, I gotta go; I want to get some schoolwork done."

"Okay, honey. Love you," she said and hung up before I could say it back. Not that I was going to.

Throwing my phone on the bed, I pulled off my shirt and jumped into the shower. I needed to wash away this day's bullshit.

Standing under the spray, I remembered Ivy's face when I stormed into the hall; she looked like a lion playing with her food. Crystal would end up with two black eyes if she kept harassing Ivy the way she was. I just didn't want Ivy to get in trouble for retaliating against the bitch.

My mind then remembered the sound she made when Wyatt made her cum last night, and my dick instantly twitched at the thought. For someone so tiny, she packed a lot of personality. I usually liked my girls, meek and big-chested. This little thing hardly had anything to fill a bra, she was too lean and athletic, but my dick didn't seem to care. Grabbing it, I gave it a few slow tugs and pictured Ivy lying on her side with Wyatt's hand between her legs. When I rolled over, I noticed Wyatt moving his hand off her face like he had been smothering her, and she liked it. I wonder if she would like to choke on my cock, too? The thought had my dick as hard as steel. Picking up my pace, I continued to think of Ivy on her knees, with tears running down her face as I forced my dick to the back of her throat.

"Fuck," was all I managed as I exploded all over the shower screen, my orgasm having come on quickly. My balls were still tingling after, a new sensation I hadn't had before. What was this girl doing to us? She had Linc's balls in a vice, and he was happy to leave them there; Wyatt was actually chasing her tail and hadn't left campus once for his regular subs at Rathbone Villa, and I was keeping my dick in my pants since she came into the picture.

This wasn't regular behaviour for any of us.

About twenty minutes later, the three of them came stumbling through the door, laughing and playing fighting. Ivy had a new Apple MacBook Pro box tucked under her arm and was beaming at Linc like he had hung the moon.

"Hey," she said when she saw me sitting on the couch watching TV.

Handing the box off to Linc, she said, "Thank you for setting it up for me; I honestly suck when it comes to technology."

"Anything for you, Petal" What the fuck? Linc had turned into a pussy whipped idiot around this girl.

Walking over to the couch, Ivy sat beside me, kicking her legs onto my lap. "What are we watching?" she asked, looking at me with those eyes of hers. They were so pretty, like stained glass, and I always got lost in them if I wasn't careful. Her scent of vanilla and honey had enthralled me, too, and was creeping up my nostrils, clouding my mind.

"Um well…" I rubbed the back of my neck, feeling my cheeks grow hot.

Wyatt answered from the other side of the room, lying on his bed, flicking through his phone. "Probably MAFS."

Ivy's head whipped forward to the TV. "You're watching Married at First Sight?" A wide smile spread across her face.

"It's his favourite show," Linc piped in from his desk.

Fuck. Thanks for that, apparent best friend.

"This show is complete trash!" She laughed. "I can't believe you actually like it!"

Holding my hands in the air in defeat, "I know, I know, but it's addictive." I might as well come clean now.

"I honestly don't think I've ever watched one episode" still laughing but not really at me for watching TV trash, "Okay. So give me the background, who is who."

Smiling at her, I gave her the information about who married who and why they don't get along. Hanging out like this with Ivy was nice, she was so damn easy to talk to. She took simple moments like those and made them fun instead of embarrassing, and all my previous anger was wholly gone again. She kept doing that.

I would just never admit that to her.

Chapter 30

Ivy Alexander

The guys and I hadn't watched another HP movie in two nights, all of us being distracted with school work, and secretly, I was glad as I still didn't know how to handle the whole Crystal situation.

On the day it happened, I was happy to go along and act like nothing had happened; I even got a bit territorial with Fox, who started to warm up a little to me. Not enough to have anything going on with him, but having him as a friend meant something to me, too. I had to wrap my head around the simple fact that I had a thing with his two best friends; I had enough on my plate. That didn't make me stop thinking about Fox in that way, though. For the first time in a few weeks, did I have the time to think about what I was doing here? No matter how I twisted and turned it all over in my head, my heart and head always came to the same conclusion. I wanted all three.

Crazy, I know, but why should I let such an opportunity go? Everyone in my shoes would do exactly the same.

Wanting to get ready for bed, I pulled out some warmer PJs; the temp here was definitely getting worse by the day when my phone beeped.

Linc: *It's cold tonight. Want to come and sleep in our room?*

I needed to be with them tonight. I missed them the two nights we didn't spend together. Pushing all previous thoughts aside. Again.

Ivy: *Give me 10.*

I am looking at my PJ selection again. Sleeping next to three not only hot as fuck looking guys but literally walking furnaces, I had to rethink my choice of nightwear.

Beep.

Linc: *Make it 15; we have some technical issues here...*

Ivy: *Okay...*

Wondering what he meant by technical issues, I decided on another pair of black PJ shorts and a grey vest top. I pulled my long hair up, scrunched it into a bun and went on to brush my teeth. I took extra time to waste the fifteen minutes away. Around the twelve-minute mark, my phone beeped again.

Linc: *Ready!*

My feet were always cold, and even though the walk down the hall to the guy's room wasn't more than mere seconds, I decided

I had to put some socks on; it really was freezing in this shitty building, and the heating was from the dark ages. The kids in our school were some hard-core fuckers, still running around in shorts and t-shirts while I added thermal leggings and tops to my online shopping carts.

I didn't want the boys to wait on me. I pulled out a big clump of socks, and by the time I was at the door, I noticed they were black knee highs I wore sometimes to the gym.

I pulled them on and up and tiptoed to the boy's room.

Having mixed dorms was an honour program for the older students. I wanted to know how many Hastings House babies were conceived on this floor.

Maturity wasn't something a school could teach kids; incredibly spoilt rich kids. But I knew money was always related to power, silence, and many secrets.

Honour system, my arse.

I giggled to myself when I reached the boys' door, remembering I was probably the worst of them all, having three waiting for me behind the door.

I knocked quietly, and it opened immediately like they were waiting for me. When the door opened further, I couldn't believe my eyes.

The guys had rearranged their bedroom. Two of their king-size mattresses were on the floor in front of a considerable projector beaming onto the far left wall, displaying the opening credits of the 5th HP movie Order of the Phoenix. LED candles lit up the room, and big blankets were draped over the mattresses with at least eight pillows strewn around. And there was a small table packed with snacks, cans of soda, and water bottles.

I stepped into the room with a big smile on my face. Fox was the one that had opened the door for me. His face was blank, not angry nor happy to see me. Man, I had my work cut out with this one.

After the *Married at First Sight* afternoon, I hoped we had at least broken the friendship barrier.

"Fuck you look hot, Wildcat!" That was how Wyatt greeted me. I blushed a little at his compliment and walked further into the bedroom. He was by his desk with a small gift bag in his hand.

"Erm, thanks, I guess" I muttered.

Linc walked up behind me and placed a small kiss on my cheek. "Sorry, it took a bit longer, Petal. Not everyone here is a good team player." He said with annoyance in his voice. He didn't have to mention his name for me to know it was Fox, he meant.

Linc grabbed my hands and pulled me onto the makeshift bed on the floor.

Fox grunted after closing the door and went and sat on his bed; I noted that his mattress had not been put on the floor the minute I stepped in. It didn't bother me as such, though Linc's comment and his going back to his bed with his stupid mattress infuriated me. I couldn't let anyone see that, though, so I let myself down on the massive bed the guys had made for us. Wyatt came over, too, and handed me the little gift bag.

"I hope I made the right choice."

I took the gift bag and sat up higher,

"I don't expect you guys to keep giving me gifts. I have my own money, enough of it, too." I declared with probably too much agitation in my voice.

Linc pulled me into his side, "Petal, we don't give you gifts for any other reason than us wanting to make you smile. The laptop was also a necessity," he threw Fox a glare, "and Wyatt got you something he thought you'd enjoy and reminded him of you."

I felt like an idiot for saying anything.

I didn't want the guys to think they had to get me stuff.

Growing up with more money than anyone could ever need but having to earn my keep to stay levelheaded made me conscious of gifts. That and the fact that no guy had ever given me gifts before.

There was Thomas McCullen in year 5 that got me a little boxing glove keychain for my birthday.

Gifts made me uncomfortable. If I needed anything, I'd buy it or ask my parents. My allowance nowadays was more than enough, and I never wanted much anyway. I never fell for the consumerism BS.

Wyatt, now sitting beside me, urged me to open the bag.

Still hesitant, I opened the bag and pulled out a scarf and glove set. It had the logo and colours, blue and bronze, of house Ravenclaw printed all over, A tiny Ravenclaw emblem on the gloves.

It was the most thoughtful gift I had ever received.

"We think that's definitely your house, Wildcat. Wit, intelligence, wisdom..." he trailed off and looked at me straight. His grey eyes gleamed.

"I love it! Thank you, Wyatt!" I said and leaned over the bag to kiss him on the cheek.

Except he turned in the last second, and our mouths collided. His lips pressed a firm kiss to mine, neither of us ready to pull away, as his hand cradled the back of my head. I felt his lips part, and his tongue came out, slowly licking the seam of my mouth. I allowed him entry, and unlike what I expected from Wyatt, the kiss was a dance of pure passion. He didn't fight for dominance. He let me set the pace willingly. It was me that turned it from sweet and passionate to hungry and rough. He pulled me into his lap, my hips immediately rocking to meet his groin. I felt him grow beneath me, his hand now firmly tugging on my hair while the other pushed at the small of my back for more pressure on his lap.

A throat clearing ripped us apart, Linc looking at us with the same hunger but more restraint in his eyes. "As much as this view turns me on, I have to mention that I did not get the same reaction when I gave you the laptop, Princess."

Alrighty then

I snaked into Lincoln's lap, up for the challenge, leaving him and Wyatt wide-eyed.

"Oh, okay," Linc gasped when I rolled my hips in his lap seductively and grabbed his head in one hand and his shoulder in the other. "Fuck…" He groaned before my mouth devoured his. My tongue prodded at his lips for entry, and this time, I wanted to fight for dominance. When my tongue slid inside his warm and slick mouth, a jolt of electricity zipped through me when I swallowed his moan.

Our tongues collided, and I felt my arousal pooling in my underwear; having reached flood levels with Wyatt, the freaking dam was now broken.

Lincoln's hands were all over my back, grabbing my arse and pushing me hard on his solid cock.

I felt a third hand caressing my lower back.

I opened my eyes slightly and saw Wyatt out of my periphery. He was right next to Linc's head.

"Come here." He whispered to me, and I did as I was told and let go of Linc to lean over and kiss Wyatt again. Linc's hands were not leaving me but getting more desperate to touch me everywhere he could. I rocked against his cock again while licking his best friend's mouth, and the groan I heard from him made my head spin.

Fucking behave! My mind shouted at me, not even having started the flipping movie yet.

I was so god damn horny, but I had to keep myself in check and these boys at arm's length; I wasn't an easy girl that gave out every night. Little excursions like we just had were okay and good, but I wouldn't be spreading my legs all the time. I slowly pulled away from Wyatt, his eyes pleading with me to return, but I didn't; instead, I crawled off of Linc's lap and wiggled myself between the two. It's the exact same arrangement we always had.

I looked up to sort my hair, and my eyes landed on Fox, who was watching the show his two best friends and I had just put on for him.

His face was unreadable, but his eyes spoke a million words. He was fighting with himself. I wouldn't look away, not this time. His intense blue eyes bore into mine, but I stood my ground. Barely breathing to keep level with him.

Apparently, he was the undisputed King of staring as he wouldn't budge, not an inch nor blink. The room's mood quickly changed to an invisible battlefield between him and me.
The other two were clearly pissed off with the situation when Wyatt said, "Get the fuck over yourself, Fox."
He pulled my shoulders, so I had to scoot down and lean against him, which made me break eye contact with Fox.
Fuck that boy had some issues.
Unsure at this point if he even liked me at all, I snuggled into Wyatt and grabbed Linc's hand to hold and to pull him closer as well, having had enough of Fox's hot and then cold again demeanour, What a dick.
The three of us settled and were about to start the movie when Linc whispered to me.
"Give him time, shit's been hard on him lately, and he takes the longest to warm up."
"Phew" I blew out, not wanting to waste any more time on Fox that evening.
Linc pressed a kiss to my temple like he understood but had to make his point, and we started the movie.
I didn't make it halfway through the film and started to fall asleep wedged between the guys. And they let me, not trying to keep me awake.

It must've been the early hours of the morning when I woke, laying on my side with my arm wrapped around one of the guys, not awake enough to comprehend where left and right was just yet. I was still tired and not fully rested.

A warm, calloused hand gently stroked my face, neck and down to my waist, then back up again. I didn't dare to move, enjoying the touches way too much.

My orientation coming back, I knew I was lying on my right side, and it had been Wyatt's hand that was caressing my skin. I was sure the other two were fast asleep from the deep breaths I heard around me. The second came from behind me, too, which meant, at some point, Fox had lost whatever battle he was fighting and had come over to lay with us.

I opened my eyes slightly, the projector still on and showing some action movie, illuminating the room enough for me to look into the most hypnotising grey eyes I had ever seen. Wyatt looked directly at me, not stopping his strokes on my skin.

I raised my hand to his face, tracing the outlines of his mouth, softly pulling on his full bottom lip. He looked so drop-dead gorgeous the way he was lying there, looking at me with hooded eyes and sleep-tussled hair.

"What are you doing to me, *to us,* Wildcat?" He sighed deeply.

I had no answer for him as I didn't know what they were doing to me either. All I learned at this moment was that I didn't want any of it to stop. I wanted to keep them all.

Chapter 31

Ivy Alexander

That morning, I woke up to Fox shouting.
"Take that, lying bitch!"
Instantly sat up and found myself tangled between Linc's and Wyatt's arms and legs, disorientated but also super alert.
"What! What's going on?" I grumbled, trying to untangle myself, but the arms tightened, not letting me move.
I turn my head to see Fox sitting up from his spot behind Linc, looking at his phone with the biggest smile I've ever witnessed on his face.
"What happened?" Reaching up, I grab my hair band, which was currently being eaten alive by the bird's nest on my head, pulling it free and running my hands through the knots in my hair.
"Mum made the school test Crystal last night!" A relieved grin on his face, "I knew that she wasn't pregnant, but now she can't

keep walking around telling everyone," he turned his phone screen towards me with the email from the school stating the test was negative.

"That's amazing!" I said. I had read the clause on pregnancies in the school policies after my thoughts about possible Hastings House babies, and they were super strict on stuff like this. Therefore, it wasn't a big surprise that Crystal was made to take a test. From a girl's point of view, she was flipping lucky she wasn't pregnant with any baby in this school at this age.

"So, you can start being nicer to Ivy!" Linc grumbled from his cocoon next to me.

Linc was clearly not the morning person of the group. I've noticed he waited until the last second before jumping out of bed to get ready.

I saw the grimace on Fox's face when Linc spoke.

"Sorry, Angel," Fox exclaimed with a shy smile, avoiding my eyes.

And just like that, all the random comments, mean digs and weird moods evaporated from my mind, and I was left gaping at him. The Fox door was ajar, and I was intent on kicking it down.

"What's the time?" Wyatt mumbled, sleep drunk.

"5 a.m."

"Fuck I gotta get up, I've got training," I wiggled out of Linc and Wyatt's hold, shuffled down to the middle of the bed and jumped up.

"I'll see you all at breakfast," I hollered, walking out the door. Swiping my fob, I rushed inside my room and got changed to head down to the gym.

These sessions had been a lifesaver; being able to take my anger out on someone who can fight better than me was like going to see your shrink.

I jogged down to the gym, throwing on my shoes and trying to get my muscles to warm up in the igloo they call a school. Rounding the corner, I saw my trainer standing at the door, waiting for me.

"Nice of you to join me." He said with a pissed-off attitude. It was only my fourth session, but I figured out already that he liked punctuality.

"Sorry, slept past my alarm," I replied with my head bowed down a little. "Okay, but don't let it happen again. Now, hurry up and let me in."

Mr Wellington, whose name made me laugh; it was such a proper English name, is the owner of a boxing chain found here in this part of England; he had belts and titles and was by far the best trainer I've ever had. He was bloody good-looking, too, in that intimidating way. For a man in his late thirties, I was sure he could still pull. His body was a weapon. I suspected that the boys were jealous of him, but they would never admit it. After my first session, they mentioned that they could help with my training and that they knew x, y and z who could train me. Last week, Linc walked me down to the gym and met Mr Wellington, and the look on his face when we were wrestling on the mat had me laughing at him for hours! He kept saying, *"It's inappropriate for a man to be touching you that way."*

My sweet Lincoln, we were wrestling, and I needed to show Mr Wellington what I was capable of; I had my legs wrapped around the man's neck, trying to get him to tap out. It's what I like to call a fun time. Linc declared then he wouldn't be watching me train anymore. Secretly, I loved that he got jealous.

"No escort today?" Mr Wellington asked.

"Nope, they are still in bed." I laughed and warmed up.

"They?" He questioned me.

"Shit, I said that out loud…" I scrunched my face up in embarrassment.

"Hey, it's okay. I was young once, too! Although it was usually two girls for me" He cackled

"Shut up," I say, throwing my water bottle at him, hoping the floor will open up and swallow me whole.

"Come on, let's see if you have any energy for training left" he cackled at me, and I wanted to throat-punch him.

By 6 a.m. I was drenched in sweat and managed to get Mr Wellington to tap out once, although it was more of a sympathy tap-out than me actually winning.

"You need to run more." He stated, not even out of breath or as sweaty as I was.

"Do you know how cold it is here in the morning?" I answered in shock.

Laughing at me, he said in a disciplined tone, "Harden the fuck up and get it done!" I felt deflated, not wanting to run in this arctic-like weather. Before he left, he spun back to me, "Now go for a run; I'll see you tomorrow!" and walked out the door, leaving me to lock up the gym.

I was going to end up looking like Harry from Dumb and Dumber when he rode that fucking scooter in the snow, I thought.

Using my feet, I started spraying the mats with cleaner and throwing a towel down to wipe them. No way was I running that morning; I would clean this room with my legs and count it as a win for the day.

I noticed movement behind me while swiping away with my feet and taking the opportunity to get in some lunges and squats. Turning around, I saw Crystal standing not far from me, with four other girls flanking her.

"I've told you to stay the fuck away from Fox," she snarled with a murderous look on her face, her eyes squinted.

Before I had a moment to get over the shock of seeing her there, she punched me dead in the face.

It hurt like nothing I had ever felt before. I felt my nose crack and blood gushing out past my mouth, the coppery tang slipping in through my lips. Professional sparring partners hit me many times in the face before, but her punch was different.

I stumbled and fell to the mat, my feet slipping on the wet surface and the towels I had used for cleaning. Crystal quickly jumped on top of me and started whaling down blow after blow, each one connecting with my face or neck. The pain was insane; throwing my hand's out in front of my face, I felt her balled-up fist connect with my hands, and that's when I noticed the bitch was using brass knuckles. I then felt kicks in my sides and other fists raining down blows on my body. The other girls had joined in. I had no chance of getting out of here, not with brass knuckles bombarding my head. Doing the only thing you could do in this situation, I balled my body up tight and covered my head with my hands, trying to shield myself from the blows.

It wasn't until Crystal connected with the back of my head that I saw all-consuming darkness.

Chapter 32

Lincoln Baker

Wyatt and I had a good talk with Fox after Ivy had left for the gym. We both could feel that she wasn't leaving him cold, but man was that guy an ice block. Hopefully, after having Crystal's lie exposed by his cunning Mother, he could start treating Ivy decently.

"Don't expect me to become a lap dog like you two." He snapped at one point.

Liar.

If anyone knew Sebastian Foxworth better than he knew himself, it was Wyatt and me.

Fox also loved to punish himself, depriving himself of good things because, deep down, he believed he wasn't worthy of anything good because of who his Mother was. We've spent years explaining to him that he wasn't responsible for his

Mother's actions and that his father, who loved him so much, would want Fox to have every dream come true.

He was worthy of more than trash and drama; Ivy was something good for all of us.

None of us expected this to go as it did, but she entered our lives like a bulldozer.

Wyatt pulled me back from my thoughts, "Let's check the cameras; she should be finished with her training."

I had some cameras installed in the gym to check in on her training sessions occasionally, not wanting to sit down there myself as I was not too fond of how that guy was touching her. I knew he wasn't inappropriate with her, but it still made me feel that way. Jealousy was funny, and I had never felt it before Ivy.

Fox had left already to catch up with his coach for something, he had told me what it was about, but it was too damn early in the morning for me to remember.

I grabbed my laptop and sat back down on our makeshift floor bed in front of Wyatt, who refused to get up, saying he wouldn't put our mattresses back on our beds and wanted to keep it that way. Fat chance.

It took less than thirty seconds for the feed to come up on my screen and less than ten seconds for Wyatt and I to run for the door.

We sprinted down the stairs and across the school grounds like our lives depended on it. And it did.

At that very moment, I had it confirmed to myself that Ivy had become my life.

I had fallen for her head over heels.

I was going to destroy anyone who dared to hurt her. Crystal and her posse of snake bitches were the first to get it.

In record time, we made it to the gym and wrenched the doors open; the screams and yells of these hyenas on top of our girl made my blood run cold in my veins.

We ran over and pulled the mob off Ivy as quickly as possible. Wyatt was so forceful, with a killer gaze in his eyes like I hadn't seen him before. He grabbed Lucy Covington, who kept kicking into Ivy's ribs by the hair, yanked her back, and then he had her around the throat, lifted into the air and literally threw her away like the piece of trash she is. I pulled Eva Richards and Lori Aldington away to reach my main target.

Crystal.

That bitch was straddled over Ivy and kept punching. I saw the brass knuckles in one of her hands and lost all control.

I grabbed her hair and, as hard as I could, pulled that bitch back. When she was finally off Ivy, I saw Wyatt in my periphery scooting to our girl. He had her. So I turned my attention back to Crystal. With one hand, I squeezed her face as hard as I could so she could look into my eyes. I hoped she saw every ounce of hatred I had displayed.

"Come near her or any of us again, and I **will** kill you!" I roared at her before I spat right into her face and pushed her away so hard she landed on her back like the fucking insect she was.

The other girls had already started to scramble away, leaving Crystal behind.

What a bunch of fucking cowards!

I took a shaky breath before I turned to Wyatt and Ivy.

I crouched down onto my knees on the other side of her. Wyatt was trying to get her to open her eyes. But I could see that she was unconscious.

The state of her face made my heart clench. She had cuts with blood pooling on her cheeks and forehead, her lips and one eyebrow busted, bruises blooming everywhere, and her left eye was beginning to swell shut.

I saw ripped-out strains of her hair beside her head.

As I gently moved her head, I saw that I had loose strands of Crystal's hair wrapped around my hand from when I yanked her off Ivy.

Good!

"We need to keep her still; I'm sure she has a major concussion."

Wyatt is forever the calmest in a storm. I wasn't freaking out per se, but I wasn't the calmest either; I had checked her pulse and breathing. Nevertheless, seeing the girl I was for sure falling in love with lying unconscious on the floor, beaten to a pulp, had me on a rollercoaster of emotions.

While I was taking in all her injuries and holding her hand wordlessly, I saw Wyatt pull out his phone to call for an ambulance.

The next call he made was the one I dreaded. Fox.

The ambulance from the private hospital that our school was affiliated with arrived in record time.

The paramedics rushed through the door that was held open by staff members.

A girl associated with the legacies brutally beaten in the gym made the rounds faster than the speed of light.

Our principal, the affable but useless guy, was green in his face when he looked at the extent of Ivy's injuries.

He watched the school nurse hover over Ivy, giving first aid, ready to puke in the next bin.

"Boys, thank goodness you found her so fast. She isn't okay, but she would've been so much worse if she was left here…"

Nurse Cam trailed off, probably never having seen a girl beaten like that before.

She made room when the two paramedics rushed to our girl; one was hooking Ivy straight up to an Oximeter and ECG machine. The other was asking questions in the small crowd around us.

I could hear the footsteps that made their way into the gym next. Wyatt's head shot up, too.

Fox stomped in a half-jog toward us, his eyes scanning the room and landing on me first.

I gave him a look, which made him slow his pace. Glancing quickly down to where Ivy's body was lying. Still unconscious and ready to be transported to the hospital.

He stopped dead in his tracks, as I expected.

He kept looking from me to Wyatt, and our silent conversation with each other had him leaving the gym, and we watched him go.

The paramedics had Ivy in a neck brace and manoeuvred onto a stretcher. They were about to leave when they stopped me and Wyatt from joining.

"Guys, you can't go with us like that. Go clean up and follow us after. She's in the right hands now."

Not used to being told what to do, we looked at ourselves stunned.

We didn't have time to dress, so we only had our lounge pants on, and it was then that we both realised that our bare torsos had blood smears all over them, Ivy's blood.

Another wave of pure rage hit me, and I saw the same in Wyatt's face. Crystal needed to be destroyed.

The skank, having fled her scene of destruction shortly after her bitches had made a run for it.

Wyatt and I sprinted up to our room, punched in the code as we left our fobs behind in a hurry, and stormed through the door to get some shirts and shoes on.

We didn't clean ourselves up. No way were we going to shower while Ivy went to the hospital.

I grabbed two extra pairs of sweats on my way out the door, and with that, we left.

We rushed down the stairs again and headed for the car park when Fox came in to view.

"She'll be gone by the end of the day" he declared in a manner that made even me afraid of him. He was so calm and collected that it gave me the chills. By "she" he meant Crystal. I nodded. He had left the gym to sort something out that would hopefully get rid of Crystal for good this time. She would get expelled for definite, but that wasn't enough.

"You coming?" That was all Fox got out of Wyatt before he unlocked his car, ready to leave.

"I'll take mine," Fox replied, and I jumped into Wyatt's car. The engine roared to life, and with squeaking wheels, we hurried away.

Chapter 33

Wyatt Forester

Running into the gym and seeing Ivy on the floor made me feel things I've never felt before.

My heart was constricted with fear. I was so anxious that I wouldn't see her again. I've not even fucked her, and I was utterly addicted to her. I honestly didn't even care anymore; I was entirely consumed by her and was all in.

She was mine, and I was gonna give myself to her fully.

If vanilla sex was all I was going to get for the rest of my life, then so be it; I just knew I needed no one but her. I knew Linc felt the same as me. It was written all over his tortured face. Between us all, we could keep her happy. There was no way Fox wouldn't be on board now; we all saw his reaction when he saw her, and he wouldn't be able to deny her anymore.

The hospital was thankfully only ten minutes down the road, but Linc was muttering nonstop about going faster and yelling at random cars to move out of the way. I got it. I was feeling the same.

Much to Linc's dismay, we arrived at the hospital and parked in the car park.

"They need emergency parking at the entrance so you can leave your car." He said, frustrated.

"They are busy saving lives, Linc, not making sure people don't have to walk across the road from a parking lot." I pointed out but understood his urgency.

"Let's agree to disagree," Linc says, taking off in a jog across the road towards the main doors and heading for the reception desk.

I managed to arrive at the desk a second after Linc.

"What is her name, and when was she brought in?" The receptionist asked politely.

"Ivy Anderson, she would have been ten to twelve minutes ahead of us and brought in by ambulance from Hastings House."

"And you are?"

"Lincoln Baker and Wyatt Forester" Linc pointed between himself and then me.

Hearing my name, she raised her face from the computer and looked at me.

"Forester? As in Doctor Micheal Forester's son?" She raised her brow at me curiously.

Stepping forward to the window, "Yes, the one and only," I smiled, causing her to blush.

"We really need to get into our girlfriend," Linc pushed.

With the word *OUR*, her browns pulled together.

"Okay, she is still in the major trauma wing at the moment; she has been triaged and is being placed on long stay until they've done more tests," and then sighed, "I can't let you in if you're not direct family." She pulled her glasses off her face and gave us a sympathetic look.

"That's okay," I smiled and grabbed Linc by the elbow to walk down the hall towards the back of Emergency. I grabbed my phone out of my pocket and called my Dad.

Answering on my fourth ring, "Wyatt?"

"Dad, I need to get into the emergency wing; Ivy has been attacked at the school," I blurted out, getting impatient.

"Where are you?"

"Ground level, walking towards the rear of Emergency."

"Okay, I'll be there in five minutes" he replied and hung up.

"He is gonna meet us at the staff entrance. It's just down there." I pointed down the hall.

"Where is Fox?" Linc looked around.

"I don't know; he said he was taking his car." I looked behind me in case he just took ages to park.

"I'll call him." Linc quickly pulled his phone out of his pocket and dialled Fox.

The automatic doors opened, and I saw my Dad walk out, waving at us to quickly walk through with him.

"I just ran into the EMT who brought her in; they just moved her to a long stay. She'll be going for a cat scan in a bit." He said as he walked us into the ward and opened the door to room 10.

Laying on the bed flat with a neck brace was Ivy. She looked even worse than she had when I last saw her. Her eye was completely swollen shut, and the cuts on her head were smeared with blood but covered with tape; her nose was also swollen and dried blood everywhere around it, and her busted lip was also taped at the outer corner.

"Oh fucking hell," I whispered and walked to her side, gripping the railing so I wouldn't touch her and cause any more problems.

Linc was still standing in the doorway, his complexion white as a ghost; turning towards my Dad, he said, "Fox is at the same doors we just came through."

"I'll go grab him," my Dad said and briskly walked off.

Another doctor walked in a few seconds later and looked at us both in surprise, "How did you get in here?" He questioned.

"Doctor Forester," I reply dryly and dare he try and kick us out. He raised his brows at me and walked over to check her vitals. My Dad and Fox walked into the room shortly after. Fox stood in the doorway and looked like he was going to vomit.

"What are her vitals?" My Dad asked and stepped next to the attending Doctor.

"She is being taken for X-rays and a CT scan now, but her vitals seem okay, her pupils are dilating well, and her breathing is unaffected. It seems she is still unconscious due to the head injury. We'll know more once the tests are done, but she is stable." He explained more to us than my father, him being a Doctor himself and understanding what was going on.

"Thank you," my Dad said as the Doctor took the brakes off the bed and wheeled Ivy out of the room.

"Sit down, boys, and tell me what happened."

Taking a seat, I listened to Lincoln tell my Dad what happened to Ivy in the gym and how we found out.

"Who is this girl to you all?" Dad asked, looking at me.

"Our Girlfriend" Linc stated, ever so casually.

"Our Girlfriend?" Dad raised his brows, looking at us, confused as hell. "As in yours? Or as in all of yours?"

"All," Fox spoke for the first time.

His answer wasn't lost on us.

"Is this the girl you were bringing for dinner this weekend?" Dad asked Fox carefully.

"Yes, that's her"

"And whose date was she going to be then?"

"All of ours"

"Okay, I don't understand, but this isn't the place for this," Dad said back, running a hand down his chin, his eyes wandering from me and the others and back again.

"I'm going to take over her care; just wait here; I'll go have her transferred to my patient list" and he walked out of the room. I knew I had much explaining to do, but I couldn't care less. I was of age and owed no one an explanation about my love life. My brain felt fried, like someone crossed too many wires, leaving me with nothing but tumbleweeds blowing around. This waiting game was going to send me insane. I've never felt so scared and worried about anyone in my life. I was too young when my Mother died, and I hardly remembered her.

Looking over, I saw Linc staring at the wall; his eyes were glassy and distant.

I looked at the door as my Dad entered, carrying two more chairs, water bottles and a stack of washcloths.

Throwing the washcloths at Linc, "Go the bathroom in there and wash all the blood off yourself before she gets back."

Placing the two chairs near Linc's, my Dad gestured for Fox to sit on one. "Sit down, son."

And like a robot, Fox did as he was told. Hell must have frozen over.

Chapter 34

Sebastian 'Fox' Foxworth

Something had broken in my head. The moment I saw Ivy on that gym floor, my brain took an invisible hit, and everything changed.

Looking at my best friend next to her unconscious body, I made it clear that I couldn't stay there. I had to deal with Crystal once and for all. They understood and let me go.

I stormed through the school looking for the conniving bitch and found her by the rowing equipment shed outside by the river.

None other, than the slimy cunt Colt Anderson cowering beside her, What a sight.

I could never figure out Colt's deal, but I got the picture when I saw them together. He was a conniving piece of shit too. The two of them make a perfect couple.

I hoped they'd both fuck off from here.

He spotted me and got up, probably trying to shield Crystal from me.

"Hey man, I get it. But you *know* that Crystal isn't well..." he started with his hand held up in a 'stop' motion.

Like fuck, mate. I thought, *get out of my way, or I'll take you down with her.*

I carried on toward them, and when I reached a defensive-looking Colt, I pushed him out of the way and instantly had Crystal by the collar. I pulled the pathetic crying shell of a woman up off the floor so she was at eye level with me.

"This is my very last warning, Crystal." I hissed with so much violence in my voice.

"This is how it's gonna go, you will pack your shit and leave the school with immediate effect; you'll go to the office and tell your parents you're too unwell for school. You have 2 hours, and I'm being overly generous here. If you refuse or think you can hide from us, be assured that we *will* find you and drag you away from here ourselves!"

She shook and whimpered, trying to escape my wrath, but she hadn't seen my wrath just yet.

Her mascara running down her cheeks from her tears. I felt nothing but disgust.

I pulled her closer to my face, Colt watching and holding on to her arm, waiting for me to hit that sorry excuse of a woman. I wouldn't give him that triumph.
"I loathe you; I'll regret the day I met you for the rest of my life. Get out of my face!" And with that, I let go, and she dropped back onto the floor, hitched breaths coming out fast from her. Colt sat beside her and put his arm around her shoulder but didn't look at me again. That's right, shithead, know your place.
I heard him talk in a low voice to her.
'You know you fucked up, you need to do as he said and leave.'
Too right.
I left them and pulled my phone out of my pocket to let my Mother know that I needed more of her help. Crystal couldn't get away with this without any repercussions.
I headed for the car park and saw Lincoln and Wyatt getting into Wyatt's Audi, ready to leave for the hospital.
I couldn't join them, not yet.
I had to make one stop beforehand.

I arrived at the hospital and was taken by Wyatt's Dad to see Ivy after a short debacle with the receptionist.
My heart was thumping so hard I thought it was about to come through my chest walls.

The minutes before I arrived here, I had to make a decision, one I never had to make before.

I decided to stop lying to myself and acknowledge that I was worth something. That something was lying in front of me, attached to monitors and beaten unconscious by the lie I kept telling myself.

Michael had asked us direct questions about Ivy, and when I answered them truthfully, I felt set free.

Yes, Ivy Alexander was my girl. She was my best friend's girl, too, and no one in this world would take that away from us, especially not myself.

The way she made me feel was indescribable. I remembered the first time she had pulled me from one of my anger outbursts without even knowing what she was doing. She and those green eyes of hers just did it.

I had no control over it whatsoever, she was just there, and like the moon pulled the tide, she pulled me back from the dark place I found myself in every time shit went wrong.

Nevertheless, the girl who had my heart in a clutch was lying in a hospital bed, beaten by one of my mishaps.

When she opens her eyes, I will tell her I'll keep her safe from now on.

I didn't need to explain in big words to Lincoln and Wyatt what was going on with me; these two knew me better than anyone else in this world.

All we had to do now was wait for Ivy to wake up.

With a hitch, though

By the next round, Michael broke the news that Ivy's parents had to be informed as she was still under 18.

They then phoned Michael, and holy fuck did they go off the rails.

They wanted to come and collect her and take her back home to Australia.

Fuck.

The three of us looked at each other with even more panic. If Ivy's parents decided that Ivy was going home, she was going home.

Fuck. Fuck. Fuck.

Ivy needed to wake up for us to be calmer, and then the guys and I had to hatch a plan.

Now that I found her, I was not about to let her go.

Chapter 35

Ivy Alexander

I've been in a few scraps before, I've even boxed in tournaments for fun.
But not once have I been so brutally bashed. The pain I felt from my head to my toes was indescribable. I could hear monitors and machines around me making continuous and repetitive beeping noises. My head felt like someone had replaced my brain with cotton wool, and my mouth resembled Alice Springs.
I could hear a faint snoring sound coming from my left. Whatever painkillers they had given me were bullshit; I could feel every bone in my body with agonising pain.
Pulling my eyes apart, I was assaulted with bright lights. Fucking pricks loved to leave all the lights on in hospitals.

Blinking my eyes nonstop until they adjusted to the light, I looked around and saw *them*. My boys are all asleep in my room.

Linc was curled up in a small plastic chair at the end of my bed, with his head resting on it; one of his hands was curled around my foot, holding it tight. Wyatt was curled up on the floor, using what looked like tracksuit pants as a pillow, and Fox was sleeping sitting up on one of the small plastic chairs, with his feet kicked up on a second one. Gosh, they were beautiful. Wiggling the foot that Linc held, I saw his body stiffen under the movement, watching his head lift up to look at me like he wasn't sure if I was awake or twitching.

"Petal," he breathed in a sigh of relief.

Jumping to his feet, he stood near my head and reached out a hand to stroke down my jawline.

"You scared the shit out of us, baby." His eyes were rimmed red, his dark hair a mess, but he was as handsome as ever.

I heard Fox's feet hit the ground as he woke from the noise and walked over to the other side of the bed.

"Ivy," he said, looking at me with so much emotion in his eyes. Fox never showed anything other than anger or lust. To see this was a little unnerving. It got me all shy.

Opening my mouth to speak proved pointless; it was that dry in there.

"Shit," Linc reached for the cup and straw on my wheel-able table.

"Here," he said as he placed the straw in my mouth so I could take a few mouths full, just enough to wash the dust bunnies down my throat.

In a croaky voice, I managed to say, "Hi."

Fox leaned close to my face and gently placed one hand on either side.

"Love, your face is a mess, but you're still the most beautiful girl." Placing the lightest and softest kiss on my lips I've ever felt. If I hadn't opened my eyes to witness it, I wouldn't have been sure it even happened.

"I'm gonna go find Michael" Linc exclaimed, walking off and leaning down to shake Wyatt awake.

I heard him grumble, "What?" Until I saw his face pop up from the floor so quickly, like a jack in the box, rushing over to my side "Wildcat!" He almost yelled and clutched the railing to stop himself from grabbing me; I could see how white his knuckles were holding the bar.

Just as I was about to say something, a man who looked like Wyatt walked to my side.

"Ah, nice to see you are finally awake, Ivy," he gave me a heartfelt smile, "I'm Doctor Forester, but you can call me

Michael; I'm Wyatt's dad." His eyes were blue, unlike Wyatt's grey. But the similarities were uncanny.

"I'm going to assume you know where you are, but do you know why?" He asked.

'Yes, Crystal attacked me with brass knuckles after my training"

"Correct. That's a good sign that you remember," he grabbed my chart and started writing it down. "Do you have pain anywhere?"

"Yes," I replied, "my ribs are on fire, and my shoulders are hurting with every breath I take."

"That's to be expected; you have two fractured ribs, a fractured cheekbone, a cracked nose and a whole heap of deep tissue damage. But thankfully, all this can be fixed with a lot of rest. Thankfully the boys found you on time." He said, looking at my guys.

"Your parents have been called, and they should be arriving in the country within the next few hours, so hopefully, they will be here soon. You were unconscious for around ten hours."

"Shit," I exhaled "that's gonna be fun." My parents would lose their shit and have a massive blowout, probably suing the school, at least.

"You're under 18, they had to be notified."

"Yes, I know, but they will not be happy."

"And rightfully so!" With an angry undertone, Michael exclaimed, "We have made sure that Crystal has left the school for good."

"How did you find me?" I asked Wyatt, who was still strangling the bar.

"Linc saw you being attacked on the security camera."

"I thought you couldn't get into the cameras?" I looked at Linc standing at the end of the bed, holding my feet again.

"I still can't, but I installed some of my own," he looked at me sheepishly.

"Why did you put up cameras in the gym?" I narrowed my eyes at him.

"To make sure you were safe," he half smiled at me, then looked down at the bed. "And cause I was jealous of your trainer…" he admitted.

How could I be mad at that confession? Plus, his jealousy might have saved me from a much worse fate.

"Thank you."

Looking up at me, "You're not mad?"

"No, I'm not mad." I smiled at him as far as my busted lip would allow, "Thank you for rescuing me."

"Petal, there isn't anything I wouldn't do for you!" He exclaimed and pushed Wyatt out of the way to get to my side.

Leaning down into my eye-line, he dropped the words, "I Love you" and gave my lips a small peck.

Pulling himself back up to standing height, he asked Michael, "Is there anything we can do now that she is awake?"

Hello, you just dropped the L word, then dismissed it like nothing had happened… I was speechless and needed a minute.

"Do you think you could eat something, Ivy?" Michael asked curiously.

"Maybe, I can always try," I said back, still trying to digest Lincoln's words so nonchalantly.

I kept my eyes trained on him.

"Okay, I'll go grab you a soup," Michael said while leaving.

Taking a deep breath, I closed my eyes.

"You okay, Wildcat?"

"No, I'm not; I need you all to sit down and be quiet for a minute. My brain needs to catch up with everything. All this is very overwhelming, and I need a minute." I rushed out.

They returned to their chairs and sat but kept looking at me.

"Do you possibly know how ridiculous you all look folded up to fit in those tiny chairs," I laughed at them.

"I think you might have brain damage," Fox grumbled back.

Smiling at him, "Possibly, yes, your ex did punch me in the face with brass knuckles." I raised my brows at him, waiting for his snarky comment.

Fox ran his hand over his face, "Yes, you're right, she did," he looked at me with so much anguish that I stopped baiting him and allowed silence to fall over the room for a while.

A short while later, Michael returned with some clear soup and a straw. "They only had chicken," he said, "drink that up, and if you can keep it down, I'll let you have something solid." Looking around the room, he noticed the boys all seated and being quiet. "Oh good, you have trained them well, I see." Then he chuckled and left the room.

Reaching out, I grabbed the cup and tried to pick it up, but my fingers were so sore and stiff from being hit while I was shielding my face that I couldn't seem to get them to bend enough to grab the handle.

A large hand came into my view, grabbed the mug for me, and brought the straw to my lips. Looking up at Fox, I gave a low "Thank you."

"Anything you want, Angel, it's yours," he dropped ever so casually.

If getting bashed by his ex was all it took to get him to be nice, I would have done it weeks ago.

After finishing the soup, I was exhausted, and the boys let me go back to sleep. Fox and Wyatt agreed they would return to the school to shower and change and bring me back some clean clothes.

Linc flat-out refused to move; he had taken his stance back at my feet.

After about an hour, Wyatt and Fox returned, and Linc had gone off to find the cafeteria to grab everyone something to eat; Micheal had agreed to let me shower as long as one of the boys helped me, and I was sitting on a shower chair.

Wyatt had volunteered for the job and helped me out of bed and into the bathroom.

He helped me undo the arse-showing hospital gown and pulled off my panties, placing me in the shower chair. If I wasn't in so much pain, I would have maybe been embarrassed about getting naked in front of Wyatt for the first time, but I honestly had zero fucks to give.

Wyatt went to work washing me from head to toe. He was gentle around my wounds and barely brushed his hands along the multiple bruises my body was covered in. He even gently washed my hair with the hospital soap. I knew I would regret that move later, but I just wanted to feel clean, no matter how many knots and tangles my hair had.

Drying me off, he dressed me in oversized men's sweats and an oversized t-shirt and jumper. Each item smelled different, making me believe they had grabbed an item from each. I could tell the hoodie was Wyatt's; it smelt just like the one I had never returned to him.

Wyatt helped me back into my bed, and Linc had a tray with carbonara pasta waiting for me.

"Micheal approved some real food, and the cafeteria had pasta," Linc smiled at me, proud of finding pasta for me.

"Please kiss me," I said to him.

Rushing over to my side, Linc lightly brushed his lips on mine, being mindful of my split lip.

"Thank you."

"Where is my Daughter!" I heard booming from the hall outside.

"Shit..." Dad was here.

Groaning, I grabbed my fork and tried to shove as much pasta in my mouth as I could before he walked in the door. I knew I wouldn't get a mouthful once he was in here.

"Ivy!" my Dad made a choked noise as he entered the room. Taking in his surroundings, he noticed the three boys occupying the chairs in the room.

"Who the fuck are these cunts?" My Dad yelled. He was a proper Australian man with a mouth to go with it.

"Dad, these are my friends from school. They are the ones who found me and got me here," I told him through a mouthful of pasta.

Bustling in behind my Dad was my Mum, trying to deflect a conversation with a nurse.

"Oh yes, Thank you that's very sweet, Sorry, if you don't mind, I need to see my daughter" then closed the door on the woman.

Turning around from the door, my Mother looked at me. "Oh, for fuck sake, Ivy, you look terrible" she yelped and threw a hand over her mouth.

Shrugging at her, I said, "Maybe I can star in one of your books now, Mum."

"Absolutely not" my Mother replied with a sigh and came to stand at my side.

"Ivy, why is your room full of boys?" Mum raised her brows at me.

With that, all three stood and held out their hands, introducing themselves.

Chapter 36

Ivy Alexander

My parent's visit went down a treat, and I was saying this most sarcastically.

In typical Aussie fashion, they let everyone know who was in charge from now on.

Even the boys heeled, and that was a sight to see.

After introducing themselves, they returned to their chairs and went quiet, watching my parents unleash a storm.

My mum was the first to mention that I'd go home with them.

The blood in my veins froze. The last thing I wanted to do was go back home; my home was here now.

I didn't plead with them yet; I had to let my parents rant and get it out of their system before I strategically worked them down.

At the mention of me having to go back home, I saw from the corner of my eye that the boys' backs all stiffened. Fox had the armrest of his chair so tightly gripped I worried the plastic would snap.

Wyatt's head lowered, and he pinched the bridge of his nose, shaking his head ever so slightly and Linc, my sweet Lincoln who not too long ago whispered to me so nonchalantly, '*I love you*'.

Well, he looked like someone had murdered his cat. Anger, worry and sadness all rolled into one.

He was the sweetest of my guys, but don't mistake his kindness and open heart for weakness; I knew a fighter lurking in his shadow.

But it would only come out to play if what he loved was threatened.

So unlike Fox

I still couldn't quite believe that I was calling him mine, too, but the minute I opened my eyes in this bleak hospital room, I felt the shift in him.

He belonged to me now.

I prayed that I could keep his alter ego with that massive chip on his shoulder in check and bring the side of him out that was the real Sebastian Foxworth. He was a guy who could love fiercely once he realised he was worthy of love, too.

And my dark horse Wyatt, ever the calm and collected. He was the personification of s*till waters ran deep.*

He hadn't shown me all of him yet, just a tiny glimpse, and I would make it my mission to go down the deep end to see what he had lurking there.

None of it would matter if my parents made real with their threat.

I understood where they came from, but that didn't mean I was in danger.

I would've, more than likely, kicked all these girls arses if I had a fair chance. The cowards knew they could only beat me if they jumped me literally from behind.

Flashbacks of the gym clouded my mind, and I had to squeeze my eyes shut to banish them.

I wouldn't let them win; I wouldn't let them scare me or my parents.

After all, I was raised a fighter, and a defeat didn't mean a loss. That's the opening line I would use to persuade my parents to leave me here.

I had to pick the right time, though. Otherwise, my arse would be on the next flight in no time.

When my parents were convinced I wasn't on my deathbed, they went out to grab some stuff for me and search for a hotel, leaving me and the boys alone again.

Fox was the first to reach my bedside.

"I pictured meeting your parents for the first time differently."
He and I both had to chuckle. Damn, laughing hurt my ribs badly. It wasn't the first time I had my ribs broken or any other injury, as a matter of fact, but usually, I wouldn't go down without a fight, unlike this time.

And that pain was worse. My body was broken, and my ego was scratched.

"You okay, Angel? Want me to ask for some pain meds?" Fox asked.

"Nah, it's okay. I should refrain from laughing, though." I replied with a flat smile.

His beautiful blue eyes were all bloodshot, and he had slivers of dark underneath them.

Still handsome as ever, though, I had that *peng* in my chest again.

I reached for his hand and pulled him closer to me. He obliged whilst being careful not to touch me where it could hurt.

I was not too fond of this already, as I wanted him as close as possible and touching me everywhere, now that he clearly wanted me as much as I wanted him.

When his face was only inches from mine, I spoke softly, just for him.

"I was waiting for you to come to me." He knew what I meant, and his lips turned into the most gorgeous smile that lit up his

eyes, and I could feel the butterflies having a dance competition in my belly.
His knuckles stroked over my bruised cheek, and he leaned closer, his lips brushing mine.
"If you jump, I jump, right?"
And then he kissed me tenderly, igniting a fire deep inside me. Forgetting about the pain in my fingers for just that one special moment between him and me, my hand was running through his blonde mane, caressing his face like it was the most precious thing in the world, and to me, it was. Giving me his fragile heart was the greatest gift he could give.

Mum and Dad returned with 'get well soon' presents, face cleaning wipes, nightshirts, slipper socks, chocolates and my favourite flowers, dyed blue Roses. And books.
Books were symbolic in our house.
Books gave knowledge, and knowledge was power.
One of the books was a special edition of, you guessed it, my all-time favourite, Wuthering Heights.
I already had around five different copies, but you always needed multiple special editions of your favourite book.
Another one was about…oh my fucking god, mother….
Polyamory. Mum had sneaked it into my lap so no one could see.

That woman's spider senses were flipping good, but I didn't need a book to tell me how I should live and love.

I felt my cheeks blush and shoved the book underneath the blanket and my painful thigh, needing to chuck it as soon as no one was looking. I gave my mum a murderous look, but she just smiled deviously at me.

Man, oh man, I knew where I got my attitude from.

And the temper from my Father, who was in that very moment trying to instil the fear of god into my guys, well, you found your matches there, Dad, I thought.

Thankfully, the boys were respectful and played along.

Dad wanted to know the ins and outs of a cat's arse from them, but when Wyatt told him his Dad was my Doctor, my Father seemed to calm down a few nudges.

Good grief, this would be the most awkward stay anyone ever had in a hospital.

When all the hustle and bustle slowed down, my parents had left for the night, and it started to hit me that I had the shit kicked out of me. A rush of anxiety went through me that turned into anger and bloodlust next.

This no holds barred piss poor attempt by these bitches to show me where I belonged in their eyes had me itching to destroy something.

The pain, mixed with anger and tinged with fright, overwhelmed me like a tidal wave.

I felt the hot tears prick at the back of my eyes, wanting release. I hadn't cried since Crystal had tipped my glass of water over my head, and I didn't want to now. But my body had other ideas, so I just had to let them flow in this moment.

Trying to cry quietly, I lay on my side, pushing my face as best as the pain allowed me into my pillow. I tried to hide my tears from my boys, who kept watching me like a Hawk.

The first sob had them all rushing to my bed in an instant; Wyatt was closest to my face, asking if I needed pain meds; shaking my head slightly; I think he realised what was going on and lightly stroked his hand over my head.

Fox, probably understanding the most, had my thigh under his palm. "It's okay, angel, we're here."

Linc was right next to Wyatt, holding my trashed hand.

Chapter 37

Lincoln Baker

Watching Ivy cry did something to my heart that it wasn't used to. My chest felt tight, and the backs of my eyes stung. She had been through something that was likely to leave some scars; whether they were mental or physical, I wasn't sure.

She was the bravest girl I had ever met.

Once her parents had gone to the hotel and we had settled Ivy down for the night, we put our heads together to hash out a plan to make sure Ivy's parents would let her stay at the school.

Fox had arranged for his mother to have all the girls who hurt Ivy removed from the school; I set for my Dad to pull out all the legal cards to make sure Ivy would be safe on campus by upping security around the place. Wyatt chatted with his Dad to see if he could offer any assistance.

By the time morning rolled around, we had slept in those plastic chairs for three nights, hoping never to see one again.

Ivy's parents arrived at the room around 6 a.m. with more flowers, stuffed teddy bears, a full breakfast spread, and a tray of fresh coffee. I usually wasn't a coffee drinker, but I gulped that drink down like it was a lifeline; my neck and body were stiff from the chair.

They had asked us all to go back to the dorms and shower after they had fed us. I didn't want to go.

I wanted to stay next to Ivy until she could return to campus. But Ivy had asked us all to do as we were told and said we all stunk and needed showers. I mean, she wasn't wrong.

Fox left first, stating he had an errand to run on the way back to school; Wyatt left his phone with Ivy so she could call us if she needed us. My heart was pulling me back towards her room with every step away from it.

"Come on, lover boy," Wyatt grumbled next to me as his hand connected with my shoulder.

"Let's get to the school and set Ivy's room up for her when she gets back." He smiled at me. "Dad said they were going to allow her to leave the hospital today."

"But what if they make her go home?"

"Then they make her go home," Wyatt shrugged. "I've heard the schools in Australia are interesting places to go to." He smiled cunningly at me, "We can always follow her."

Taking a deep breath, "I'm in love with her" I told him.

"I know, we're all falling for her ."

"Even Fox?"

"Oh, Fox has fallen; that poor girl is in for it now," he laughed, "he's let her in, and he will never let her out."

"Come on then, let's buy out the florist on the way back." I would fill that room to the brim with every flower they had.

After arriving back at the dorm, Wyatt had set up Ivy's bed, so it was easier for her to climb in and out of and moved all her furniture around so she would be comfortable for however long she needed to rest. I went to work filling every free space I could find with flowers. The local Florist delivers them, So far I had managed to get two van loads in, and they were unloading the last one downstairs. Fox had popped his head in the room to tell us his mother had won, and that all 4 girls were all being removed from the campus today.

"That's the last of it" The delivery driver stated as he handed me the last vase of roses.

"Thank you," I said and walked up to her room.

Walking in, I heard Wyatt talking on my phone.

"No worries, Wildcat, see you soon!"

Looking at him, I saw him smiling, "What happened?"

"Ivy's parents said she can stay but will need daily phone calls and updates." His smile was huge. I don't think I've ever seen him that happy about anything in his life. I understood; the butterflies were having a rave in my gut, too.

"Her parents are filling out the discharge paperwork now and bringing her back." He continued. His happy face was a new sight for me, and I would lie if I said I wasn't happy for him. I wondered if we'd never had a girlfriend before because we had never looked for only one to share. We were as close as brothers and knew we'd always stay together, no matter the job or whatnot, but it never occurred to us that we would only need one girl between us. Until Ivy came along. She was the missing part of us. No way would our future hold three different girlfriends, let alone wives. It was us three and our love, Our Ivy.

At that, Fox walked back into the room and looked around at the forest of flowers I had filled Ivy's room with.

"I hope she actually likes flowers," he smirked at me, "I mean, what if she has allergies?" He pointed out.

"Don't take me for a fool. I've checked her file." I quirked an eyebrow at him.

"Of course, you have her file."

"Dude, you should see my internet browser now! After what her mother said to that nurse, I had to dig into her background and find out who her parents were."

"Who are they?"

"Her Mum is actually a big deal in the book world; she is an international best-selling author of crime and thriller novels. Her Father is in property development, not like your Dad was, more like the buying and flipping for profit type."

"That's why the guy is so big and scary!" Wyatt interjected.

"Glad I wasn't the only one who felt emasculated around him." Fox chuckled.

"Come on, let's get outta here and leave Ivy to find this when she returns." As much as I wanted to see her face when she walked in here, I wanted her parents to feel like their little girl was taken care of; I wanted them to see she had three guys here, willing to do anything to make her happy and safe. Which was what we're going to do every day from now on.

Chapter 38

Sebastian 'Fox' Foxworth

Ivy had healed and rested well over the last few weeks. We were all proud of her, and she was basically back to normal.

The first week back on campus was tough for her; she woke a few times at night, sweat-drenched and screaming.

Her flashbacks wound her tight. She was used to being this indestructible girl, a fighter.

She knew there was nothing she could've done to defend herself, and lately, she seemed to accept that fact. The nightmares had stopped the second week of being back.

Her usual snarky, feisty and fun side was coming back.

That's why the guys and I decided to take her to the school's annual Halloween ball.

"Only if I can wear a paper bag over my head." Was her snarky answer

"Don't be silly. You look beautiful. The battle scars make you look tough." Linc, the soppy git, told her.

It turned into a whole debate, and in the end, I told her that we would sort her costume and surprise her with it.

She was happy enough to agree, trusting we wouldn't make her look foolish.

So, Linc and I went on an online shopping spree.

Wyatt was the one to choose ours.

He got us all excited with the ones he got for the three of us.

We picked a spin between The Grim Reaper and Red Riding Hood for Ivy.

She was our sexy black riding hood with a cape and deep hood, and for her self-conscious side, we got her a lacy gothic masquerade mask to cover up what she thought was the worst she'd ever looked.

None of us thought she looked awful; she was as gorgeous to us as any other day.

We also got her a velvet black dress, fishnet stockings and biker boots.

Just imagining how she'd look had me having to readjust my dick constantly.

Being this new version turned me from a horny guy into a 24/7 horn dog for the girl, My girl.

While healing up, she kept teasing me, knowing we couldn't do anything until she was entirely okay again.

Which brought me to at least four jerk-offs in the shower every day!

Linc and Wyatt were affected the same, heading for the bathroom just as much, thinking I was stupid and didn't know what they were doing. We basically stood in line to get in there at this point.

I walked in on Ivy and Wyatt making out heavily the night before the Halloween party, and it had me so hot that I told Wyatt to fuck off out of her room.

He just laughed like a crazy guy and walked out with the words, "Not long, brother…"

The sexual tension was heavy in the air, and even Ivy kept rubbing her thighs to no extent when she thought no one was looking. But we saw everything.

She told us to stay away from her room to prepare for the party, and we reluctantly did.

By nine p.m., as agreed, I rapped my knuckles on her door.

You could hear a pin drop when she opened it, as she took our breaths away with how incredible she looked.

If she were what waited for us when death came knocking, we would be happy to follow her to the end of existence.

Her long black hair fell over her shoulders under the hooded cape, and her eyes under the mask had dark make-up to cover what minor discolouration she had left. It made the intense green of her eyes boom out like a beacon.

The dress complimented her beautiful figure, and those damn biker boots with the fishnet stockings accompanying her look turned me on to no end.

She looked sultry and mysterious.

At first glance, you couldn't recognise that it was her under the costume, and that was essentially what she had wanted.

"You really delivered with this outfit." She said while pointing her hands to herself.

I caught the tremble in her voice, clearly affected by how we had dressed.

Black jeans, black shirts under black hoodies and half-skull masks covering the bottom of our faces.

"Fuck, you guys are the most sexy entourage a reaper could ask for."

Her reaction was what we had hoped for.

"I love your eyes! You are all sex on a fucking stick." She declared to us.

"Let's go before this becomes a party for four." She said while weaving her arms between mine and Linc's, Wyatt leading the way.

The party's theme was Haunted House, and the school's party committee delivered. The party itself was good but not as good as the one us seniors organised by the sports sheds.

The faculty's staff was fully aware of the shenanigans of their students. Money overruled the staff members, though, so they turned a blind eye.

Sending twice during the night our security guard down there to tell us with nothing behind it to wrap it up. This was purely to log it and to see that none of us had passed out pissed paralytic.

Ivy, still with sore ribs, took it easy during the official party, but she was chugging from our flasks; we had to be careful she'd make it to the second one come midnight.

She had stopped taking her pain meds, and I had a feeling that she was using alcohol as a substitute.

By 11 p.m., we ended the official party with the typical haunted maze.

"Come on, Angel…of death." I joked, taking her hand to lead us down to the maze.

"No way I'm not going to scream blue murder if anyone scares the shit out of me." She said, laughing with truth in her voice.

"Why, when you are the one to take their souls?" Lincoln said jokingly and kissed her on the forehead.

I always thought when I finally found a steady girl, I'd be the sort of jealous guy, but sharing her with my two best friends came as naturally to me as sharing everything else with them. I saw how she affected them and how they affected her, and I knew that's exactly how this had to go, and it worked. The three of us were what she wanted.

The maze had been pretty decent. The efforts of the kids planning it all had paid off.

And yes, Ivy did scream, but only once when a flipping good clown got close to her from behind in the pitch black until we were under some blue lights, and his face popped up next to hers.

None of us expected her to lash out and punch the guy in the nose.

It was poor Vince from drama class. He was, however, so intimidated by Ivy and most certainly us that the idiot apologised to us for scaring Ivy.

The legacies found a girl that was fit for the role.

Down at the after-party, the music was much better, and the light was incredible and fitting for Halloween. I made a mental note to donate a little extra to the party committee.

Ivy asked for water, telling us the buzz she had from before was enough to last the night. The guys and I were sticking to whiskey.

The party was in full swing, and we noticed Ivy finally letting go and enjoying herself.
Some girls from her art and photography classes came over to chat with her, and eventually, she ended up on the dance floor. The three of us watching her closely, not because she was in danger, but because the threat was eliminated, and the rest of the school either did not have an issue with Ivy or accepted her as part of the legacies now, which meant untouchable. We watched her because fuck me, that girl could move.
Had she told us how she could move, we would've turned our room into a dance floor a long time ago
Clearly, she could feel our eyes burning into her; she turned around, facing us and moved in a way I had never seen before. Holy shit, we had to be careful that we wouldn't come in our pants from just watching her.
Her hips swayed in a way that made me want to touch her without wasting another second. I gave Wyatt my glass, and he chuckled. "Knew it would be you that would go first!"
I went over and grabbed her hips from behind, still careful not to hurt her injuries.
I started moving to the beat with her, and when she laid her head back onto my chest, looking up at me with that mask on, her eyes shining like emeralds, I was done for.

I leaned down and gave her the most resounding kiss I had in me.

Her mouth instantly opened for me, and when my tongue touched hers, I felt the vibration of her moan. The zap, like an electric shock, raced through my body down to the end of my balls, and I knew then that tonight I wasn't going back into that shower; I was going to claim what was mine. The way Ivy looked at me proved that she knew it, too.

The DJ played 'Cry Little Sister' from the Lost Boys soundtrack, and all hope for me and my two best friends was lost.

She beckoned the other two to join us, and when they did, it was the most exhilarating feeling I had felt in a very long time. That girl, our girl, knew what she was doing.

Thankfully, the lighting was dark enough so no one else could see us; it was our own private Ivy show, without her having to take any of her clothes off. She was that good.

After five more songs, she turned to me and stepped on her tippy toes to whisper in my ear.

"Take me to bed." She demanded.

The three of us left and quietly walked to our room together. I was not expecting anything but hoping for at least a sleepover after the party; the guys and I had placed our mattresses, yes, mine too, on the floor again. We had the LED candles back on and added more pillows and blankets that we had ordered online. Knowing Ivy was the Queen of comfy and cosy.

Wyatt unlocked and opened our door so Ivy could step in first, taking in what we had prepared for whatever she was in the mood for. We even had the projector back up.

Ivy stepped into the room and looked at the huge floor bed, noticing that my mattress was there, too.

She turned around and took the hood of her cape off, then the cape itself.

We stepped in behind her and closed the door.

No words were spoken.

As in a trance, we just stood there watching her.

She grabbed her hair, laid it over one shoulder, and unzipped her dress.

It fell to the floor, and what we saw would bring any guy to his knees.

The lace underwear, matching her mask, with the fishnet stockings on a suspender belt and those damn boots made her the sultry, sexy goddess she was to us.

She stood there for a few silent seconds, filling our eyes until she walked toward us. I stood unintentionally in the middle, Linc to my right and Wyatt to my left, all with our masks still on.

She stepped up to Lincoln and kissed him like her life depended on it without hesitation, pushing the mask into his hair. He growled, and I thought he'd take her there and then. However, Ivy breaks the kiss to step into Wyatt.

Giving him the same seductive kiss, pushing the mask back down after she was done with him. He, too, sounded like a man in beautiful pain. She was communicating with them.

Then she paid attention to me for the first time since we left the party. She stepped up to me, but I didn't get the expected kiss. Instead, she leaned over to my ear. "I said, Take… Me… To… Bed"

She looked deep into my eyes, and the dam broke. I gripped her under her arse, her legs wrapping around my middle.

I walked her to the bed and gently let her down.

Her head came up to kiss me, one hand of hers pushing the mask up the same way she did with Linc and Wyatt, and if I thought the kiss at the party had me, I was lying.

This one right here cost me my soul.

Her legs parted, and I laid in between; when she broke the kiss and her head went back, I kissed and licked a trail from her collarbone to her chin, only to go back down and blow on the slick mark I had left. She groaned, and it was the single best sound to me.

One hand holding her steady, the other moving to her back to unclasp her bra. I will forever regret making the shitty comment about her small tits, cause in reality, they were fucking perfect, and I needed to show her.

My head went down to take one of her perky nipples into my mouth, sucking and nibbling until I had her writhing under me. Another groan from her threatened my dick to explode for the fiftieth time tonight. When I paid attention to her other nipple, I felt her need growing to an unstoppable level; she breathed out, "Don't anyone dare take their masks off unless I let you kiss me." She commanded.

Anything for you, Angel, I thought and realised that Wyatt and Lincoln had sat on the bed too, far enough to give us the space we needed but close enough to see everything of her.

With my mask pushed into my hair, I took the opportunity and moved further down with my body, Ivy seemingly in agreement.

I kissed my way down her belly, bit her hips until my teeth gripped her panties, and in one swift move, I had them off.

I pushed her legs further apart, and her intoxicating smell drew me in like a drug.

I placed a soft kiss on her pubic bone, and she shivered with anticipation.

I went further, and holy fuck was she wet.

I inhaled her scent, and it drove me insane. Her usual vanilla and honey mixed with her arousal was nearly too much for me, and I had to wait a second before I stuck my tongue out and licked an opening path into her pussy. Her moan had the three of us growl out. The other two were still not touching her, just watching with their masks fixed on their faces.

I placed a kiss in warning on her clit but didn't give her time to adjust before I sucked it into my mouth. Her back arched off the mattress, and I pushed her back down with one hand on her tummy. *You're not going anywhere, Princess.*

I drew tight circles around her clit before I trailed down to her opening and glided in as far as my tongue would let me. Her moans grew louder; I went back up to her clit and used two fingers to push deep inside, curling them, and stroking her quivering walls. She wasn't far off, and her back left the mattress again while her hips bucked in rhythm against me. One stroke, two strokes and she exploded under me. Her pussy clenched my fingers so tight, pulling them in further.

I didn't leave off, though; I stayed right there, my fingers buried inside her, my tongue still teasing her clit. She was shaking and gasping for air, and I couldn't wait any longer myself. Withdrawing my fingers, I looked up at her and sucked them clean, another moan escaping her.

I went up to her face, leaned down and kissed her letting her taste herself on my tongue.

She closed her mouth off to me, pulled my mask back down and went to unzip my hoodie and unbutton my shirt. Her hands explored my bare chest, but her eyes were telling me to lose my jeans. I did her bidding.

I would be lying if I said I wasn't nervous about taking the next step. This incredible woman who was lying underneath me, waiting for me to have sex with her, did things to me that I had never felt before in my life.

I looked at her, wanting her to know this wasn't just fucking, this was about staking my claim.

She smiled her seductive smile and parted her legs again.

Slipping between them, I guided my cock to her core. Her legs trembled.

And while looking deep into her eyes, I pushed into her with a hard thrust.

Chapter 39

Ivy Alexander

I've used sex as an outlet for a couple of years now, never really putting a lot of stock into the action, just using it to get off and move on.

But sex with these boys wasn't anything I had experienced before. They made me feel things I hadn't before; they also weren't selfish lovers and had my legs quivering and twitching every time.

Looking into Fox's blue eyes as he pushed himself all the way to the hilt, creating a connection between us, I didn't want to let go. I wasn't one to get attached or involved with boys, but these three were mine. I was done running away.

I was a girl with three boyfriends, a girl's-wet dream, and I wasn't about to let them go for anything. I would sink my claws into them and demand they stay with me forever.

Fox pulled out and pushed back in, making my back arch and toes curl.

Turning my face towards Wyatt, I saw him palming his dick through his pants while he watched us.

"Touch yourself while I watch," I purred at him, then turned my head towards Linc and asked him to do the same.

Snaking my arms around Fox's neck, I shoved his mask back up and took his mouth with mine, allowing him to swallow my moans as he fucked me slowly. I could feel my orgasm starting to build again, but I wanted Linc and Wyatt to join me.

Pushing Fox back up with my hands on his chest, I pulled his mask back down and tilted my pelvis upwards to match every thrust, giving him a view of his dick being swallowed by me. Hearing him groan with every thrust had my pussy walls squeezing him tight, over and over again.

Fox reached his hand down and started rubbing my clit, making the dam burst inside me. My pussy clenched him so tight it was hard for him to pull out and push in. I felt his body stiffen.

"Fuck angel, that's it, cum for me," he speared me as he grabbed my hips and started to pound in hard and fast, fucking me through my orgasm.

I heard Linc move closer towards me as he moaned and came all over my chest, his ropes of cum hitting my breasts and leaving hot wet marks all over me.

"Oh fuck," I heard as Wyatt joined Linc and painted me white, some of it hitting my chin and lips. Snaking my tongue out, I licked, curious what he tasted like.

The action seemed to trigger something in Fox as he went as stiff and growled, "Fucking hell, Ivy" shooting his release deep inside of me.

Bracing himself with his arms beside my head, "You look so fucking hot covered in cum, Angel."

Smiling at him, fully sated and exhausted, I heard Linc get up. He came back with a wet towel in his hands and wiped my chest and face. Fox pulled out of me and looked down.

"Holy shit, that's hot," as he watched his cum leaking out of me. Wyatt leaned down to kiss my lips, unaffected by the leftover traces of cum.

"Come on, Wildcat, let me wash you up," he snaked his arm under my bent legs and shoulders, lifting me up to carry me into the bathroom.

He placed my feet on the floor, turned on the shower, and pulled off my stockings and garter belt. He quickly undressed himself and put me into the shower with him. With a body-wash-laced shower puff, he went to work cleaning me. We stayed silent as he washed me clean, pushing my head under the water to scrub my hair last. I noticed he was using the same hair products that I had.

"When did you start using Vanilla scented Shampoo?" I looked up at him and squinted the beads of water off my eyes.

"Since we knew it's your favourite, we stocked up for you" he smiled and kissed my lips. "Now turn around and let me finish," he said and gave my head a massage.

I groaned into his touch, willing my libido down.

"Come on, babe, I'm tired and need some rest," he announced after rinsing the shampoo off.

I returned to the bedroom with just a towel around me. Fox came over to me, pulled a massive white top over my head, and whipped the towel off me at the same time.

"Go climb into bed, angel"

Tapping my ass with his palm, I climbed onto the mattress and the millions of pillows. I curled up on my side and felt Wyatt slide in behind me. I heard the shower turn back on, assuming that Linc and Fox were getting ready for bed, too.

I fell asleep to Wyatt, drawing small circles on my thigh.

The following day I woke to a hand snaking between the folds of my pussy, circling my clit.

I had no idea who it was, but I wouldn't stop them.

Lifting my leg up higher to allow better access, I felt a hand cover my mouth and nose, restricting my airway and instantly knew who was playing this morning.

"If you stay quiet and very still, I'll let you cum," Wyatt whispered into my ear.

Nodding, I felt him push two fingers straight into me and hook them to touch that spot that made me squirm.

Rolling over onto my back, I spread my legs to allow Wyatt as much access as he wanted and ran my own hand down towards his crouch, palming his dick through his boxers. Shit, this guy was big.

He was the only one I hadn't had yet, and I was not even sure he would fit into me without stretching me wide.

Reaching into his boxers, I wrapped my hand around his dick and started to run up and down, making him moan with every movement. Leaning into him, I whispered, "If you make a noise, I'm not going to let you cum either," wickedly smiling at him.

With one side of his mouth curled into a devious smile, Wyatt moved out of my reach and slid under the duvet to settle between my legs, licking up the seam of my pussy lips and slowly spreading them apart.

Sliding two fingers into me, he moved them in a slow torturous rhythm, licking away at my clit. With his other hand, he pushed down on my abdomen so he could reach my sweet spot more easily.

Slowly, he picked up his pace, and I felt that familiar tingle in my toes working its way up. Feeling myself tightening around Wyatt's fingers, he added a third digit, and I fell apart. A hot gush left me and soaked Wyatt's face, leaving me squirming and moaning loud enough to wake everyone up, so much for following Wyatt's order to stay quiet.

He quickly sat up and pushed the white shirt I was wearing up over my tits and gave his dick a few pumps before coming all over my belly. His rugged breath accompanying his release had my head spinning. All three made the most sensual noises, and I couldn't get enough.

"Holy shit, Wildcat," he said with my release glinting on his mouth and chin.

"Did you know you could squirt baby?" He licked his lips, "It tastes sweeter."

"What? No?" I looked down between my thighs and saw a puddle had formed on the mattress "Holy shit'"

Looking to my left, I saw Linc and Fox looking at me with hunger in their eyes. "I think I just came in my boxers," Linc said wild-eyed.

"Shut up," pink tingling my cheeks. I was actually shocked with myself.

"Don't be embarrassed, Wildcat." Wyatt leaned up between us and kissed my lips, "Now that I know you can, I'll make you do this every time," he smiled into the kiss.

"I think I'm gonna shower again," I said and jumped out of the bed and raced to the bathroom.

Chapter 40

Colt Anderson

Going to a Halloween party was the perfect opportunity to stay incognito. I dressed as a Voodoo Witch Doctor with a top hat, coat, contact lenses and full face paint; no one knew who I was.

I hid in plain sight, watching these assholes with Ivy. These pretentious pigs thought they owned this place and everyone in it. But soon Ivy would see what they were about and that none had genuine interest or feelings for her. She was another nudge on the headboard for them, a conquest nothing more.

They'd drop her like Fox dropped Crystal, having found a shiny new toy to play with.

I didn't know exactly what their deal was, but I was sure she wasn't sleeping with all of them like a whore.

When the senior's party kicked off by the river, I stayed close to them, watching Ivy with friends from her classes, enjoying herself.

I felt terrible for what Crystal had done to her, but I understood Crystal's motives. I hoped Ivy could see it too someday. Her wounds were superficial, whereas Crystals ran through her veins.

I moved further to the back, the dance floor getting more crowded, and settled in a dark corner near the back.

That way, no one could see me at all, but I saw everyone, and most of all, I had a perfect view of Ivy and the three bastards. Ivy had left them to dance with some of her friends, and she knew how to dance like a seductive slut. It ground on me how explicit she was and how she kept looking at these dicks like she wanted to invite them to a fuck fest. Damn, Ivy, I might have to interfere sooner than I expected. I needed more time, but I saw that they had her in their trap already, making a sluttish fool of her.

When that prick Foxworth started to dance with her, my hand gripped that stupid voodoo staff that came with the costume and snapped it. I could no longer watch this foolishness and stormed out of the place.

Chapter 41

Lincoln Baker

I had my fair share of girls since I busted my first nut a few years back, but what I had now was like nothing else I ever experienced. Sure, Fox, Wyatt and I had shared a few times, but this thing with Ivy was new, something I didn't know I craved. I never had sex with feelings involved, despite having the reputation of being a ruler with an iron fist yet caring enough to never leave carnage in my wake.

I knew at some point I wanted to settle down and have a girlfriend and eventually a wife and family, unlike the other two. But I thought it'd hit me differently, and definitely not while still going to fucking school.

Along came Ivy and changed all that.

She changed us.

Waking up to see her cum as Wyatt worked her body was insane.

I knew one thing for sure: she would be mine that night.

But first, I had to finish some work for my business class; my Dad was hot on my heels as he wouldn't accept anything less than top tier.

People thought being a legacy was all fun and games, sex and parties.

That couldn't be further from the truth; our parents rode us hard. If we flunked in class, there was some hell to pay. Fox was the only one who had it easier; when his Father passed, he inherited his money and a sort of disinterest from his mother, which allowed him the free pass. He didn't slack, though; he worked harder for himself, but without a whip at his back and doing things at his own pace, Wyatt and I felt a sense of envy. Though we still had at least one parent that gave a shit, so I wasn't sure who should envy who in the end.

We still hadn't figured out what to do about the upcoming marriage of Dr Forester and the Foxworth widow. We were so absorbed by Ivy that we got sidetracked. Maybe we could involve her somehow?

My train of thought made me forget about my schoolwork yet again, as it always wandered back to Ivy.

When she came out of the shower and engulfed the room with her scent, I knew I had to vacate or not get any work done.

She strutted over to me, wrapped her arms around me from behind, and rested her head between my shoulder blades.
"You got schoolwork today?" She asked in a husky voice, making me want to throw her down on the bed.
"Yep, but I need to go down to the study hall; I won't get anything done around you."
"That's not very nice" she replied with fake shock in her tone, "Go and work; I need to get some physio in and then hit the books myself. Let's meet for lunch?"
"Deal," I gave back and pulled her over for a deep kiss before I got up and headed downstairs.
I shut the door behind me and bumped into none other than Colt, too close to our room like he'd been lurking, the fucking creep.
"Anything you need, Anderson?" I gave him a look so he knew I wanted to punch his lights out for simply being around.
"No man, all good, Just heading down to the gym."
This all-American football quack gave me the weirdest vibes, and I made a mental note to look into him again; something would pop up about him somewhere. I had that gut feeling. Giving him a dismissive nod, I waited for him to leave before I followed the same way downstairs.
But when I reached the last step, he was already nowhere to be seen, and unless he ran like someone was chasing him, he

should still be around here somewhere. Like I said, something was off with him, and I was going to get to the bottom of it.

I studied for hours, not even stopping for some water, let alone food. It was nearly time for lunch, so I started to pack up, knowing Ivy would be down here soon.
Wyatt and Fox joined me to get some work done a little while after I arrived, telling me Ivy told them to use the day for school.
All packed up and having a casual chat about the Halloween party, I wanted to grab my phone to call Ivy and tell her to move her sweet butt down here as we were starving, More for her than actual food.
I looked around in my pockets and bag and couldn't find my phone anywhere.
I asked the guys if they had seen it.
Fox just finished telling me he had last seen it on my desk before I headed out when I caught sight of Ivy. Her face was furious. I had never seen her so mad. Her emerald eyes were wet and bloodshot, and we all shot up to come to her aid. Thinking this time we'd kill anyone who upset her.
She practically ran across the hall, and when she reached us, her voice hitched, and she snarled with a pain-filled voice, a finger pointing at me and my friends, "I hope you enjoyed wasting my

time! I'm sorry, Wyatt, that you didn't get fuck me for the ***bet!*** Stay… The… Fuck… Away… From… Me!"
Holy fuck. My heart sunk into my stomach.
Ivy took a deep breath, turned to the table next to her, picked up some books, and threw them at us immediately. Stunned, we just stood still like statues.
With one last glare at us, she turned around and left.

Chapter 42

Ivy Alexander

I swear physio needed to be renamed torture sessions. I mean, how often do I need to pick something up and put it down? Or twist to the left, then back to the right. I knew I had to be here; they needed to clear me to return to training. Mr Wellington had texted me daily for updates. I suspected he felt terrible that it had happened after training.

I returned to my room to get changed out of my gym gear so I could go down and meet the boys for lunch. I also needed to finish my history assignment; I had only managed a few thousand words on William the Conqueror and his Battle of Hastings. Usually, I loved history, and it was something that fascinated me. Still, my mind had been a bit of a muddle after the Crystal incident, and I was finding it hard to concentrate on my school work and didn't want to let my grades slip.

Arriving back at my room, I quickly showered and changed into something comfortable to study in. I was grateful we only had to wear the uniform on school days and only during school class hours; they were super uncomfortable. I wasn't a massive fan of them.

I quickly pulled up my emails so I could shoot one off to my mum to let her know that physio had cleared me to train again, and she needed to clear it with Mr Wellington as he wouldn't come back until my mum had approved it.

Seeing I had a random email from someone I didn't know, I debated whether to click it. Spam was a massive issue these days, and I wasn't keen to fry my new laptop.

It was just the subject line that had me pausing on the delete button.

"The lie the boys have been keeping from you."

Did they mean MY boys? No one knew we were all together, no PDA, yes they all doted on me in public, but we didn't group kiss or anything. Clearly, curiosity was riding me hard, and I clicked the email.

It shattered me.

The email was full of messages between the boys; they all looked like screenshots from Linc's phone, as the texts were to Wyatt and Fox.

They had made a bet when I first arrived at the school to sleep with me. The first one to sleep with me won, and then they'd use me for the rest of the year between them. Like their own personal fuck doll.

I felt like a fucking idiot.

I had allowed this to happen; I had allowed them to force their way into my life, and then I'd gone and fallen in love with them. They were good, I had to give them that. I had fallen for every word they said to me; I had fully believed Linc when he told me he loved me. I had fallen for Fox, suddenly warming up to me and letting me into his heart. It was all a lie.

By the time I read the last screenshot, I was crying. My heart was shattering into tiny pieces. This was all my fault; I had the root-and-boot motto for a reason. And this was why! But I had allowed them to worm into my life, and now I was reminded why I didn't let anyone in.

Re-reading the screenshots, I grew angry, so I needed to confront them. Grabbing my fob and sliding it into my pocket, I headed out of my room and raced down to the study hall, seeing them all sitting at the table waiting patiently for me.

Nope, I was done. They wouldn't wait for me anymore.

Storming over to them, I yelled, "I hope you enjoyed wasting my time! I'm sorry, Wyatt, that you didn't get fuck me for the **bet!** Stay… The… Fuck… Away… From… Me!"

Turning to walk away, I spotted a stack of books on a nearby table, instantly picked them up, and started throwing them at the boys.

I was done.

Oh, so done

Turning on my heel and heading straight back to my room, I didn't want to see anyone in the state I was in.

I could hear Wyatt calling my name and running after me. I quickly sprinted back to my room and slammed the door behind me; grabbing my phone and pulling up the door lock app, I pressed the emergency lock button, which meant you couldn't use a code or fob to open the door.

Wyatt started pounding on my door.

"Wildcat, it isn't what you think! Just open the door and let us explain."

"Ivy baby, please talk to me."

"Petal! Please open the door. Let us talk to you!" Linc had joined in.

"Fuck off!" I yelled back furiously.

"Seriously, Ivy, open the fucking door!" I heard growling through the gap. Fox has joined, too.

"I said fuck off, or I'll call campus security!" I screamed back. The next thing I heard was a loud smashing noise like someone was mad enough to kick over the ugly plant they had in the hallway.

"Fox go to our room before you get into shit for trashing school property," I heard Wyatt yell at him.

"Fuck!" Fox screamed back, and I heard his heavy footfall retreating.

"Petal, please open the door," Linc said through the gap.

"I'll open the door if you can tell me one thing," I said confidently.

"Anything" Linc and Wyatt replied in unison.

"Tell me it isn't true, and I'll open the door."

I was met with silence, silence for so long confirming the fact that the bet was real.

"Petal..." Linc whispered.

"Linc, I want you to leave, go the fuck away, and stay the fuck away from me!" I started to cry, but my anger was pushed into my voice.

"Everyone warned me about you; they said you were cruel, they said you were man whores." Leaning my back against my door, I slid down to sit.

"I should have listened" with resignation in my tone.

"Petal, it might be true, but things changed; we don't care about the bet; we want to keep you forever."

"It's too late for that, Linc, and I am **not** a fucking object to keep." I sighed, "Please go away; I don't want to see any of you again!"

I could hear his footsteps retreating away from the door, then a low voice, "I'm going to my room, Wildcat, but I'm not leaving you. We not done, and I won't allow you to leave us; I'll fix this" then Wyatt's footsteps followed Lincoln's.

Curling up in a ball at the base of the door, I cried myself to sleep.

Chapter 43

Ivy Alexander

It had been three nights since I found the messages. Three nights for me to pull myself together again and face this shithole of a school with its fuck head male students.

My heart broke at the thought of the three who were the most giant fuck heads of them all. It hurt. But I couldn't let it get to me. I didn't have that long left. I could manage that and then get the hell out of here and never look back. What a fool I was for letting them lure me into their trap; I was just as much to blame as them. In the end, I was the idiot that fell for it all.

It was nearly 7 p.m., and I had ordered my dinner and ate a little. I have not been feeling up to eating much these past few days. 7 p.m. meant that the knocking would start any minute. That's what they had been doing every evening since the truth came out. From 7 o'clock, they hounded me, pleaded and even begged. I wondered what their game plan was and why they kept coming back telling all these lies.

What enjoyment could that give them? Sickos!

7:01, and I heard the first knock.

"Ivy, Are you ok? I promise you, if you let me in, I can explain. You will be able to see what happened." Lincoln pleaded.

I could put my headphones on and tune them out.

Ha! I was a masochist, though, and listened to every word they had to say, Staying stock-still behind the door, breathing as quietly as possible.

Then Fox's knuckles rapped along my door; I could tell them apart by now.

"Ivy, you will open this fucking door, you hear me? We need to know you are ok!"

Fuck the hell off, I wanted to answer, but the words were stuck in my throat, knowing they wouldn't go away anyway, Not until around 8 p.m.

"Listen, what you and I have is real, for fuck sake! You know that as well as I!" He continued.

Lying bastard! He knew this was all a game; I knew nothing.

At last, Wyatt piped up after Fox's usual slap against my door.

"We won't leave Wildcat, you know that, we know that and the whole fucking school knows it."

Mind games were Wyatt's forte, I figured out.

Eventually, they would leave, though. They'd go when this cat and mouse game got boring, or they found a new toy.

Until then, I'd hide in here and let them play their act out. I had excused myself from classes, doing remote work.

Like clockwork, around 8 p.m., they left after saying goodnight and hoped I would change my mind and that I could always come to their room, the code still being the same.

I went to bed and cried.

The following day, I decided that I couldn't hide in my room forever, and after a few texts from my friends from class, I made plans to meet them and Colt for breakfast in the coffee lounge.

I was cautious not to bump into the arseholes and even had Lucille come meet me outside my door.

Thinking about the friendships I could grow here instead of falling for these cunts, I pulled my big girl panties on and headed out. Friends always lasted longer than boyfriends, and as I had neglected the former since the boys waltzed into my life, I was eager to be more sociable from now on. It would give me the much-needed distraction, too.

Lucille promised she had seen the boys in the dining hall, so we headed to the coffee lounge.

I got excited as Lucille was an exciting personality, and spending more time with her would be fun. She had so much knowledge about art since her Father was a curator at the New York Museum of Arts and Design. I was desperate to pick her brain. She even mentioned taking me to New York to see him and show me the best places there.

I had been to NY, but only for Christmas; Mum loved it there. I wasn't a fan; there were too many people, but the art scene was unmatched.

Of course, none other than Fox, Wyatt, and Linc crossed our path when we arrived at the bottom of the stairs and headed outside for the food court.

They were a good few meters away, but I felt their gazes without looking in their direction. My body stiffened next to Lucille, and she took the cue and hooked herself under my arm, ready to drag me away.

In the end, I looked up at them. Their faces were strained, their eyes focused on me.

We all kept walking in the opposite direction of each other, staring at one another.

I knew they wanted to come over to me, but the sternness on my face told them enough to stay away.

We kept walking until Lucille and I reached the coffee lounge; that's when I allowed myself to breathe.

"You all right?" She asked, concerned, feeling how hard I had to push my body to keep moving forward.

It hurt like hell seeing them, more than I wanted it to hurt. I tried to be strong, having learned my lesson and moved on. Yet my heart had other ideas. It wanted to hurt and mourn.

"Yeah, I will be," I replied quietly, and Lucille's hand squeezed mine lovingly.

We walked over to a table with two other classmates and Colt. Two extra coffees for me, and Lucille was already waiting with two muffins.

Colt texted me earlier when he arrived at the lounge, asking if he could get our order.

He was a thoughtful guy. He's too nice for my liking despite the bad guy looks, but as a friend, I'd sure accept him.

He'd never lied to me. He'd never betrayed me. In fact, he was the one warning me to stay away from the notorious legacies of Hastings House.

I owed him an apology someday.

Lucille and I sat and were immediately involved in the conversation.

It felt good to wrap my head around something different from the three boys who had broken my heart.

By the end of our breakfast session, Colt had invited us all to a party in London the following weekend for a charity ball. A family friend of his happened to host one. Colt showed us the online invitations, and for a small donation, we got ourselves in.

Something to look forward to and get me away from here.
Excited to go dress shopping, Lucille, another friend, Mika, and I planned to go to some boutiques the day after next.
I thanked the universe for helping me here and putting good things in my path.
I hoped that all the distractions would also help me heal my heart.

Chapter 44

Wyatt Forester

I had never tried to win over a girl before. In fact, I never had to, but Ivy was different. She was the Rose between our thorns; we needed her like the air we breathed.

Since she found out about the bet she had taken to barricading herself into her room, she was still using the app to lock the door, making it impossible for us to get in. I was grateful the lock worked so well, but now I wished she had a regular one we could pick.

Linc had chosen 7 p.m. to be the time we all approached her nightly; he said if we turned up at the same time every day, she would come to see we were vigilant in our approach to win her back. Dependability and reliability are the key points. He wanted to prove to her that even though she was mad at us now, we would still turn up daily. As sweet as the gesture was, it wasn't working. Fox's 'take no prisoners' attitude also wasn't working. Every time he screamed and pounded on the door, I could hear her quick intake of breaths from behind the door when he started.

We only needed to get her alone for a few minutes to make her see reason.

All we had so far was the death glare she threw us when she had walked to the coffee place with her friend. She had managed to get her friends to shield us from her daily, and it was starting to get on my nerves. I needed to talk to my Wildcat and explain to her what she meant to us all.

Linc had hacked her laptop from his the night it happened and found the email sent to her. He had been trying to trace who had sent it for days now, but he wasn't having any luck; it just kept leading back to an email address that was brand new and had been made on campus the day it happened.

The email had yet to be used once since making it, which made it impossible to pinpoint who the user was. He had placed a tracker on it so we could trace it back to the owner the next time someone logged in or sent an email. Linc had also managed to clone her phone and was able to read every message and text she was receiving. It was a complete invasion of privacy, but having lost Ivy was tearing him up inside. It did make it easier for us to be in the same place as her all the time, making it almost impossible for her to avoid us.

Everything just needed time, and time was something I needed to improve at. I hated waiting. It made me anxious.

Ivy was back at training; her mother had cleared her after physio, and the Doctor gave her the green light. I had planned to use the gym simultaneously to finally get a moment to talk to her.

All was going well when I turned up and sat and watched her train. She was terrific; I was curious about why she didn't compete.

When her training was done, and the trainer had left, I offered to help her clean the mats.

"Let me help you clean?" Ivy just gave me death daggers and threw me a towel.

"If you're going to stalk me, then you might as well help,"

"I know you didn't believe us when we said things had changed, Ivy, but they did."

Spray and wipe.

"Yes, we made the stupid bet, but that's what we do; we make bets between us for fun, and even though it started out that way, it wasn't how it stayed."

Spray and wipe.

"After we met you and got to know you, we stopped caring about the bet and just wanted to get to know you."

Spray and wipe.

"We wanted to keep you safe from Anderson initially, too."
She whipped her head towards me and stalked right up to me.
"You say you wanted to keep me safe, but Anderson was the only one being honest with me; he told me you were all horrible, and he was right," she said with tears in the corner of her eyes.

"Ivy, there is something off about the boy; we could see it from miles away. We wanted to keep you safe from him, but you are hanging out with him again." I pleaded.

"Wyatt, I don't think you understand at all," Ivy said, taking a deep breath.

"I fell in love with every single one of you," she admitted with a tear trailing her face.

"I believed you all felt the same, but you were just acting to win a stupid bet."

"Wildcat, we gave up on the bet ages ago; we fell in love with you, too! We had forgotten about the bet and realised we wanted only you!" I said as I reached out to grab her hand.

The second my fingers touched hers, she stiffened and stepped back.

"DO... NOT... TOUCH...ME..." she bellowed, her eyes scanning mine.

"I'm sorry" holding my hands high, "I miss you"

"I miss every single one of you. My heart shatters a little more every day when I see your face, but at the end of the day, you used me for a bet; you lied and manipulated me. Even if things changed, you had the opportunity to come clean with me for weeks, but you chose not to; you chose to keep deceiving me," she sighed heavily, her eyes watery, "and I just cannot forgive you for that."

"Wildcat."

"No, please Wyatt, Just leave me alone," she turned on her heels and walked out of the room, leaving me to finish cleaning for her, which I gladly did as a simple act of penance.

After cleaning the gym and returning to our room, I found Fox sitting on the edge of his bed, looking into space. He looked like a lost puppy. Fox didn't let people into his heart. But he allowed Ivy in; he allowed her to see his most vulnerable side, and now, with her gone, he was lost.

He turned to look at me as I entered the room. "We had training today."

"I know I didn't go" I gave back, uninterested.

"I know," he was looking at the floor, "I didn't go either. I wanted to wait for you to get back."

Walking over to my bed, I sat on the edge and clasped my hands in my lap.

"I think we really fucked up," I breathed a sigh, "she is really hurt." Her words played on repeat in my mind, making my heart clench.

"I don't know how to win her back." Fox looked defeated. He couldn't regulate his feelings at the best of times; I waited for the explosion.

"I don't know if we can" I admitted to pouring fuel on his fire, but unwilling to lie to him.

"I don't know what to do with myself now. Do I move on? Do I let her go? Do I keep fighting?" He looked at me for answers.

"We keep fighting!" Linc walked into the room from the bathroom.

"We need to prove that we meant it when we said we would protect her!" Linc stated as he sat next to me on my bed.

"If we move on or let her go, then we are doing exactly what she accuses us of." He carried on.

I knew he was right. I knew what he was saying was true, but I was starting to feel like letting her go was the easier option. I couldn't take fighting for her to never forgive us.

"I'm in love with her; no other girl is good enough; I can't even get my dick to twitch looking at another girl," Linc declared and stared daggers at his crotch like it mortally wounded him.

Fox pulled one of Ivy's t-shirts that she left in our room out from under his pillow and held it in his hands, "I can't sleep without her smell." This was huge for Fox. He didn't even allow us in this deep.

"I have no idea what we can do to get her back, though," I said in defeat.

"We just keep doing what we're doing," Linc said, like it was that simple, "we keep showing up, we keep pleading with her, we keep in the shadows behind her and keep her safe at all times; eventually, she is going to see we mean it when we say we love her, in fact, let's tell her we love her every single time we see her!" He smiled then, "lets kill her with kindness until she believes every single word we say."

"So, in other words, we stalk the shit out of her and declare our love at every chance" I looked at Linc like he was insane.

Shrugging, he said, "Why not? I don't give a shit who knows my feelings for her, She is *OURS*, and that's what the rest of the school is to understand, I will not share her with them, and they cannot make a move on *OUR* girl" his gaze was darkening with every word he spoke.

Fuck. What if someone else made a move on our girl while we were here licking our wounds?

NOT A FUCKING CHANCE!

*Chapter 45*

Sebastian 'Fox' Foxworth

Keep fighting for Ivy.
That's what Lincoln said we had to do. It had been over a week, and none of what we did worked.

She was so closed off to us. Remnants of her scent on the t-shirt she left behind faded quickly.

I never dreamt of girls, but I dreamed of Ivy most nights. I dreamt of her smile. Of the night of the Halloween party when we had slept together and how she looked at us after finding out about the bet.

The fucking bet. It was supposed to be like any other, quick and easy with a bit of fun.

Ivy was anything but quick and easy. She burrowed herself deep into me, and now I felt something I thought impossible: heartache.

I betrayed her, and the remorse and guilt were all-consuming. If that's what love was, I wasn't sure I could take it.

But I wanted Ivy at all costs.

I wrecked my brain to the point of a headache, trying to find a solution. A way to win her back.

I only just got her.

The stares she gave us at the dining hall were murderous.

Surrounded by her friends and that absolute cunt Anderson.

Acting like the three of us didn't even exist.

That hurt the most.

Ivy pretended that we were invisible to her while she was the centre of us.

I trained more than usual and ran four times a day instead of two. I realised running was helping me clear my head. I wasn't built for shit like this. Girlfriends, break ups, pain.

The only pain I knew was the physical type when I pushed myself to breaking point in the gym or in the boat.

The coach had picked up that Wyatt and I were off, pushing and pushing ourselves until nothing was left.

He told us he'd suspend us for the next race if we didn't get our act together. He didn't support reckless fury in the boat when we needed to be a team that worked with strategy and strength, not rage and anger.

That made me more angry, and I stormed off, letting Wyatt take the brunt.

I ran instead, not wanting to randomly punch something for some unknown reason.

I ran towards the forest that belonged to the school, thinking that's where I'd be alone. Reaching the pathway, I saw a small figure ahead, stretching and bending.

I got closer, and my heart started thumping. It was Ivy. She was heading out for a run herself.

By the time I reached her, so did someone else, Fucking Anderson.

They laughed and joked together, clearly blind inside their bubble to even acknowledge me.

So I ran up to them faster, racing past them in their casual jog and barged into Colt's shoulder as hard as I could. Not so much of an All-American Football player, I thought as he went tumbling and landed in the dirt. I chuckled, the first time I felt a sense of humour since Ivy left.

"Such a childish arsehole!" I heard her shout at me, but I didn't turn around. I didn't want to look at her. The mood I was in, I would probably throw her over my shoulder and, take her back to our room and never leave.

So I ran, ran as fast as my legs would take me, and then a bit more. My lungs hurt from the hard breaths I forced down, not at

all breathing right as I could not get this fucking girl out of my head. Seeing her again with Colt pushed all my buttons. Anger was cursing through my veins.
Reaching a clearing, I was drenched in sweat, and my gut had enough of my shit and violently expelled its contents.
I spewed and spat, my body exorcising its demons.
When I was sure I had nothing left, I sat on the wet grass, my legs stretched out.
Thinking about what I had going through my mind earlier.
I pulled my phone from my shorts and texted Linc and Wyatt in our group chat.

An hour later, we met up in the study hall. They both commented about my state, but I was too hung up on the plan I had come up with.
"I love her, Fox, you know that, but this plan of yours is borderline insane. And that's coming from me!" Line declared.
"It could work with decoys and lies..." I reiterated.
"Yes, and that's what got us into this mess in the first place. Fox, LIES for starters." I know Wyatt was right, but what other choice did we have but to basically kidnap her and take her to a remote vacation spot and have her hear us out? No way for her to run away, lock us out...

"I'm desperate; I never had a girl that wouldn't be at my beck and call with the snap of my finger, let alone one I liked." I gave back, feeling defeated and run down.

"You *like* her, all right!" Wyatt chuckled sarcastically, "Let's come up with something less insane, more reasonable and diplomatic. I'm pretty sure at this point she had her fill of our shit."

I hung my head between my shoulders, one hand weaving through my hair, pulling it to feel something other than the pain in my chest, and wondered how long I could go like this before I snapped.

A hand on my back made me jolt and turn around, hoping it was Ivy.

No, it was Katie Tasller. She was a friend and a legacy, too. She was a pretty brunette but was all over Rhys Bowen since we were in the primary. The power couple in our school.

"I have some news that might interest you guys." She said in a hushed voice like she was a spy.

Lincoln leaned in closer, and Wyatt looked up at her. "Spill."

"Mika told me she and some friends are going to London this weekend for charity. Ivy is going with them."

Fuck. Ivy wouldn't be here this weekend at all.

"Thanks, hun," I said with my face still down to the floor, nodding.

"Anytime, shitheads" She chirped, and as quickly as she came, she was gone again.

Linc sighed. "We should use this weekend to devise a plan for Ivy."

"I don't like that she's going to London without us…" Wyatt said, his hand wiping over his face in worry.

"She'll be ok; remember we have her phone tracked," Lincoln said confidently.

"I know, but it still irks me."

I listened to them go back and forth, but ultimately, there wasn't much we could do.

We thought about going ourselves, but then we agreed that would piss Ivy off to no end. We'd give her that weekend and have a plan by the end.

Making a plan that's what kept me afloat. Putting all our hope into a plan to bring Ivy back to us.

We managed to get through two more classes that day and arranged to meet for dinner at six.

I went down to the dining hall at half six, notoriously late.

I closed the door behind me to see from the corner of my eye that hers opened. She stepped out, giggling with Lucille and non-other than fuck face Colt in tow, My blood boiling instantly. She spotted me and froze. I held her gaze, the tightness in my throat threatening to choke me.

She had a faint smile before Lucille grabbed her arm; walking away, they had Ivy in the middle like she needed a security detail. I was her damn security detail. I protected her. Now, she acted like she needed protection *from* me.

Raging, I returned to our room and took it out on the wall mirror by the door.

Splitting my knuckles with the almighty crash from the shattering glass.

Chapter 46

Ivy Alexander

It was getting easier every day now. Seeing the boys in the hall no longer made me feel sick. Instead, I had started to long for them again.
Colt was making it clear that he liked me a lot more than being my friend only. I might have jumped him at the start of this school year, but now everything was different. My body craved Lincoln, Fox and Wyatt, as did my soul. I missed them. But I wouldn't forgive them. My heart hurt, and I couldn't forget what they had done.

Lucille and I had gone out to a few boutiques the day before, looking for the perfect dresses for the Ball. I had picked a tight black glittery number that showed off my boobs and hugged my ass. I had decided to embrace my small boobs; I mean, they weren't going to get any more significant at this point.

We were heading to the Ball tomorrow, and I was super excited to be doing something off campus. I had only managed a few trips into town and one into London since I arrived. I would have to persuade my parents to allow me to stay after graduation so I could travel UK more. I really wanted to head to Scotland for a weekend trip.

I could live in an apartment so I could explore this place for a little while.

Colt and Lucille always popped over at dinner to pick me up so I didn't have to walk down alone. It was lovely of them; I had told them not to bother. That I could walk alone without them as my guard dogs. Lucille and Colt disapproved, mainly because the boys hadn't backed off at all. I had started to soften a little to their constant tries. We could try to be friends. I wasn't sure my heart could take being friends, but I also wasn't sure it could handle not seeing them.

Linc went as far as to say, "Petal, I love you. Don't you forget that?" Every single day. I don't think he has missed one yet. I wasn't 100% sure what game he was playing, but whatever it was, it worked. Colt and Lucille could see it, so they doubled their efforts to ensure I was never alone around them. At times, it was hard work.

On Saturday morning, Lucille knocked on my door at 9 a.m., declaring we needed to prepare for the Ball. I had only just gotten back from training. One of the boys turned up at training every morning and watched me; they helped me clean the gym. They had stopped trying to talk to me, just silently helping. I hadn't told Colt or Lucille this; they would only turn up too, and honestly, I secretly loved the boys being there. Call me a masochist.

"Lucille, it's 9 a.m.; we have eight hours to get ready." I laughed at her but secretly wished she'd go away to let me rest.

"Oh no, we don't. We have six. Colt is taking us to dinner before we go to the Ball, and I want to look better than I have ever looked." She blushed and fiddled with the drawstrings of her hoodie.

"Hang on a minute," I smiled knowingly, "do you have a crush on Colt?"

Her blush deepened, "Maybe, Is that okay? It's obvious that he has one on you, but you're still so clearly in love with the boys, so I thought if he looked my way for just a minute, he might see me?" She replied shyly

"Lucille! Omg! Of course, it's okay; I do not like him that way!" I said, giving her a reassuring hug.

"Let's make you look a million dollars so he can see how beautiful you are!" I exclaimed. Excited to have some girly fun.

Lucille beamed at me, "Yes!"

For the record, it took us 6 hours to get ready; we danced around in our underwear for ages, put curlers in our hair and took extra time for our make-up. I ran down around lunchtime and grabbed a few sandwiches; Lucille was too embarrassed to run down with curlers in, so I did the quick dash.

On my way back, I ran right into Wyatt, nearly bowling him over in my pursuit back to the bedroom.

Thud, "Oh shit, sorry, Wildcat" he exclaimed. His scent of sea breeze infiltrated my senses. He looked so hot, wearing slung black sweatpants and a hoodie, the hood pulled deep.

"It's okay," I said, blushing from being so close to him again. I hated how my body language betrayed me still.

Picking the sandwiches up for me, "Let me carry them for you," he offered.

"I'm fine, thank you, though," reaching out and grabbing them off him, "I can manage four sandwiches."

"You look adorable with those curlers in," his grey eyes glowing at me, his lips showing off his handsome smile.

"Thanks, I gotta go," I said.

I quickly turned and walked off before he could see how affected I was by him.

My heart was thumping a mile a minute. They had really worn me down since everything had happened. After the Ball, I could entertain hearing them out. I had never met boys who made me feel this way before. Plus, I was sure my heart couldn't handle being away from them any longer. I just needed to figure out if I would be strong enough to offer them friendship or if my heart would let them back in fully and heal it.

By six, we were dressed and ready to leave; Lucille looked beyond amazing, and I offered to hide in the bathroom for a few minutes when Colt arrived so he would only see her, not me.
"You look magnificent," I heard Colt say to Lucille through the crack in the door.
"Thank you," she replied shyly.
Taking that as my cue to enter, I walked out of the bathroom and grabbed my little clutch bag sitting on my couch.
"Okay, let's go, everyone," I stated, eager to leave and start the night.
"Holy shit Ivy," Colt whispered to me.
"What?" I said, looking around like there might be an issue with my dress.
"You look amazing," he said and fucking blushed at me.
Shit, that's not good. I could see poor Lucille's face fall.
Dammit, you idiot, can't you see she likes you and I don't!
Deciding to nip this in the bud.

'Well, you look nice yourself, Colt," I replied in passing and slipped my hand through Lucille's arm.

"Let's go and get us a man, girl!" I winked at her and pulled her through the door.

"Yes, let's!"

Chapter 47

Wyatt Forester

Seeing my Wildcat with those curlers in her hair, getting ready for a good night, warmed my soul. She deserved a good night out; I wish it was with us. Definitely not the sleaze bag Colt, but as long as she was happy, safe and having a great time, who was I to deny her any of it?

However, we made sure that we'd be downstairs in the foyer to see her off, desperate to catch a glimpse of her dressed up and beautiful. Lincoln was sure we were wearing her down and that it wouldn't take much longer until she'd crumble and at least talk to us about what happened.

Fox had the most challenging time. He struggled with Ivy not being around and was highly pessimistic about us being able to wear her down. I spent a lot of time convincing him that it'd work and boosting his self-confidence, which had taken a hit since Ivy treated us like we were invisible to her.

He'd come around and made daily efforts with her, too, and the three of us made an impact.

She had started talking to us, not much, a word here and there, but the fact that she acknowledged us and gave us the time of day showed it was working.

Every night without her stung, we held on to her coming back to us….Hopefully soon.

As we walked down the stairs to see her off, I felt the tension in the air. We weren't nervous but a little on edge, enough to make Fox pace up and down the ancient rug on the foyer floor.

"They will come down soon. Jesus, sit down, Fox, you're making me nervous." I snapped at him, brushing my hand through my hair, trying not to pace myself.

Linc, with his back straight, ready for whatever, was a confident calm in the storm. Calculated. He was so level-headed lately; it was sickening. He leaned against the closest wall to the staircase, playing with his phone like nothing important was happening. Usually, that would also be me and Fox, but since Ivy dug her claws into us, we were practically changed people. Not gonna lie, as I was the one that never had sex with her and staying abstinent from any other pussy even before she fell for us was part of why I was a bit of a wreck. Fox used sex for his anger. Fuck or fight. Lincoln just loved sex of any kind, but it wasn't that simple for me.

The act itself wasn't enough to satisfy my complex needs. Sure, I got off, plenty in the shower by myself, thinking of Ivy too, but *just* fucking would never fully satisfy me. She had already changed that to a degree in me; I was more concerned about making her feel good, testing how far I could push her and seeing her writhe made my dick near explode, but I was desperate to have my needs met again.

I was so occupied with my kinks that I nearly missed Ivy and Lucille walking down the stairs, Colt trailing behind. Fuck, she was stunning. She was a natural beauty anyway, but in that frock, with her hair and make-up all done, she looked exactly like the Goddess she was.

My heart was racing at the sheer sight of her. I'd give anything to go with her tonight, and judging by the look on my best friends' faces, they sure thought the same.

We didn't approach her; we wanted her to see us in the distance to ensure she thought about us that night. And hopefully, missed us. I did catch a faint smile on her face when she glanced our way, and I was hopeful that she would think of us.

As my eyes trailed from her to Lucille and stopped at Colt, who completely ignored us, something in my gut went on alert. His face had a devious look, and I didn't like it, not one bit.

It was probably jealousy, which I wasn't accustomed to feeling, that he'd be with her all night instead of us. At least, that's what

I hoped it was. I never liked the guy, let alone having him spend a night with our girl out on the town, but there was something so off that I usually didn't see in him.

The guys and I headed back upstairs when the doors closed behind them.

We talked about how incredible Ivy looked, but no one said anything about picking up a weirder-than-usual vibe from Colt, so I kept my mouth shut, convinced it was my jealousy.

Ivy, what are you doing to me? I thought.

Linc was busy watching the feed of the tracker he had installed on Ivy's phone, and Fox kept bouncing a flipping ball back and forth against the wall. His main pastime activity since Ivy had gone. He used to do it as a kid, mainly when he was a nervous wreck. Hence, I did not comment on it now. It was way better than having him demolish our room on the regular.

At one point, I was sure all his inheritance would go on new furniture at a weekly rate.

Since Ivy, we didn't need to buy anything new; she kept him steady, which made Linc and I love her even more. She was precisely what Fox needed: a rock in his stormy seas.

Love. I knew deep down that I had fallen for her and that I loved her, even if it scared the shit out of me.

We were all a little uneasy about Ivy not being on school grounds, so we eventually kept checking her whereabouts on

Linc's phone. He was working on his computer. His tech mind astounded me daily. It would be a colossal waste if his parents forced him to become a lawyer. So much talent wasted. He got us out of more parking tickets than I could count.

"What are you working on?" I asked him while flipping through the TV to find something easy to watch, Fox still throwing that poxy Ball around the room.

"The sender of the email that was sent to Ivy. I think I'm close."

"Good, Let me know when you've got it," I replied with an absent mind, though, as I landed on HP, and it brought back all our memories with Ivy. Man, I had it bad.

"They have arrived at Park Lane." Fox declared with Linc's phone in his hand.

We nodded.

I thought it must be Grovner House; that's where they usually host these significant events. Having attended many in the past ourselves.

I decided on rewatching some Peaky Blinders, and it wasn't long until Fox joined me. I was glad the bouncing was over; it was starting to give me a headache, but I wouldn't have stopped him.

Lincoln never joined us, too deep into his work. He was like a dog with a bone. Hammering away on his keyboard, doing all sorts of stuff I could never understand.

Fox declared that he wanted pizza about an hour later, and I felt peckish, too. Lincoln grunted from behind his monitor; we took that as a yes and ordered Uber Eats. By the time the pizza arrived, Lincoln had become unapproachable, which could only mean he was close to figuring out what he wanted to know, and Fox had nodded off on the sofa. That left only me to go downstairs to get our food. I kicked the couch to wake Fox up and told Linc I was heading downstairs when he shouted at the top of his lungs.

"Fucking got you cunt!"

Bingo.

He found the person responsible for the shit show we had found ourselves in.

Chapter 48

Ivy Alexander

I had never actually been to a ball before. You would think having the parents I had, I would have at least attended something similar. But in Australia, Balls were not a big thing; we held fundraisers and whatnot, but they were like beachside parties, not fancy events that took hours to prepare.

Colt had driven us to a fancy place for dinner, now fancy restaurants I was used to, having attended a few with my parents back home.

What I wasn't prepared for was the way Colt was acting. He kept trying to hook his arm through mine or reaching out, touching me the whole time. It started making me uncomfortable, but I tried to shrug it off as best I could. The fact that I had such deep feelings towards the boys that any touch from another male just made me uneasy.

Thankfully, dinner went by quickly, and Colt walked us across the road to the Ball; it was so beautiful. I wanted more of these in my future, that was for sure; I felt like Cinderella, except I had no Prince or Prince's.

"Oh my", Lucille giggled as we walked into the place. "It's so fancy", she said, covering her mouth with her hand as she looked at the ceiling and chandeliers hanging everywhere.

"Well, Princess, may I have this dance?" I joked, held my arm to her, and pointed to where people were dancing. They were doing some crazy waltz thing I didn't know, but I would try. Colt had been approached by four people already, asking about his Dad and family, the American star. He would be fine on his own; this was a world he knew well, and we were just along for the ride.

We danced for ages and drank fancy drinks that were walked around on silver trays. It was all regal; Colt had joined us at some stage, making a funny waltz impression. The kid actually knew the dance but was pretending he didn't. He introduced us to the rich and famous people he knew, and we found he always led with who my Mother was in conversations.

Yes, my Mother was an International best-selling author, well known for her books, and had a huge fan following, but she was also my Mum first, not just an author. It was something Colt felt was necessary in introducing me to people.

"Hello Archibald, it's great to see you; let me introduce my guests tonight. This is Lucille. She attends school with me at Hastings House, and this is Ivy Alexander; her Mother is Lilly Alexander, the author of Bones in the Woods and Skelton in the Boot; you might know them."

Blah, it made me all wanna vomit. The longer we spent at the Ball, the more I disliked the people there. Once you take the fancy dresses and make-up away, it was just a bunch of rude, money-hungry twats all trying to measure their dicks.

One giant dick-measuring competition.

This was more than likely why my Mother didn't attend these events, she had zero tolerance for bullshit, and my Father had no filter whatsoever; he would probably say something super offensive and piss everyone off.

Lucille and I made a game to see how many guys we could get to give us their phone numbers. So far, I had four cards tucked into my bra, and Lucille had five. The looks Colt gave us every time someone handed us one was fantastic! He was so jealous. Hopefully, he would see that Lucille was a total catch-and-go for her. After seeing the couples dance at the Ball, it made me want to hear the guys out. I needed them back, even if we were just friends.

At around midnight, Colt declared we should make our way home.

Thank fuck, as I was so done, and my feet hurt. Colt brought our coats, and we only had to wait a short while for the car to be brought around to the grand entrance of the building. London was definitely gorgeous at night. With its glitz and glamour, I wanted out of these heels and to get comfy in my bed, preferably with some junk food.

"Wow, that place was amazing!" Lucille gushed when we climbed into Colt's car.

"Did you have fun tonight, Ivy?" Colt gave me a half smile and kept looking at me weirdly.

"Yes, and no; I mean, the place was beautiful, and getting all dressed up was fun, but some people were real snobby and only interested in where your money came from." I gave back.

It had felt amazing to get out of the school for the night, and even if the place wasn't entirely to my taste, I still had a blast with my friends.

Lucille and I kept chatting about the boys she had gotten numbers from and how and when to text or call them on the journey back to the school grounds. We giggled, and I felt happy and content. Colt mainly kept quiet, just looking at me every now and then.

Once we had arrived at the school, Colt declared we would walk Lucille back to her room first, as she was a level below us, and then he would walk me back last.

Made sense to me.

Giving Lucille a quick hug at her door, she said, "Thank you for coming with me tonight; you looked amazing! You definitely need to call someone from the cards you collected." I told her and playfully patted her bra.

"I will if you do," she winked at me.

"Deal" and with a high five, we said good night.

"Come on," Colt grumbled as he grabbed my arm, steered me towards the stairs and walked me to my room.

Swiping my fob, I turned around to thank Colt for the night again, but he pushed past me and walked into my room. "A little nightcap before we turn in?" He asked, holding a little flask that he had stashed away in his jacket.

Not wanting to be rude, as he took us to London, I nodded and took the flask he held in front of my nose. I took a big gulp, the whiskey burning nicely in my throat and heating my rather cold body up instantly. I held the small bottle out to him, but he declined and asked to go to the bathroom first. Suit yourself, I thought and took two more gulps before Colt returned.

"Can I talk to you for a quick moment?" he asked, sitting beside me on my bed. I felt a little dizzy, and comprehending his words took me a while.

"Sure" I mumble, not feeling myself at all.

Colt reached out with both hands and grabbed my face to force a kiss on my lips. My hand barely managed to lift, and I tried to push him away.

"Fuck Colt," I slurred, my head spinning, and I felt the intense need to lay down and go to sleep. Something was not right here.

"Why don't you like me?" Colt's voice was like an echo ringing in my mind, hazy and distant. I had to stay awake; shock gripped me when his words started to form in my brain. I needed to focus and steer clear of this guy. My gut shouted at me to leave the room, but my head and body wouldn't move quickly enough. Stay awake, I yelled inside my head! Stay the fuck awake. And I did, but my limbs went droopy and floppy. I could not get off this bed.

"Just remember this is all your fault." I heard Colt sigh. He came close to my face, my lazy eyes trying to zero in on his features. Then his hand, I assumed, crept up to my throat, and I knew what he wanted.

Holy shit!

He pushed me further onto my bed, my weak body fighting, but it wasn't enough. I had no strength in me. I tried to scream but to no avail. No way, I shouted, but the words were trapped in my throat, unable to reach the surface. But I forced my eyes to stay still on him.

I saw him reach for his zipper with his free hand, the other still on my throat. Not enough to restrict the airflow but hard enough to keep me in place. I willed my body to move, to do anything to get away from his hold. I wriggled as hard as I could. His hand around my neck slipped. He was too occupied trying to unzip his pants. When he realised I had some strength left in me, he quickly grabbed me around the chest and flipped me over. I was lying on my stomach, my head pressed into my sheets, and I took longer than intended to move my head to the side so I could breathe. I clung to consciousness.

I couldn't let him do this. I willed my brain to shout, and a garbled voice I didn't recognise as my own whispered as loud as I could, "Help." Over and over, I tried to get my voice to comply, to shout louder and by the third try, I managed to get out somewhat of a yell. Colt gripped me at the back of my neck, trying to smother me into the mattress.

"Shut the fuck up slut." He growled in a menacing tone. "I hoped it wouldn't come to this, but as you are whoring yourself out already for those bastards…" He trailed off, too busy trying to push my dress over my backside. My legs and hips wiggled as hard as I could make them move.

"If you had just shown a little interest in me, I wouldn't have had to do this!" He sneered, his spit hitting my exposed shoulder and the side of my throat. I wouldn't give up.

I felt the lace of my undies tear at the sides as Colt tried to rip them off my wiggling body, making it a minute fraction harder for him. But eventually, they gave way and left a burning sensation on my hips where the lace pulled tight before giving way.

I continued to form screams. But still, nothing viable came out.

Crossing my legs at my ankles took more effort than I could spare, but I managed it, clamping my legs shut as best as I could.

"I said shut the fuck up, no one will hear you now anyway." Colt hissed and punched the side of my face; my body went lax for a moment again.

With the last flittering strength I could conjure, I bucked and writhed, but he was too strong, and the darkness wanted to pull me under once more. But then I heard a bang. It was so far away, yet it felt so close.

I tried to move my head and saw with hazy eyes that my bedroom door flew open, right off its hinges and landed with crash. I thought I saw Fox storming in, but my eyes were too heavy to stay open.

Chapter 49

Sebastian 'Fox" Foxworth

I jumped up from my slumber the second I heard Lincoln shout. He'd found the person who'd sent the email to our Ivy. My heart was racing, eager to find out who it was and confront the piece of shit.

"Hell fucking no! I knew it!" He shouted next.

"Show me," Wyatt was beside him, eyeing the screen. I went over, too, but couldn't make heads or tails of what we were looking at.

"This cunt! This fucking cunt!" Wyatt growled through gritted teeth.

"Who is it for fuck sake? I can't see shit," I asked impatiently, wanting in on the anger radiating off them both.

"None other than fucking Colt Anderson," Linc said in a deathly tone.

Oh shit, he's gonna get it! I thought and went to put my shoes on that I left by the door.

"Let's ransack his room." Lincoln declared, and with that, the three of us were out the door.

It took less than twenty seconds for Linc to open Colt's door. We flew in like a pack of vultures. The anger in me clawing at my insides, waiting to be set free. I gave in a little for now, tipping over and throwing things around in his room that caught my eye on the way over to his desk.

Linc switched on the lights, and that's when there was no holding back. The two walls by his desk and bed were plastered with pictures of Ivy. Every move she made in this school was there, on his walls, a small silver necklace was pinned to the wall with the photos.

I heard Wyatt on my left, "Fuck, man. This bastard is another level."

I brushed my hands through my hair, not quite believing what I saw here. He was a motherfucking stalker. "We have a problem here." I heard Linc say.

"I scanned his browser history." He sighed so heavy I knew shit was about to hit the fan.

He then turned the screen to us. There was a newspaper heading from somewhere in Texas. Colt's face was in the centre, and my blood turned to ice, my fists trembling, and I was about three seconds from going nuclear.

"Teenage boy cleared from rape charges has the town in an uproar."

I turned around and had his room upside down in a minute. Wyatt pulled me around just as I was about to throw one of his chairs through the closed window. "We need to go. We need to find Ivy. Come on."

Ivy.

She was with him in London, nearly two hours away from us. Like in a trance, I let them move me out of Colt's room, catching eyes peering out the rooms surrounding Colt's room. "Nothing to see here." I heard Wyatt declare to the crowd as he pulled me toward the stairs.

On autopilot, we ran to our room to grab car keys.

When I say my blood turned to ice when I read the heading of the news article, I didn't know how to explain what it turned into when we heard muffled voices coming from Ivy's room as we ran past it to get to ours.

No time to waste here. I rushed over, and with one swift kick, the door flew out of the frame.

With tunnel vision, I took in the scene unfolding before us. Colt had Ivy on the bed, her dress up to her waist, with her underwear ripped away. His pants were unzipped and lowered.

Everything from then on happened so fast. Linc got to them first; he practically flew on top of Colt and served him with severe punches to the head. But as quickly as he had hit Colt, he was on his knees, pulling Ivy up and into his lap. Ivy's muddled sounds will forever haunt me.

I caught my breath, my lungs on fire, and only one thing on my mind. I lunged for Colt, who tried to scramble off the floor. I swiped his legs, and he tumbled back; before he could blink, I was on top of him. I heard Wyatt shouting somewhere next to me but didn't take in what came out of him. My mind only focused on Colt and how I had to end his pathetic existence.

I pounded on his face over and over again. His blood poured out from all different places. He turned his head at one point, and I caught his throat with a devastating blow. I had his hair in a tight grip and kept on punching his face until my knuckles spilt, and he started going limp underneath me.

"It's enough. Fox, STOP!" Wyatt's voice made its way into my head, and that's when I realised he was trying to pull me off of Colt. Reluctantly, I let go of the unconscious form under me and looked sideways to spot Ivy. Her face looked like she was high. The cunt had probably drugged her. I scrambled to my feet and staggered over to where Linc was still holding her in his lap. Without a word, I scooped her into my arms and held her close.

Her eyes were dazed, but low sobs rippled from her chest, coursing through me like a wave, I came back to my senses through her quivers. She shook in my arms uncontrollably, and I just held her tighter, desperately wanting to make it all go away for her. "Shhh, I got you, Angel. We are here." I whispered into her ear. Her face was buried into my neck, her tears dripping down.

"The police are on their way." I heard Wyatt slowly brushing Ivy's hair out of her face. "Let's get her away from here." He said, leading the way out of her room. I caught Wyatt from my periphery kicking Colt with all his might in the ribs on his way out for good measure.

I carried Ivy downstairs to the nurse's office; students were everywhere on our floor at that point. Principal McRowan was just a shell of a man overlooking what had unfolded in his school. Nurse Cam was hot on my heels downstairs, telling me I should be careful with Ivy. No shit Sherlock! Our screams and ruckus, within a matter of two minutes, had this place on its feet. I was halfway down when Nurse Cam came rushing toward me. How McRowan, the fat bastard, got there so quickly will always be a mystery to me. Unless he was in Nurse Cam's room, hers was only one floor below us. His was ground level and around two corners. "Take it easy, Sebastian." She said again.

One more word out of her, and I would have Wyatt put her to sleep. Ivy was safe with me, her heart slowing down in my arms, her breathing evening out. Her arms were wrapped around my neck, holding on for dear life. But her usual strength wasn't there, I was sure she had something in her system.

"We are leaving here and going home," I told her in a gentle voice.

"You're the strongest and most brutal girl I've ever met, but no one stands a chance against psychopaths, and apparently, there's too many here." I declared. The plan formed in my head as I walked her into the nurse's bay. Ivy managed a slow nod and answered with tiny, hitched breaths.

"Please, take me home." Her voice was so quiet, barely reaching me.

As I was laying her down on the wheelie bed, I heard the sirens of the Police and Ambulance in the distance. Lincoln and Wyatt were beside her with me; we knew this was it. Ivy changed our lives in the shortest amount of time, but one thing was clear: no way would we spend another day without her, for as long as she would have us. We'd follow her anywhere. When I told her I'd take her home, I meant it. I would take her back to Australia myself, and we'd stay with her. Fuck this place.

The nurse was trying to push us out of the way and getting Ivy to check her over, swearing at us and threatening us with all sorts of things. "If you three won't let me get to her, I swear I'll knock you over the head with my bat." I admired her compassion, but I wouldn't budge.

Ivy tried to say something, but again, her voice had left her; she was in a dazed state, so I crouched down to her to hear her slow whisper. "He didn't..."

The relief that ran through me at that moment could not have been sweeter.

He didn't get all the way; we took him out before the perverted waste of fucking space had a chance to follow through with his sick plan. I sighed deeply, looked at the others, and shook my head. They understood, and relief was painted on their faces. I looked back at Ivy and stroked loose strands of hair off her beautiful face. She tried again to speak, so I leaned close again, "No hos...pi...tal." She breathed weakly. "She doesn't want to go to hospital," I announced, not knowing if that was the right call, given her state. Nurse Cam piped up, "Sweetie, I think you need to, I'm afraid. It seems like you've been drugged, too." Cam said, but Ivy kept shaking her head slightly. She really didn't want to go back there.

Before this could turn ugly, Wyatt grabbed Nurse Cam's arm and pulled her close, explaining that Colt didn't get all the way.

She thought briefly and turned back to Ivy with closed eyes and a scrunched nose.

"I'll see if I can get them to leave you here. But someone will have to….Have a look at you."

Ivy's eyes closed, and we let her but kept a close watch until the paramedics stormed into the room. We filled them in, and without hesitation, they administered an injection, which they said would hopefully reverse whatever the cunt had given her. Then we waited. In the meantime, an on-call doctor who often attended the school for non-emergency cases arrived. After checking Ivy's vitals, he was okay with her staying here. He was sure Ivy had been given a low dose of diazepam as she was not convulsing, just tired and hard to keep awake and moving. He did, however, need bloodwork done. When the needle penetrated Ivy's skin, she was jolted awake and shouted, "Fuck is going on. That hurts!" I was never as relieved as when I heard her swear in her usual voice. The Doctor and Nurse, Cam, worked on Ivy for a while, ensuring every step was followed and she was continuously stable to avoid going to the hospital, which was against her wishes. "Doc has to take your blood, petal," Linc explained to a shocked-faced Ivy; In return, she giggled. That girl was high as a kite. Wyatt had called his Father to inform him briefly of what happened, and he promised to rush Ivy's bloodwork through. The paramedics left soon after the blood was drawn. The perk of wealth is that it gets you special treatment in the worst cases.

Ivy went back to a low slumber. In and out, she jerked out of most of them and nearly jolted out of the bed twice. The Police understood that Ivy was in no state to give a statement but was happy to take ours and to take the Doctor's okay that she'd be fine, being left here in our care. Before they left, Colt already having been transported away, they made sure we understood that Ivy had to give a statement at some point when she was better. When she woke again, she seemed clearer, her voice near normal again. "Thank you." She said into the room, not really looking at any of us. It was just the four of us in the room at that moment, and I was glad, not wanting an audience when she came to, and memories returned to her. We also didn't want her to waste energy, so we said nothing. Just stood there and smiled at her.

But then Ivy's hand came out, and she grabbed for ours. We all stood close around her bed, not having moved unless necessary. We held her hand together, and silent sobs emerged from her tiny form. My heart shattered.

Chapter 50

Lincoln Baker

Seeing Ivy cry like this would haunt me for the rest of my life.

I wanted to go back upstairs and throw that waste of space out the fucking window. The Principal was going to have a lot to answer for, allowing a rapist into the school.

Reading the title of that news article had my heart sinking into my goddamn shoes. I had broken out into an instant sweat. My beautiful sweet Ivy was hurt by someone who should have remained a fucking wank stain.

Thankfully, the Police were okay with the private on-call Doctor and Nurse Cam doing the checks on her and even allowed Cam to do the swabbing once Ivy was awake and alert enough. Even though Colt hadn't managed to force his way into her, he still managed to drip his DNA all over her butt cheeks. The nurse could swab it all for them when Ivy was stable enough, thankfully solidifying Colt's fate. Ivy kicked up such a fuss about us leaving that Cam gave in and let us stay, not wanting to upset our girl further. But she made us scramble to Ivy's head, pulling out drapes, pads and all sorts to give Ivy some privacy for the invasive procedure.

Ivy had sobbed throughout the whole thing. She held on to Fox so tightly that her knuckles had turned a permanent shade of white. She settled somewhat when we all had a hand on her. The Police had seen Colt's room before coming to speak to us while Ivy was sleeping off the drugs and meds. I pulled out my phone and sent them the security video footage of outside Ivy's room that I had set up earlier in the year. It didn't show much, but it did capture Colt being in there. It also showed Fox kicking the door off the hinges to get to her. When everything calmed down, and Ivy was as okay as she could be given the circumstances, we discussed our next step.

Conveniently, Fox had bought an apartment in the city a couple of weeks ago, stating he didn't want to move into Wyatt's Dad's house when we graduated in three months, and it would give us all a great home base for when we went to University. The biggest hurdle we'd face with that was Ivy's parents. They would go more than nuclear, despite her daughter being of age. Maybe Fox's initial plan, us all going to Australia, would come to fruition instead. I saw only a slim chance of her parents leaving her again, especially with what happened this time. Only time will tell. At least, as Ivy was 18 now, no one had to inform her parents immediately. That gave us some time.

Time we wouldn't waste here. For a quick fix, we decided to go to Fox's apartment, let Ivy heal, and choose when and what to tell her parents.

"Wyatt, can you run up to our room and grab all of us a change of clothes," Fox asked as he scooped Ivy up into his arms. "We'll walk out to the car and wait for you there."

"On it." Wyatt jogged out the door.

"Fuck I don't have any car keys on me," patting myself down like they might magically appear in one of my pockets.

"I grabbed mine when we were in our room," Fox replied, "they are still in my pocket."

"Will you roll the top down for me?" Ivy mumbled into Fox's chest, still a little groggy.

Fox gave her a broad smile, knowing full well Ivy was having a dig at him for his choice of car. She loved to pick on him for owning a convertible in the UK, where it's raining more days than not. She also stated in Australia, only girls owned convertibles and always asked to see his vagina.

My heart warmed at her attempt to have a dig at him now. Our Ivy was still in there.

Fox carried her out to his car and placed her in the back seat, where I could pull her into my lap and hold her tight. I honestly had zero regard for a seat belt at that moment; I just needed to keep her close, bury my head in her hair, and breathe in her scent.

We had lost her, and then Colt had tried to take her from us with force; I could guarantee there wouldn't be a moment in her future that didn't have one of us glued to her side.

The passenger side door opened, and Wyatt jumped in with two duffle bags stuffed with clothing, a handful of mobile phones, and all our laptops.

"I had no idea what we need," he shrugged, "so I just grabbed what came to mind."

"Good thinking," Fox replied as he backed out of the parking lot and headed for the city.

"I wasn't allowed in Ivy's room, so I just grabbed extras of our clothes for her," Wyatt stated, turning in his seat to look at her. Leaning back, he reached his hand out to touch her. She shifted her body so she was able to reach her calf.

"We'll be at the apartment in just over an hour, Wildcat," Wyatt looked at her with glazed eyes.

The adrenaline was wearing off of us all, making us feel the repercussions of the night. Ivy was shivering, and her teeth had started to chatter.

"Fox, turn the heating on," I demanded, holding her even closer to my body.

"Thank you", Ivy just about whispered into the silent car.

Wyatt squeezed her leg, which he was still holding on to.

Fox remained quiet, the night having ridden him the hardest. Fox didn't do feelings well, but once he felt them, he experienced them so strongly it was hard for him to turn them off again.

Ivy had flicked that switch with him.

Over an hour later, we arrived at Fox's apartment; scooping Ivy up into my arms, I walked us from the underground car park to the lifts. She complied, too exhausted and damaged in many different ways to be able to protest.

Fox used a unique code for the elevator and the apartment, then opened the apartment for us to walk through with Ivy; it smelled like it had been locked up for a while, so Wyatt opened the windows to allow the morning breeze to blow through.

"I had two Mattresses ordered and delivered last week, they are still in the plastic. But we'll make it work."

Walking off, I heard Fox grunting and groaning as he moved the mattresses around in the room next to us. Walking down the hall, I located the bathroom and opened the door. There, I found a vast bathtub and an equally big shower cabin. Still holding

Ivy in my arms, I placed her on the closed toilet and started running the bath for her.

Wyatts walked in and placed her shower products on the bench, clearly thinking ahead when he grabbed stuff from our room.

Filling the bath to the top, I asked Ivy if she needed help or would rather be left alone. She shook her head vehemently and said, "Please stay." She had a bruise blooming on her cheek that made the anger rise back up in my chest. I hoped Fox gave the fuck-wit brain damage!

Unzipping her dress, I found minor bruises peppering her back, arms and wrists. I was as gentle as possible when helping her undress.

Helping her into the bath, I grabbed her body wash and asked if I could wash her. She nodded absently but gave me a faint smile, too. I made sure to mainly let her soak, only washing her back and hair.

Some time through my methodical washing routine, Wyatt had walked in and settled himself on the floor next to the bath. I suspected he needed to be close to her like myself.

"I think I'm clean, Linc," Ivy looked at me with big, sad eyes, her voice small.

Wyatt jumped off the toilet and held out a big fluffy towel for her to sit on.

"Fox ran to Tesco to grab some bedding for the mattress and some towels." He smiled as he wrapped her burrito-style in the towel, then scooped her up into his arms.

Carrying her out of the bathroom, he placed her on the makeshift bed Fox had created on the floor. "Do you want us to go so you can get changed?" I asked her, but she shook her head, "No, please stay. I'm okay. Just drained, and my brain is still fuzzy." Wyatt proceeded to rub her hair and legs with a second new towel. Fox then walked over, pulled a t-shirt over her head, and held a pair of sweats out for her to step into. Once fully dressed, Fox scooped her into his arms and sat on the mattress on the floor with her in his lap. "You okay like this? Tell us if you need us to stop being close or touching you." His voice was laced with anguish for her. "I promise I'm fine, With it all." She gave back and snuggled her head into the crook of his neck. Fox then began to slowly stroke up and down her back with his hand in a gentle pattern.

"I love you, Ivy," he whispered to her, "I have for a while."

Chapter 51

Wyatt Forester
3 months later…

We had settled in nicely at Fox's apartment, attending online classes as much as possible. We wouldn't have set foot in that school if we could avoid it.

Colt had been dealt with, and thanks to some excellent connections, Fox didn't have to face any charges either. He had done a number on Colt, we all had. Linc punched him as he first reached him and kicked him hard in the ribs as a goodbye present. But no one saw the kicks I delivered in that night's chaos. It didn't satisfy me that he was still breathing, but a nice stint in the ICU would suffice…for now.

He was then transported straight to jail, and I hoped he'd find justice there. If not, we'd be waiting for him regardless.

McRowan nearly lost his position as Principal when the school board started their investigation. However, Lincoln had uncovered that Colt and his family had connections back in the States, and everything that would've prevented him from entering the country was wiped clean. His Mother, though, was facing charges for aiding and abetting, document fraud, and the list went on.

Ivy attended therapy and had upped her training sessions, feeling guilty for not being able to fight Colt off or the ambush from Crystal. Thankfully that one was finally locked up in a Mental hospital now.

It took Ivy a lot of time in her therapy sessions to come to terms with the fact that she was not at fault for the things that happened to her, and she couldn't have fought any of them off. They took advantage of her in vulnerable situations or put her in vulnerable situations by drugging her. But she came back stronger. And yes, more fierce, too, even though we didn't understand how that was possible. Her sassy attitude was on another scale. The most significant development was that she forgave us. After we nursed her back to normalcy, we had a very long and heated discussion. We had to come clean to her about everything; Linc even admitted to cloning her phone and hacking her email accounts.

She put us in our place, and we'd probably be grovelling for the rest of our lives, but we would do so happily.

Then there were her parents, that was a whole other ball game. Fuck, these Australians were cut from a different cloth.

Her Dad alone scared the shit out of me, and that's saying something. It took two family therapy sessions between Ivy and her parents to agree that she could stay. But it came with stipulations; she was to live in the apartment with us and only attend school for exams. She had unavoidable daily checks in with them, and always via FaceTime, text messages, and emails would no longer suffice; they wanted to have eyes on her daily to make sure she was all right. I was totally on board with this idea; if I was in a different country, I would demand the same from her.

That she was of age apparently meant shit to her parents, who also kept sending us online brochures for Universities in Australia; they really wanted her to move back and were trying to persuade us all to come too.

She didn't feel completely put off by them at first, having asked Fox to take her home that night. He promised her we would, though that was just her shock speaking, as she still wanted to travel, explore and live in the UK. We were young and indecisive at the best of times; we didn't know where we would end up. Yet we all knew we would go together.

Fox had several meetings with my Dad and also with his Mum, still trying to avoid a catastrophe in the making. My Dad was a hard nut, though; he knew all about Vera's past, and it didn't bother him. He'd fallen for her madly. Vera seemed a changed woman, too; watching her be anything but a socialite gold digger was pretty eery.

By the end of summer, Fox and I were to become official brothers. Dad had Vera sign a prenup, which shocked us all. Crazy times.

Ivy and I also had sex for the first time. I'd never live down how fucking awkward I was, it was like it was my first time. In a sense, it was. I never had a lot of interest in vanilla sex, but with her, I did. I was a complete nervous wreck, praying I wouldn't ruin it for her. In the end, I didn't, as it turned out. My Wildcat was just that, a Wildcat with many kinks, and I happened to be the one to fulfil her most desired ones.

What we hadn't explored yet was sharing Ivy between ourselves simultaneously. We didn't want to rush anything with her at all after what happened with Colt.

Again, therapy had helped her so much that one afternoon, while she made us watch Twilight…under duress, she blurted out that we needed to take her to bed.

Emphasis on the *we*.

I nearly busted a nut just hearing her blurt it out.

"Are you all going to just sit there and stare at me like I've grown an extra head?" She asked, arching an eyebrow at us. Fox was the first to move, jumping up, scooping her into his arms and running for her room. Fox had given Ivy the main bedroom in the apartment, claiming one of us would always be in there with her nightly regardless of whose room was who's. So far, he had been correct; we all managed to squeeze into bed with her nightly, refusing to allow her from our sides. Ivy never once complained; in fact, she made Fox find her the most giant mattress known to man. She had done some reading in that book her Mother had bought her. We had all seen it and just pretended like we didn't, but we noticed a few pages had been dog-eared when she moved her stuff off campus and into the apartment. I was sure Linc was secretly reading it when no one was looking, as he had many new and exciting ideas for us on the regular. I wasn't complaining, some of them were fantastic.

Chapter 52

Lincoln Baker

Fox placed Ivy on her bed and grabbed the waist of her leggings, pulling them off her in haste.

"Careful, Fox, someone might think you have been waiting for this to happen?" She smirked at him.

"Wildcat, can I restrain you?" Wyatt asked as he leaned over her and kissed her senselessly.

Gasping for air, Ivy replied, "Yes, please."

Wyatt looked like that cat that got the canary.

Racing from the room and returning with a soft white rope, Wyatt placed intricate knots in the rope and secured it to the headboard; he showed her how to slip free from them if it got too much. Shibari was more of an aesthetic illusion than an actual restrain.

Wyatt sure loved his Wildcat. He hadn't pushed her for anything in his kink basket, simply asking her if she would be interested and then still giving her the watered-down version of it. I think Wyatt might be scared to hurt her or have her, thinking less of him. Not having his usual kinks hasn't seemed to affect him like it would have a year ago; maybe all he ever needed was Ivy?

Once Wyatt had her arms tied to the headboard, Fox started placing small kisses up the inside of her thighs, right up to her underwear; she was already squirming in anticipation underneath him. We couldn't deny that how she looked, softly tied to the headboard, was the sexiest sight.

Wyatt pulled her singlet top over her breasts, licking her nipples and blowing on them, making her shiver and moan.

I hooked my fingers in the hem of her panties and slowly pulled them down her legs. Her intoxicating scent of arousal filled the air.

Fox did not waste a second, and his head went down to lick a line from her arse to her clit, where he stopped and drew tight circles. Ivy's moans grew louder.

'Oh fuck, Fox."

I watched as he pushed two fingers inside her, pumping a few times only, and then he shoved his soaked fingers into Ivy's mouth. "Taste yourself." The sight drove me insane, and I discarded my clothes in record time, holding the weight of my rock-hard cock in my palm, giving it a few pumps. "Be a good girl; come for us, angel," I heard Fox whisper against her clit, and it was her undoing. She came with ragged breaths and loud groans. Her legs quivering, and her bound arms flailing. Fox let Ivy ride her orgasm out on his tongue. Once her legs stopped shaking, Fox moved away from between them to make room for me.

Hooking my arms under her legs, I lifted her butt off the bed and lined her up with my cock. Slowly, I thrust forward until I bottomed out. Fox had made her so nice and wet for me.

"Fuck, Petal, you fit my cock so good," I moaned and started to plunge deep into her.

Fox shuffled up to her head with his cock in his hand and rocked it up against her lips. She opened for him instantly, licking a line from the base to tip, making him moan and fisting her hair.

Wyatt was still licking and sucking her nipples as I made my slow assault on her cunt; when I felt her getting closer to the edge again, I glanced over to Wyatt. He understood and peeled his remaining clothes off.

I felt my balls tighten, but I didn't want this to end so quickly. So instead, I pulled myself out and smirked at Wyatt to trade places with him.

Chapter 53

Wyatt Forester

I traded places with Linc, sliding my cock straight into her dripping cunt.
I could feel her walls gripping me like a vice, and it felt like heaven. Pumping my dick faster, her walls growing tighter and tighter around me, placing my hand on her clit I rubbed tight circles, making her orgasm build higher. She was panting, choked by Fox's cock, and I gave her clit a quick squeeze, and it threw her over the edge. Her cunt grew so tight when she came, making it hard to pull out. Fucking her through the orgasm, I gave Fox a slight glance, who looked about ready to bust a nut in her mouth.
Pulling out of her quivering pussy, all swollen and pink, I leaned up to slip her wrists free of the ropes and flipped her onto her hands and knees. She had no time to catch her breath. With her arse up in the air, I had the perfect view of her tight,

puckered hole and ran a finger through her soaked pussy to slick it up, circling her hole I pushed my finger into her ass gently.

"Relax and push back, Wildcat", I commanded

Moaning, she pushed onto my finger, and I slipped two knuckles deep.

She was desperate and took my finger so well that I gently inserted a second, stretching her for more.

"Linc, slide under her," I instructed. I grabbed Ivy's ponytail, the movement causing her to jolt in pleasure, writhing, needing more. I yanked her into a kneeling position while Linc slid in between her spread legs; once he was settled, I shoved her forward with my hand between her shoulder blades. Her mouth connected with Linc. I guided her body to line up with Linc's hand that was holding his cock straight for her to sink down on. Guiding her cunt to take the tip of him in, I held her hips steady.

"I'm going to fuck your arse now, Wildcat, all right?" I breathed out, consumed by the lust for her.

"Yes," she whined into Linc's mouth.

Lining myself up, I slowly pushed in.

"Relax baby, push back a little," I said to her with gritted teeth, finding it hard to compose myself.

I needed to be inside of her, all of her. Feel her strangling my cock. She stilled her body and shimmied back slightly, allowing me to pop the head into her arse. It was so fucking tight I wasn't even sure I was going to fit. I released a growl, overcome by my senses. She gripped around me and practically sucked me in. My head felt dizzy, and I needed to push and pull.

I looked up to see Fox climbing up to the side of Linc's head, grabbing Ivy's ponytail and pulling her face off Linc's mouth and guiding it towards his dick. She took all of him with a sultry gagging sound.

Chapter 54

Sebastian 'Fox" Foxworth

I grabbed Ivy's ponytail and guided her mouth back to my dick.
This girl's mouth was made for me, so wet and warm.
I needed to see if she could take all of me.
My blood was pumping through me like lead, time slowed down, and I had tunnel vision. That's what that girl did to me. She was my girl; I don't think I'd ever let her go. Her mouth closed around my cock, and I had a hard time trying not cum right away. Watching my two best friends pound into her whilst her eyes were all teary from swallowing me got me all fuzzy in the head. My fist tightened in her hair; I needed her to look at me. When her eyes met mine, I found nothing but love and devotion. "You take me so well, Angel. Fuck!" I groaned, knowing that she loved the praise. Her hands fisted the sheet beneath her, and her back arched in a nearly inhumane way, and

I knew she was close to falling over the edge. Wyatt's groans got louder, too, and I pushed deeper into her mouth. I was very close to following her but stopped myself at the last minute by pulling out.

"Shut…her…off, Fox", Wyatt demanded between heavy breaths. I kneeled next to Linc's head, stroking Ivy's face before my hand covered her mouth, and I pinched her nose between my thumb and the middle of my index finger. Ivy's eyes grew vast and wild, she was so into this. "You gonna be a good girl for us, Angel?" I spoke softly to her, "Do not close your eyes, baby; I want to see when they make you come." It didn't take long before her eyes rolled into the back of her head for a second, and she exploded around us, trying hard to keep her gaze on me. I felt the pressure of her screams and hot, wet exhales under my hand. Lincoln growled with pleasure, "Fuck Ivy, I can't hold on, you are so tight…." But apparently, he did; he kept fucking her through her orgasm. However, his pace slowed down. When I let go of her mouth, she collapsed with the sweetest moan, her body trembling. Her head fell in between my knees and Linc's head, gasping for air.

She looked back up at me, and with hitched breaths, she said, "More!"

I grabbed her under her arms and slowly pulled her off Linc and Wyatt. I sat with my back resting against the headboard and pulled her into my lap, immediately entering her tight core. Wyatt came up behind us and grabbed her arms to hold them tight behind her back; his other hand went to her throat and squeezed gently. "Scream for us!" He demanded, Lincoln coming up next, stroking hair out of her face and kissing her temple and forehead only to grab her ponytail and tug.

"Now," he whispered into her ear.

I bucked my hips up into her, and her groans became louder. Six more pumps and she fell, screaming in absolute pleasure.

"Lay on your back, angel," I said to her, placing her next to me on the mattress. "Open wide" tugging with the tip of my thumb on her bottom lip.

She opened her mouth with her pink tongue poking out, the three of us crowding around her head. We pumped our shafts until we spilt everything we had inside her mouth. She was still writhing underneath us, still hungry. Linc and I went back a little, catching our breaths, but Wyatt, who was straddling her, leaned over, stroked her face and closed her mouth with his thumb. "Swallow."

And we saw her throat bobbing.

We all collapsed on the bed; Ivy managed to wriggle her body so that she was tangled up with all three of us. Her head was on Linc's chest, and I saw her smile growing into something sultry and devious. "Let's do that again, but I want you on chairs, and *I* will tie you up this time!" She exclaimed in her most seductive voice. "I'll give you half an hour," she scrambled up and walked into the bathroom.

Epilogue

Ivy Alexander
10 years later…

Tilting my face up to the sun, I let my skin drink in the heat, I loved the summer sun on my face.

"Ivy," I heard Linc calling me.

"Out here" I called back and listened to his footsteps as they closed in on my location.

"There you are," Linc laughed and slipped his arms around my waist to rest his hands on my belly.

"When will you let me put a baby in here, Petal?" Linc sighed, "I wanna be able to wrap my hands over a swollen bump."

Shaking my head at him, I leaned my body back into his. "I miss this weather," I announced, not answering his question. "Maybe we could move back to Australia?"

"I don't think Wyatt would survive the heat," I laughed, "He starts whining the second we fly in every year, complaining that we have arrived on Mars." I giggled, Wyatt's voice echoing in my mind.

"He really does hate the heat, doesn't he," Linc nuzzled his nose between my ear and neck, "but he would move here for you, Petal."

"I know, but I'm happy in the UK with you," tilting my head back to kiss him.

Linc leaned his face down and kissed me softly. It had been ten years since I decided to move to the UK for good, and I haven't regretted it once. I had thought a polyamorous relationship would be a hard one to maintain, but it was the opposite. We settled into a comfortable lifestyle that really suited us; even when we all attended University, we stayed together, living in the apartment Fox bought all these years ago.

Once Fox and Linc had graduated, we bought a loft closer to the hospital so Wyatt could do his residency without a commute. We were currently in the process of selling and buying a new one.

I wanted a bigger one for storage and projects, using the excuse of needing at least two spare bedrooms. I was curious if they bought my lie. I could have done better at lying. In the past six months, Linc had doubled his efforts in begging for a baby; I was beginning to think he knew. The others were all on board with having a kid, but they didn't harass me as much as Linc did.

I found out I was pregnant four weeks ago and was now 8 weeks along. Despite not being very good at keeping a secret, I thought I had done an excellent job hiding it.

I wanted to wait until we went for Christmas in Australia to surprise them all with the news, you know, killing two birds with one stone. My Father's acceptance of my lifestyle had taken ages, while my Mother had been cheering me on since day one. Because I was unable to marry or be married because I refused to only marry one of them, I had my Father all out of sorts.

Five years ago, the boys had changed their names to mine. They were all currently Alexander's, which had my Dad changing his tune eventually. And now I would be dropping the most giant bomb on them all. I was pregnant and didn't know who the Father was. I was also not going to find out and would never allow anyone to find out.

"Petal, your parents are waiting for us to open presents," Linc said in my ear, "I mean, I don't mind making them wait a little longer" rubbing his growing dick against my arse. I was surprised that I took so long to fall pregnant, considering my three boyfriends had a never-ending sex drive.

"Behave," I laughed, "I thought men calmed down with age."

"My dick is hard for you every damn second of the day." Linc kissed my neck, "All I have to do is picture your ass in the air as you suck off Fox or ride Wyatt, and it's as hard a steel pipe." He continued to grind his cock further into me.

"As much as I agree with Linc on that comment, it's time to open presents."

Turning around, I saw Wyatt standing there with his arms crossed and a smirk on his face, "Plus, it's like a million degrees out here, and I wanna go back inside."

"Come on then," I smiled at Linc, who was sad that he got cockblocked, and at Wyatt, who thought twenty-one degrees Celsius in the morning in Australia was too hot. I tapped him playfully on the shoulder, "Next year, we're back in snowy London for Christmas, so don't get too stressed, babe."

Walking back inside, I sat on the floor by the tree and handed out everyone's gifts, making sure I left mine to last.

Once everyone had opened their presents, I pulled out the ones I had hidden under the tree and handed them out to everyone in the room.

"Now, before anyone opens them, I want you all to wait and do it together," I smiled at them all.

"So... no chance of it being something naughty then?" Linc pouted.

"Mind out of the gutter, Lincoln," my Dad growled at him, and we all burst into laughter.

"Okay… Ready…Set…Go…" I hollered and watched them.

My Mum instantly squealed and jumped up and down, my Dad looked confused, Linc had gone dead still, Wyatt had a look of pure shock on his face, and Fox's face turned white as a sheet.

"Surprise!" I bellowed.

"Petal, please tell me this isn't a joke," Linc looked at me with huge round eyes.

"Wildcat? Are you sure?"

"Yes, Wyatt. I am."

Fox's senses came back the fastest. "There's two dots on there, Angel. Does that mean…."

I grinned at him, and he flew off his feet and grabbed me tight.

My Mum was doing a happy dance around the room behind them all. She was holding up the mini jumpsuit with two stick figures on the front with the writing, *'We can't wait to meet you, Nanny'*.

Linc, having processed everything, jumped up and crashed into me. "This is why you wanted two spare bedrooms," he laughed and kissed me senselessly.

"Omg, Linc, don't shake her around too much," Fox rushed over and took me out of Linc's arms. Placing me back on my feet and cupping my belly like it was made of glass. "We gotta be careful now," he stated, looking down at my stomach with pure love.

Turning to face Wyatt, who was still sitting with a look of shock, you would think being a doctor meant he could keep a cool head. But two small dots on an ultrasound could make the poor man speechless.

I walked over to him and placed my hands on his shoulders, "You okay?"

Looking up at me with those perfect grey eyes, I said, "This is possibly the best Christmas I've ever had. I love you, Wildcat, you know that?" He said, with a single tear running down his cheek.

"Oh, sweetheart," I sighed and climbed into his lap.

"Clearly, this is how we ended up with two of them," my Dad muttered.

"I don't think that's how it works, dear," Mum trying hard not to laugh at him. "Do you need a beer?" She offered him.

"Yes," was his only response.

"You okay, Dad," I asked, climbing off Wyatt's lap to walk over to him.

"I'm gonna be a Poppy," he stated wide-eyed with a massive grin.

"Yes, Dad, you're going to be a Poppy."

"Thank you," he said quietly, wrapping his arms around me.
"Aw, Dad, I didn't know you wanted grand-babies." I laughed and hugged him tighter.
"I love children and wanted a whole football team, but your mum wasn't able to have more after you, so I always thought I would be able to surround myself with grand-babies instead," he says as he kisses my hair.
"Well you're gonna have 2 in 8 months"
He turned his head towards my Mum as she handed him an opened beer bottle, "I think it's time we moved to the UK."
My three men circled me in when Dad went on to hug my Mother.
Each gave me a kiss on my lips. A kiss that proved one thing: their love for me and mine for them would never falter.

The End

Discuss the book with other readers in our FB group:
https://www.facebook.com/groups/1241372387265018/

We're also on Instagram:
Cassandra Doon:
https://www.instagram.com/doon_co/
J. N. King
https://www.instagram.com/author_j.n.king

Printed by Amazon Italia Logistica S.r.l.
Torrazza Piemonte (TO), Italy